This book is a work of fiction. Any references to historical events, real people, or real locales are used fictitiously.

Jonathan Bloom
The Nudist

Cover photo © Tricia Laughlin Bloom
Cover art / book design by Heather Kern, Popshop Studio, popshopstudio.com

ISBN-13:
978-0692113455 (Toothy Chum Press)

ISBN-10:
0692113452

For my parents, Nancy and David Bloom.

The Nudist

*"I've heard that the son must bear
the burdens of the father,
but it's the daughter that's left
to clean up the mess."*
- Cowboy Junkies

Four Years Ago

Chapter One

Harold Gomberg splayed his legs out as far as they could go. He dug his heels into the moon shells, winged kelp, and warm sand, hunching over the book he was reading, a screed detailing the failures of the federal government. The breaths from his head came infrequently and loudly. They sounded like snores but were whispers of the words he was reading. He occasionally picked his nose as if he were the only person on the beach. And, as always, Harold was naked. He wore nothing but aged, suntanned skin loosely resting over fat and bones.

None of this was new to Gloria Gomberg. She had dealt with her father's nudity for decades by simply fixing her eyes elsewhere. Quietly hosting her white wine hangover, she tried to read an article in the *Vineyard Gazette* about the swearing in of a new Register of Deeds. At forty-three, she had no job, no relationship prospects, almost no money, and she was good with it. The hangover felt appropriate given her station.

"Did we bring any water?" she croaked.

Her father glanced around at the sand before him, grunted, and continued to read.

Gloria twisted her body to look at the house. It stood close enough to make out missing roof shingles and the tie-dyed sheet acting as her father's bedroom window blind, but it was still too far. Drinking water would have to wait. She craved a cigarette as well, but she had blazed through her only pack the night before. In lieu of these comforts, she bit her lip, closed her eyes, and tried to sleep.

Being the Thursday before Memorial Day weekend, the crowds had not yet arrived, but one pioneer family staked its claim on a patch of sand near the still-frigid North Atlantic. Gloria watched the young mother and father with their two children. The mother appeared to be New England stock, raised on horseback and educated at Smith. Her freckles were not blemishes. They were subtleties. She sat in a sand chair, Barbara Kingsolver momentarily cast aside while she pulled tuna fish sandwiches out of a public radio bag for her two little ones. They were beautiful children. Olive skin and long blond hair, boy and girl alike. As for the father, he stood in the middle of his family, young and tall, a center of gravity around which the others revolved. In his eyes, Gloria saw dropped college date rape charges and secure retirement funds. He was complete. The entire family was complete. The sun over their heads was not yet at the crest of the firmament and the days before them were long and many.

Gloria was so engaged in conjuring the family's mental life she was late to notice the father's gaze. He was not taking in the sparkling sea, nor admiring his wife and children. His focus was directed at Gloria's father, naked and spread-legged in front of desiccated sea grass and collapsing dune fences. The young man appeared to be calculating the situation and considering all angles. The math apparently completed, he began to walk toward Harold, but his wife reached for his ankle.

The wind blew north and carried the woman's words right to Gloria's ears. "Don't," the woman said squinting up at her husband. "The kids don't even notice." But she did not hold his ankle with much force and he was on his way again.

'Cigarette cigarette cigarette cigarette cigarette' was all Gloria's mind could produce. She did not like conflict, and she especially wanted to avoid it now with her headache and excruciating nicotine fit. She reached for her purse and searched pockets for the possibility of a loose Camel Light. Nothing. The young man had already closed the distance. He stood over them, white Polo shirt, grey cargo shorts, and thick black hair that was far too manicured for a day at the beach.

Gloria noted that her father was still reading.

"Dad?" Gloria said.

Harold Gomberg looked up from his hardcover library book and then back down. He dug his feet deeper into the sand.

As was always the case, Gloria felt the need to apologize. Saying she was sorry was her signature move, her conversational ice breaker, her repetition compulsion. Back when her mother was alive, she often ribbed her daughter about the child's profuse apologies. She liked to tell people that when she gave birth to Gloria and the doctor slapped the newborn's back, the infant responded "Entirely my fault." Now Gloria wanted to apologize to this stranger before he had even made his intentions clear.

"Hi there" the young man said, as nice as could be.

Harold finally changed his focus to the person before him but did not return his salutation.

As casually as possible, the young man squinted up at the first cloud to roll in. He stuck his hands in his pockets and rocked back and forth from heels to balls of feet. Gloria took it to be a poor pantomime of jaunty.

"Nice day" he said to the sky.

Harold was perfectly still, peering through his glasses atop his sun-blocked nose. Where the sunblock had sloughed off in sweaty droplets onto his pot belly, the nose was pulsing red with sunburn and scotch intake. His breathing was still slow. The eyes did not move off the young man and rarely did they blink. When they did, the event was unhurried.

14

Done admiring the sky and making small talk, the young man now focused directly on the old man's face and spoke quickly. "Look, I know the nude beach is really close and I'm a pretty liberal guy, but that isn't where you are. This is Aquinnah Beach and I'm pretty sure Jungle Beach – where you should probably be," he pointed to the west, "begins about a quarter mile down." Then he paused for a response. Nothing. "Normally I wouldn't mind, but my kids are *right there*." He lifted his other arm and indicated the spot where the boy of no more than four was dumping sand into his sister's diaper. "So if you could do me a solid and move down the beach a bit, I'd really appreciate it."

"Sorry" Gloria intervened. "We'll move."

Harold looked at his daughter but said nothing.

The young man did not seem to hear Gloria. He was taking in the sight of Harold. A distant seagull screeched. Then, following a pause that was too long for Gloria's tastes, Harold let out a sigh, closed his book, marking the correct page with a wadded up cocktail napkin, and placed it into his Eastern Airlines duffle bag. He pushed an empty six-pack collar and emptier pair of gym shorts deeper into the bag to make room for the book. He groaned as he lifted his aging frame from the beach chair.

"Thanks, bud. Much appreciated" the young man said as he turned. What started as a walk back to his family became a jog and then a run as he scooped up both of his children and carried them down to the pounding surf. The kids screamed and laughed. Gloria remembered those joyful screams from her own childhood. The certain terrors of the deep mixed well with the uncertain safety of Dad. The three of them splashed in the stinging water as their mother watched.

15

Gloria had had enough of the sun. Her head hurt. The shadow of a cloud cooled the air for a moment and it felt good to her. "I'm going in, Dad. I need water and sleep." She began to walk. Upon reaching the splintering wooden path at the foredunes, something made her look back, and she wished she had not. Instead of finding a spot further from the family, her father was lumbering closer to them. Now twenty-five feet away instead of fifty, he put down his duffle bag, unfolded his chair, and settled in. The book was pulled from the bag and opened to the correct page.

Gloria saw the young father put his children down where the waves rolled up the beach. He walked back towards Harold Gomberg, briskly this time. Gloria watched the young wife yell at her husband stomping past. "Kevin!" she called sharply enough for Gloria to hear, but Kevin did not change his gait in the least. "Kevin!" This second call from his wife did not make him waver, but it did catch Harold's attention. The corpulent old man closed his book and tracked Kevin's approach.

More clouds arrived and the waves strengthened. Whitecaps grew in number and size. The ocean's hue darkened. No ships broke the continuity of its troubled, green expanse. A breeze picked up from the west, forcing a cotillion of terns to adjust their direction.

"Dad!" Gloria yelled, walking back onto the beach. "Just come back to the house please." No matter how many times the old man embarrassed her, she never grew accustomed to it. Every single one of his public displays twisted her stomach equally.

Kevin reached her father before Gloria did. Even before he was done walking up to Harold, he was already speaking. "What's the big idea?"

16

Harold went from sitting to standing with the overwhelming force of the nearby sea. For that moment, his body defied the weathering that life had administered for the better part of a century. He was a springing leopard. A phony snake in a peanut brittle box that Kevin had accidentally opened. Harold was much older than Kevin and nearly a head taller. And he was wide. And overweight. Kevin was dwarfed on every metric. Harold began to move forward, forcing the younger, smaller father to inch backward.

The sun was slipping in and out above a carpet of clouds. Waves crept up the shore. Harold was still advancing. He spoke. Rather, he yelled. "I will *tell* you the big idea, sir! The biggest of all ideas. Downright cumbrous!" He poked Kevin's chest at this moment. Hard. Kevin continued to walk backward to avoid being stepped on. "Three pillars, runt. And they are as follows."

Here come the pillars, Gloria thought.

"Shed clothing. Shed government. Shed God. Do those in order. Your petty frustrations will cease. Until then, be gone, gnome!"

Gloria had arrived at the skirmish, planning to intervene, but fear got the better of her. The look in the men's eyes was alarming.

In the shadow of his outsized adversary, Kevin said, "Don't touch me, man. I'll call the police."

Harold replied through a scowl. "Ah! You reminded me of another thing. You are on *my land*. Uninvited! So call the police, those mindless lapdogs of the Leviathan. Not only will the law favor the naked today, but I could just *not* wait for them to arrive and beat you silly right now in front of your family and claim self-defense. This is my beach. You, sir, are an interloper! I cast you out, vile imp!"

"But Dad," Gloria started.

Harold did not turn to meet her gaze but held up his hand and said, "Stay out of this, young woman."

"Kevin, he's-"

"Dup dup dup! I said stay out of this!"

Sweat was visible on Kevin's brow as his eyes darted about, taking in his environment. "Your beach?" he asked. Kevin looked back at his family. Then to the dunes, and then the water. "But I've been here before. I could swear." There were no signs saying this was Aquinnah Beach, but then again there were no signs saying it was private property either. He stopped scanning, locked into the eyes of his aggressor and said, "I'll be damned if I know what you're talking about with your three pillars, but you are not a good man."

Harold smiled. "I am not a good man. That is a fair and correct assessment. But tell me, Kevin...that is the name your spouse bleated, correct? Tell me, Kevin, what kind of man is it that walks off and leaves his two small children to do battle with ocean waves just before the arrival of bleak weather?"

Kevin's eyes grew wide. He was sprinting to the water before Harold had completed his question. The children were peacefully playing in the surf. Their father threw his arms around them while yelling at his wife for not keeping an eye on their children. "Were you even thinking, Linda? Were you thinking at all?" Linda slapped her husband with Kingsolver. Hard.

Harold sat back down, situated his buttocks in the sand chair with much agitation, and licked his finger to find the proper page of his book.

There was something in this action, the licking of the finger, that caused Gloria to time travel. The curtains of the world thrust

18

open, moving the day's drama to the periphery, and a memory so precious and fragile superimposed itself onto the landscape that it caused Gloria to gasp.

She was eight or nine years old and sitting on this very beach. Her hands and arms before her were small and smooth. A temporary tattoo of a butterfly from a Crackerjack box peeled on her wrist. Sand crunched between her teeth. Her brother Seth sat next to her on the family's makeshift beach blanket, a torn blue bed sheet. With a straw, the boy struggled vainly to extract more liquid from an empty Dr. Pepper can. The sun torched them from a cloudless sky.

Gloria and Seth's backrest was their mother, lying on her side in a red, skirted one-piece swimsuit, fast asleep.

The children watched as their father structured wet sand into an ornate castle, replete with battlements and buttresses. He crab-walked around the castle as he worked, all the while whistling a tune unknown to Gloria. He wore a straw hat, plain white t-shirt, and khakis he had cut short at the knees using scissors.

The construction completed, he sat down next to Gloria, causing their mother to squirm in her sleep, and wiped sweat from under his hat. "Chateau Gomberg is open for business," he said.

"Who's Chateau Gomberg?" asked Seth.

"A brother of mine who you have never met, my boy. Big teeth. Smells like onions."

Her father reached behind him and picked up the small book he had been reading since the morning. The white lettering on the green cover read *Ralph Waldo Emerson: Circles*. Gloria rested her head on her father's shoulder and opened the book in his lap before he had a chance to. Her eyes scanned the page and fell upon some words at random. She struggled to put them together.

"'Under every deep, a lower deep opens.' What does *that* mean, daddy?"

He kissed her on the head and said, "You are the princess and the poet of this family. You tell me what it means."

She struggled to make sense of it but her mind could not piece it together. Was it a good thing? A bad thing? She came up empty.

Her father spoke again. "One needs to think on these things a good long while before drawing a conclusion. Take a feeling from it for now, my dearest, rather than a meaning."

He licked his finger and turned the page. The memory evaporated and the clouds returned.

Kevin and his family were packing up now. Tuna sandwiches, Kadima rackets, plastic pails and shovels, a blanket, and dog-eared reading material; all accounted for. Beach chairs were placed under arms. Gloria saw that the family's exit would require two trips to their overheated car, and the second one would be terribly awkward for this Kevin person as he would have to return to the place where he was brought low.

Gloria yelled to the family as they began their first trip to the car. "Sorry. Please stay. My dad and I are leaving."

"My daughter has early onset dementia," Harold said to the family.

"I do not," she responded.

"She is confused and we are staying."

"Would you both just shut up?" Kevin yelled over his shoulder.

"Can you believe the nerve of him?" Harold asked. "Offended simply because I am unwilling to cover up my mentionables." Looking over his bifocals at the family's remaining items, he mumbled, "It is beyond my ken."

"Your ken must be the size of a pea." Gloria said, fingernails digging into palms and head still pounding. "You don't think his frustration was even a little justified? Where are you going?"

Her father was tiptoeing toward the family's cooler.

"Stop whatever you're doing" Gloria pleaded. "Why are you tiptoeing?"

Harold opened the cooler and extracted a tuna fish sandwich in plastic wrap. Peeling back the wrap, he sniffed the sandwich and inspected it. His eyebrows lifted as he said, "Bibb lettuce. And a red onion! It is a thoughtful sandwich."

"Dad," she said. "Please." She watched the dunes closely for signs of Kevin's return.

The bite he took was enormous and it was followed by slow, savoring chews. "Merciful Jove!" he exclaimed.

Kevin's head appeared among the beach roses.

"Dad dad dad" Gloria said like staccato gunfire.

"Shit." Harold closed the cooler and placed the sandwich on top.

"Inside" Gloria hissed. "Put it ins-"

Harold began to run back to the cooler but was out of time. He reversed his trajectory again and sprinted to his beach chair. He fell into it more than sat, Gloria standing beside him.

When Kevin got back to his beach blanket and cooler, he immediately picked up the sandwich. He turned to the naked man, who was silently mouthing the words of his book while he read. Gloria looked down and saw that there was a gob of mayonnaise stuck in her father's chin stubble.

"Really?" Kevin asked. "Did you take a bite of this?"

"I suspect a seagull." Harold replied too quickly.

"Listen," Gloria said. "Can I give you five dollars for the sandwich so we can just move on?"

Kevin was still staring at Harold. He asked, "Who the hell are you?"

Harold answered. "You, in two weeks, if my words sink in. Remember them." He removed his glasses and pointed them at the young man as if he was casting a spell. "Shed clothing. Shed government. Shed god."

"Up yours!" Kevin snapped as he went to grab the remainder of his family's items. Then he was gone. The clouds and the naked man had won.

Harold and Gloria were alone now. The air was cold and breezy. Still standing, Gloria stared down at her father, wanting to say a thousand things but choking back all of them. He was all she had since Mom died, and he was not enough. He cupped his hands against the building wind and lit a joint. With a slow inhalation, the old man took in the grey sky, the seagulls bolting leeward, and the waves crashing on the Aquinnah shore.

"You don't own this beach" she finally said to him.

"Fair enough. But Kevin did not need to know that."

"Your nudity disgusts me," she blurted out.

"Forgive me for making a statement."

"You're not making a statement. You're posing a question, and the question is 'What the fuck is wrong with me?'" She waited for him to respond but he was silent. "I'm going back to the house" she said. "And I think I'm going to go back to New

York early. I'll catch a ferry tonight. The visit has been delightful."

"Safe travels," he said through lungs full of marijuana, still admiring the sea.

And then he spewed improbably large clouds of smoke into the salt air, and uttered nothing more.

Gloria, 'the princess and poet of the family,' walked along the wooden planks to the house, hangover screaming, promising herself she would not visit her father again until it was to mumble his brief eulogy.

Thursday

Chapter Two

Gloria rode in the passenger seat of her fiancé's car, on her way to visit her very much alive father, yet again. She was physically present in the old Volvo wagon but her mind was everywhere else. And while flitting about as it often did at times of stress, looking for purchase on a memory or new idea, it now landed on something her father once said. Most of the ideas that emptied from his mouth were parboiled absurdities, but on occasion, he would accidentally let a careful thought slip through.

He had uttered it in his usual way, devoid of contractions and peppered with words that only appear in writing, like he was misquoting literature. He had said, "At times life feels like a trip across America eastward. When you are in the middle of the trip there is so much road ahead, but all the beauty is behind you. There is nothing but flat land and straight interstate. The charge of the mountains and canyons is not even in the rearview mirror anymore. All that waits for you is the eternal mundane."

Now, at age forty-seven, driving eastward through the infinite pines of Rhode Island, she felt those words more than she wished. The big decisions of her life were now done. It was time to just ride them out. The problem of the moment and perhaps all coming moments was that she regretted every decision she had ever made. To take a corporate job. To smoke so much. To drink so much. To quit drinking. To get married so late in life. Most of all, she regretted the decision to make this trip to visit her father. The spring sunrise glimmered through the windshield, but it could not fool her. The immediate future was going to be dark.

27

Her fiancé Scott whistled a pop song at the wheel. The car smelled of the bacon, egg, and cheese sandwiches they had picked up at a rest stop and consumed gracelessly on their laps. Scott's old Rottweiler, Logan, slept in the back among the roller boards and backpacks. Done considering the landscape, Gloria stared at a magazine but did not read it. She did her best thinking while staring at an unread New Yorker. She thought about her family, incomplete and scattered. She thought about her mother, sixteen years dead and buried. She thought about her younger brother, Seth, an escapee of the family's clutches, living a blessed life in San Francisco. And she thought about her father, probably out sun-burning his naked body at that very moment, unaware of his daughter's impending arrival.

Gloria turned to Scott, took his hand lovingly, and smiled.

You poor bastard, she thought. You have no idea that you are the hammer with which I am going to bludgeon my father.

They had arrived at the docks of Woods Hole. She looked past the windshield wipers which were stopped halfway through their sweep and focused on the ferryboat boarding in front of them. They were several cars back in the boarding line. "Get your keys out, hon" she said. "Our lane is going to board soon."

This request got Scott to stop tapping on the steering wheel to the beat of a Steely Dan bootleg long enough to search his pocket for the keys. His tapping was replaced with his singing. "*Any major dude with half a heart surely will tell you my friend,*" he sang but also grunted as he stretched and twisted to get his keys out. "*Any minor world that breaks apart falls together again.*" Logan pricked up his pointy ears and whimpered in the back of the station wagon.

Gloria thought about how much she loved this man. She grabbed his arm and squeezed. The hold she had was problematic because this was the same arm he was using to fish in his pockets. After some deliberation, Gloria decided to say what was on her mind. "I love you," she whispered with a smile. To be sure, this was not the first time she had said it. She knew that she tended to over-say it. Uttering the words was a kind of compulsion, driven by the fear that if she stopped saying it, the magnetism that held them together would dissipate.

It took all of Scott's concentration to get his keys out, to the point where he was scrunching up his face. He jerked his whole pelvis up away from the seat to make the angle of entry into his pocket more straightforward. He said through his frustration, "You know I feel the same."

Gloria looked back out at the drizzle. "God, I hope the weather picks up. It was so nice this morning. I *cannot* be on the island for a whole long weekend if it's going to be like this. Especially if we're dealing with Dad. Did you check the weather forecast?"

"Nope. As you requested, I'm not checking the news or checking my email. No technology the whole weekend. So who knows? We could get clear skies or we could get a tsunami."

"The weather report wouldn't tell you if a tsunami was coming."

"Good point."

She loved him despite his being clumsy with thoughts.

Having finally gotten out the keys, Scott started the car and she went from holding his arm to stopping his hand. "Don't start the engine yet."

"I thought you said start the engine because our lane's gonna board soon."

"No. I said get your keys ready. You shouldn't start the engine until the cars in front of us are moving. Why idle and belch more shit into the air than we need to?"

He rolled his eyes and took his hands away from the ignition.

She loved him despite the fact he was a Republican who doubted the science of climate change, and that he was a weapons designer for Lockheed Martin. Marrying a Republican would have been unthinkable when she was younger, but now in her forties she wanted stability. She was liberal to the marrow, but he was kind. He was handsome. And they shared deeper bonds. They had both lost their mothers; hers gone more than a decade and his dying when he was a boy of nine. Gloria decided to brook the right-wing worldview, which for the most part, he kept to himself. What's more, she had the feeling that old-school Republicans were evil on a global scale, but one-on-one were mostly solid people. She felt like her fellow Democrats – maybe even her - tended toward the opposite: super concerned about the world but total heels in person. She would have no problem with George W. Bush watching her kids for an hour (if she *had* kids), but wouldn't trust John Edwards to watch her movie theater seat while she went for popcorn. It seemed to balance out nicely. Some people are awful globally, others locally. She would rather marry a man she could tolerate locally. It is okay to despise welfare mothers to your heart's content, but treat Gloria Gomberg right.

As for Scott being a designer of weapons, at least, as he put it, 'If you accept that weapons will always exist, then you want to build them well because fewer innocent people die if they are precise.' Using this reasoning, he framed himself as a

30

humanitarian. She did not frame him as such, but tried to respect the logic.

Logan was still whimpering. Scott looked back at him, and the dog returned the gaze, his eyes darting between the humans.

Scott said, "Maybe we should let him out for a minute before we get on the ferry. Maybe he needs to pee again."

She loved Scott despite his overabundance of empathy (empathy for those around him, that is. One does not design daisy cutter bombs if one has empathy that expands beyond one's social circles). His ability to sense the discomfort of others made him act irrationally. The Rottweiler had fouled the sidewalks of Woods Hole when they walked him not twenty minutes ago. Had it escaped Scott's mind? How could it? They had forgotten a waste bag and had to use an unmailed holiday card from the bottom of Gloria's purse to claw and dispose of the turd. Perhaps, Scott himself had to use the facilities and he was just projecting onto the crying dog.

"He doesn't need to go," she said. "His bladder is tapped."

Logan gave out one last whimper that sounded almost human before slumping his head down on top of Scott's backpack.

The trip returned to the forefront of her mind. She could not think of it as a "vacation" because the weekend ahead would involve spending time with her father. Measuring six feet four inches from thinning white hair to toe, his heart beat but once per minute. That heart was coal-fed and belched out black, polluted sentiments. At least that was Gloria's take. Perhaps the things he said were objectively neutral and sufferable, but for her they inevitably stung. They stung with neglect or, when his neglect was spent and he turned his focus on her, they stung from insight. "Vacation" was not the right word at all. "Trip" would have to do.

"Are you nervous about meeting him?" she asked Scott.

"Meeting who?"

"Cesar Chavez." She looked at him for a while. "My Dad."

"No. Not at all. You've certainly warned me about him, but I think you experience him differently because he's family to you. The quirks of a parent are only aggravating to the child. To me, he'll just be entertaining."

"Quirks? This weekend is going to have a body count."

Scott looked at her. "A body-? That's strong talk."

"Literally. A body count. God, I want a cigarette and a drink."

"You're done with both of those. Hundred seventy-five days. You're almost at a hundred eighty days. Almost half a year. Better pick up a crossword and a soda instead."

She loved Scott despite his sobriety. He had had his last beer in college and never looked back. This cessation was not even due to a drinking problem. He was just done with it. Total pragmatism. When Gloria first met Scott, she was drinking enough for both of them. At that time, she had thought she was drinking because she had missed her chance to bear children, and because she had not landed a six-figure job. Then in therapy she came to an epiphany. She was drinking because she *did not want those things*. Not in the least. All she wanted in life was to come home from her job as a convention organizer for the American Organization of Plastic Surgeons, pour multiple glasses of wine, and binge-watch something. That was it. No kids. No eighty billable hours a week. Just her small job and peace. And that ushered in the shame. Her lack of motivation led to her shame which in turn led to her drinking. Very simple and sad math.

With the recent removal of booze from her life, she could more clearly see that she was a shame addict. She would do anything to justify that feeling. Being with Scott kept her sober to work on that shame. Her hope was that once she untied the shame knot, she wouldn't want a drink anymore for good.

But why did I quit smoking at the same time, she thought. She had the urge to smoke ten Camels at once, like someone in a photo from Ripley's *Believe It or Not*.

"So?" Scott was asking.

"So what?"

"I've been talking to you for like a minute and I suspect you didn't hear any of it."

"I did. You reminded me that I had almost a hundred eighty days."

"That was over a minute ago. Emotion management. I was giving you an emotion management tip my boss taught me. The thing where you focus on an object in the- you know what? Forget it. Not important. The only part I care about now is my last question. If seeing your dad is so awful, why visit?"

"I've said it before. To get some sun, to shake off the winter, to dip our toes in the saltwater, to read on the beach. To take a day trip to Nantucket, to see if we spot James Taylor in Oak Bluffs, to ask ourselves 'Do we really need to go back to the city?', to see the cliffs, to bask in the shade of old sea-worn cottages. And, of course, to announce our engagement to my father while we're at it."

"I still think a phone call would have sufficed."

"He doesn't have a phone. Hasn't had one in years."

"A letter in the mail?"

She sighed. "Listen sweetheart. You'll see. I want you to see. It's just not that simple. I need to tell him in person. He *is* my dad, and this is big news. A daughter, an only daughter, marrying for the first time? It'll make me happy to see his face. To see him show some emotion and have part of it be pride and happiness, and to know I caused it. That's a rare event. Do you understand?"

That was all true, she guessed. But for all of her sharing, she was not sharing everything. She wanted to go to Martha's Vineyard because she had a murder mystery to solve. She would have to summon everything she had learned as a psychology minor to find the clues and parse them into a solution. She would channel Hercule Poirot and Miss Marple. All that she understood about deductive thinking would be brought to bear on the key question: Who had murdered her father? Actually, that was not quite right. She already knew that it was her father who had murdered her father. Harold had utterly destroyed his old self and stolen his form and his name. The reasonably well-adjusted, regularly clothed, only mildly misanthropic giant who had hugged her as a child was now in cinders. No, the mystery was not who had murdered her father. The mystery was why had the crime been committed? She wanted her father back, and she would sail the earth for an answer to his deathless death. But a world journey was not necessary because the beast was only miles away on the island of Martha's Vineyard.

Gloria would not allow this weekend to come and go without an answer. Harold Gomberg would spill his guts all over the deck. And if he did not, Gloria would spill them for him.

And there was also her plan to agitate the piss out of him with her choice of husbands.

Get answers, hurt him with Scott, and leave. Nothing to it.

"I understand." Scott said. "You want his blessing in person. Totally cool. Get it."

"Thanks, Sweetie. Plus, I think we could both use a break. I've been working non-stop lately. Oh, shit. Start the car."

Through the pouring rain, the taillights of the orange Honda Fit in front of them lit up. Its exhaust pipe belched to life. Through the Fit's windshield they saw the blurry outline of an SUV starting to move. Scott put the key in the ignition and the engine engaged. Logan barked with as much excitement as he could muster at the complaining of the old loud car beneath him.

"You got the boarding pass?" Gloria asked.

Scott dug into his right pocket. And then his left.

"Ssssshit." he whispered loudly.

Gloria watched him. She loved him despite his forgetfulness. But that love was straining now. Maybe Logan did not need to pee, but she did. Plus, she was hungry. What was more, absolutely nothing stressed her out more than being dependent on others when a task needed to be completed quickly. Moments from now, the horns of cars behind them would begin honking. She could already hear them in her head. And she could hear the voices of impatient drivers and passengers as they cursed them out.

The brake lights on the car in front of them went off and it began to move forward.

"Scott," Gloria said, her voice low and fast, prepared to rise in pitch the next time it was used.

"I know" Scott said as he reached over her and opened the glove box. Scattering registration, moist towelette wrappers, and a cracked Grateful Dead CD jewel case, he eyed no boarding pass. "Shit shit shit" he was hissing.

"Scott." She was a little louder this time.

"I know, I know, I know." He looked in the back seat. Logan returned his gaze.

The first horn honked and the resulting stress in Gloria's stomach was more appropriate for someone about to get keel hauled than for someone being asked to move. But it was real to her. So, she did what she always did at times of stomach-dissolving stress. She spoke. But the talk was fear-driven and probably unfair. "Scott Simon. If you do not find that pass I am going to lose it. Just lose it totally. I don't see it in my purse and I don't see it in the cup holders. Not on the floor. What about- no it's not there. Did you leave it at home? Please tell me you didn't leave it at home. Pull over to the side and we'll ask them to print you a new one inside."

Another horn. Then several.

She continued. "Oh c'mon it has to be here somewhere I know I saw it today when we left at noonish right we saw it…it was on the printer oh shit don't tell me you left it on the printer…" She wanted a cigarette now. "The printer right that's where it is."

"Leave it at- no. No," Scott retorted. "I gave the guy at the booth the printed thing and he gave me the ticket. But where the heck is it?" He checked his pockets again.

Gloria groaned. "Could you at least drive up to the ferry entrance and resume looking for it there oh no here comes the guy…" A man in a red shirt, yellow mesh vest, and knee-length shorts emerged from the rain. He held a clipboard and a walkie-talkie. If he was angry it was difficult to tell because his entire face was squinting to defend against the weather.

Her mental model of people who traveled to Martha's Vineyard involved high-born ladies and men of the finest etiquette. Scholars and diplomats. Soft spoken and humble but brimming with intellect. None of them would dare lose their tempers; none would consider even tapping a car horn or yelling.

That mental model was now shattering. And even worse, she herself was one of the people visiting the Vineyard and she was no scholar or diplomat and she could feel any etiquette she had flaking and peeling off as if under sudden high heat.

All it took was Scott saying, "It's okay. We'll figure it out" and her next words came like a flash flood. "Godammit Scott are you fucking kidding me? It is not okay. Are you brain damaged or something?" She heard herself say this and was disgusted. "The guy is coming to chew us out. We're missing this boat. Stellar. Just stellar." And then it slipped out. "Idiot."

Scott had stopped searching for the ticket. He was still, looking at her, dumbfounded. She returned his gaze. Logan had begun to howl in response to the car horns. None of the din mattered for a moment. They had hit some new plot twist in the story of their relationship. It was taking time to sink in. Not even the knocking of a clipboard on the driver side glass and a muffled voice saying "Sir can you roll down your window" seemed to break their concentration.

At that moment, the sun just over the ferryboat burst through the clouds and rain and overwhelmed the scene. Scott, released from his stupor, shielded his eyes with one hand and lowered the sun visor with the other. Down floated the ticket.

Gloria watched it land on Scott's lap and gave out a humorless laugh.

No words were spoken as the massive white ferry consumed their car and darkness once more held sway. A chubby steamship employee with an expansive grey beard directed them to their spot in the hold. With the car stopped, Scott reached over the seat, found the leash, and snapped it onto Logan's collar. Not once did he look at Gloria. That was fine because Gloria was

37

staring out of the passenger window. A family of kids approached their car, hopped on the hood, and scooted across to reach the doors to the ferryboat deck. She barely registered this.

"Are you coming up?" he finally asked.

"No" she responded before he was even done. Whatever came out of her a few minutes ago was as unexpected to her as it probably was to Scott. The next step was going to be tricky. How would they negotiate this new tension? Up until now, their fights had been more of the bickering kind, and if she had to be honest, somewhat entertaining. They had bickered when Gloria used his toothbrush and Scott admitted that that sort of thing grossed him out. They had bickered when they had experimented with a trip to the rodeo and Scott was turned off by the brutality. Even their political disagreements unfolded with smiles on faces. All of it had seemed emotionally removed, as if they were watching it on a sitcom but they were starring in the same sitcom. The words were humorous and scripted, missing only a laugh track. What had just happened on the dock was altogether different. No studio cameras were watching. What was the next step? There was no script. She needed time to plan. The car was as good a place as any to mull it over.

Then the next step introduced itself. The ferry worker who had approached their immobile car earlier approached again. He rolled up to Scott who was now standing outside of the driver's side door with Logan close by.

"Listen man," the blockish ferry worker said. "Next time, have your ticket ready. We've got a schedule we need to stick to. Please."

Gloria yelled out the door "Why are you bothering him? I was the one who couldn't find the ticket. You just assume the man is in charge?"

"You get my point" the guy said and he walked off toward the bow of the boat, shaking his head and beard.

Scott looked back inside the car. Gloria smiled at him.

"You didn't need to do that" Scott said. "I'm not helpless."

With that he slammed the door and walked toward the steps that led to the upper decks. Gloria was alone. She brought her foot up and kicked the dashboard. "Fuck!" she yelled.

It was her father's fault, she thought. He is still about ten miles away. But it is his fault. The heat. The grim energy. It was emanating from the island. From his fat soul. The weekend ahead would have a body count. She knew it. Hopefully her father would be one of the fallen.

Chapter Three

Asphalt gave way to wet sand as the Volvo pulled into the driveway. Rocks crunched beneath the tires. The beach house of her youth rose before them under grey skies. Scott parked at the foot of the stairs and killed the engine. When Gloria got out and stood in the drizzle looking up at the house, the whole structure listing slightly to the west, she felt like she was looking at the husk of something. Any memories had left this place long ago.

Like most coastal construction, the house rested on stilts; one great box in the air. It appeared – and was - top-heavy. The structure had been quite modern and groundbreaking in its heyday; the architects and engineers had employed cutting edge strategies to put most of the load-bearing burden on the land-facing side. This allowed the beach-facing side to be mostly glass.

All of that had gone to seed. Neglect was the caretaker now. Wood splintered. Glass cracked. Roof shingles blew off. Mildew infested. The award-winning house could fall over at any moment. It almost did during Hurricane Isabel. The local police knew Harold's family and were kind enough to call Gloria just before the storm hit. Harold had apparently decided to tough it out, they said, even though a local police officer had stopped by requesting he evacuate. The officer speaking to Gloria on the phone explained, "We told him to leave, but he indelicately told our officer to 'fuck right off' even though we had sent Officer Houghton, who's a woman. Just wanted to let you know he's taking a big risk, ma'am." That had been within the first year of Harold's move to the island as a "year-rounder," and the police had not yet learned about the belligerent nudist he had become.

40

Now, out of courtesy to the female officer, the chief only sent over police of the same sex. Officer Houghton had not asked for that courtesy and on the contrary had wanted some excuse to return and bring a truncheon down on the naked oaf's skull.

Gloria climbed the front steps and opened the weathered screen door. A splinter caused her to flinch. She was bleeding. She sucked her finger, blaming her father, and knocked loudly on the door.

There was silence except for the large waves breaking nearby and the sizzling sound of light rain on the sand and rooftop. The air smelled of ocean.

The door opened and in front of her stood her father. He was wearing Bermuda shorts and nothing else. His mop of hair seemed whiter and his paunch saggier, but otherwise he was the same. Many things seem smaller when you see them as an adult. Not her father. He still seemed enormous.

"Hiiiii" Gloria said as Harold pulled opened the door. This was joined by a smaller, shadow "Hii" from Scott who stood back, loaded down with bags and a big dog on a leash. The utterances were not accompanied by any change in bodily position on anyone's part.

Harold smiled and said "Look who it is." Nobody said anything for a time. Logan barked.

Gloria walked over the threshold and hugged her father. She then pulled away and reviewed him head to toe. "You're wearing pants" she noted. "No shirt but pants. Have you maybe..."

He spoke at an unnecessarily loud volume. "No I have not changed my ways. I put these on because you may have been the police. I have learned that things never go well when I start a conversation with the police while naked. And who is this, Glor?" he asked, looking down his bifocals at Scott. Then he

41

looked even lower at the leashed dog, whining and struggling to run down the beach. "And this?"

"Dad, this is Scott Simon, my boyfriend. And Logan. Scott, Logan, this is dad. Harold Gomberg."

"Hello sir. It's great to finally meet you." Scott reached out his hand through the entrance. Her father seemed surprised by the gesture, but he put out his own hand. After guiding Harold's hand through two impotent shakes, Scott let go. Harold's arm dropped away as if it were only bone with no connecting tissue or muscle.

"Come in," Harold said as he turned.

Gloria followed her father's lumbering gait toward the center of the room but Scott was still standing outside. He cleared his throat in a loud, intentional manner, drawing Gloria's attention. He gestured down to Logan.

Gloria asked, "Dad, is the dog okay?"

"Sure." Harold was taking off his pants as he spoke.

Gloria had briefed Scott about this, but as Scott's stare attested, no amount of preparation could make this normal. She know that context is king when someone publicly drops their pants. Seen in a YMCA locker room, one does not flinch. Seen after an introduction in a stranger's home, the experience can be unbalancing. After a stunned moment, Scott and Logan ventured inside the house.

The old smells were what hit Gloria first. It was redolent of garlic, mildew, and stale bong water. She was used to it, but Scott was wrinkling his nose. Then the visuals kicked in. The main room was wall-to-wall books, records, and windows. There seemed to be no exposed wall save one patch near the kitchen and even that was partially covered by a framed, autographed photo of Ron Paul and a smaller newspaper clipping of Murray

Rothbard shoved inside the same frame. Every table and counter surface was taken up by detritus. In the kitchen, egg shells and cut vegetables mixed with puddles of water splashed from the sink. The water drenched unpaid utility bills. On the dining table, which straddled the kitchen area's tile floor and the pile carpeted living space, a newspaper with a half-finished crossword sat atop a plate containing a half-finished omelet. A candle, wax droplets, and a single burnt match took up the center of the table. Next to that a bottle of white wine sweated while some of its contents in a neighboring glass did the same. The ancient, unmatched chairs and couches of the living area ringed a steamer trunk turned coffee table, covered in a tie-dyed bed sheet. Jazz records leaned against the trunk and were stacked on top of it in piles and non–piles.

Near the door was a wood-burning stove. It too was covered in jazz records and political books. Gloria had seen the stove once before. It had been installed two years ago despite the warnings of an engineer. That was another phone call Gloria had received. Apparently, the engineer had told Harold that the floor was rotted in that area of the room and might not be able to carry the burden. The engineer had also been concerned his men wouldn't be able to get the largest parts up the narrow flight of steps and into the narrower door. They could bring them up through the sliding doors on the beach side but, as he explained to Gloria on the phone, "that house looked like it was gonna give way just holding the two of us." That was when Harold had apparently whispered to the engineer "I know who could probably carry the stove. Ten Ben Franklins." This statement had been accompanied by the sudden appearance of cash in Harold's right hand. "I told your dad to keep his money. I said I'd install the stove if I wasn't held responsible for what happened. So, I'm just warning you about the situation. Something might happen."

Nothing had happened.

Then there was the translucent blue bong. It was taller than the kitchen table. For a four-foot-tall water pipe, it was rather understated. No Deadhead stickers on it. No skull-shaped bowl. It was a straight blue cylinder. Upon seeing it again, Gloria recalled the bong's back story. An island glassblower had assembled it as a joke, but her father had not seen the humor in its height and bought it full price without haggling. The bong was now an axis upon which the surrounding house spun towards entropy.

The house used to be so elegant, Gloria thought.

Scott was pulling two very large roller bags. "Put our stuff anywhere?" he asked.

Harold did not respond. He moved some dishes around in the sink with no apparent intention of cleaning them. Then he asked, "Did you contact me about your visit? It is acceptable that you are here. I just do not recount the information ever being fired across my bow."

Gloria stopped walking. "Across your bow? Isn't that the terminology people use to describe a warning shot? Why do you need a warning shot when your daughter's visiting?"

"Maybe that was the wrong metaphor. Let me try again. I did not hear any trumpets sounding from on high. Should I have known you were coming?"

Gloria sat down on the couch but not before inspecting it for ashes and spills. "Yes. I called Dick and Prissy. Dick answered and said he was going to stop by to let you-"

"Whoa whoa whoa," Scott interrupted. "What were those names?"

Gloria helped. "Dad's neighbors. Richard and Priscilla Hoyt. Those aren't nicknames people use behind their backs; Dick and Prissy call *themselves* Dick and Prissy. It's some kind of preppy thing, I guess."

"It is some kind of affected faggotry is what it is god damn if it is not," Harold added. "Dick and Prissy. *Please.* They employed the wrong side of the human anatomy. It should be Asshole and Asshole."

Scott laughed at this and Harold shot him a grim look. This was the first time he had made eye contact with the young man. "Funny, is it? You try living near those garish twits. Drinking cocktails with their five thousand friends, playing their precious bridge games on the deck, laughing like seagulls in the middle of the night, and then Dick is up at sunrise with his ridiculous metal detector scouring the beach for god knows what. Maybe the key to the prison cell he is stuck in. I swear their very flesh is whale-patterned."

"Dad's upset because they complain about him being naked all the time."

"Precisely," Harold said. "So why did you ask *them* to get in touch with me?"

"What other choice did I have? Ask the police? Would you have preferred a visit from them, Doctor Giant Bong? You see what I was talking about, Scott? No phone. No computer. Not the easiest guy to reach."

Scott admired the cluttered room and then said "Mr. Gomberg, I'm so sorry you didn't know we were coming. I just assumed Gloria-." He stopped and turned to her. "Why didn't you send him a letter?"

"Dad doesn't look at mail. It goes against his principles."

Harold pointed at both of his guests. "The United States Postal service is the hind-part of the tick that is the federal government. And that makes mail a tick-borne illness."

Gloria continued, pointing at her father. "And that is the reason I had to call Dick and Prissy. They are the last remaining method by which I can reach you. But I guess Dick screwed up and forgot."

"Dick cannot even look at me let alone speak to me. Of course he would conveniently forget to pass along the message. But you are here and none of that matters now. Something to drink? Eat? Wine? Omelet?"

Gloria felt elation come over her. She smiled so extensively that her large brown eyes were crushed shut and her cheeks ached. "I'm starving, but I want to wait and take you out for a celebratory dinner." She looked to Scott and held out her hand. "Sit next to me." Scott put down the suitcases and walked over to the couch, taking up his fiancé's hand and inspecting the couch before sitting down.

Harold was the only one standing now. His hands were clasped behind him; this was his go-to stance due to lack of pockets. He gazed down his face, under his glasses, at the young couple seated before him. Logan was sniffing his naked bottom.

The voice Gloria heard coming out of her own smile was young, hopeful, momentarily ignorant of all past pain or disappointment. It was unrecognizable to her. "Dad, we've got exciting news." She cleared her throat. "Scott and I are getting married!"

"I am as well."

"What?"

"Me too. I am getting married as well."

46

Gloria looked around the room. "What are you t-... to who?"

Down on one knee now, Harold was bonding with Logan the dog, scratching his neck. "Her name is Nika Bugorski. I met her at Jungle Beach. She is not a nudist, but she respects my nudity."

"Congratulations, Mr. Gomberg!" Scott exclaimed.

"When were you planning on telling me, Dad?"

"I do not know. At some point. Maybe in a few weeks when we planned to go to the courthouse and officiate our nuptial intents. Why are you sounding angry?"

Gloria stood up. "I'm not just *sounding* angry. I *am* angry. And I'm not sure why. But let's start with the fact that you stole my moment. Do you know how excited I was to walk in here and knock your socks off? And when I put the big news out there, what happens? A congratulations? A hug? A handshake and celebratory bong hit for Scott? No. 'I am as well.' Jesus Christ." She was walking to the bottle of wine.

Harold raised his voice a notch. "How long have you been here? One hundred and twenty seconds? And you are already splenetic? You could not make small talk for twenty minutes? Nor could you ask if I had heard from your brother? How is the convention planning business going? Plastic surgery is no flagging market."

"Small talk? With you? You lose interest if the dialogue is anything less than Chekov. And why would I ask you about Seth? How would you know about anything besides yourself in your ramshackle sensory deprivation tank by the sea?" Picking up a dirty glass on the table, Gloria poured. Sobriety was irrelevant at that moment. Her mind hardly registered the struggle of the past months to not have a glass of sauvignon blanc – a struggle that had dogged her every waking moment. The struggle was no more than a momentary flash of awareness and it was humorous to her, like a bittersweet memory of a childhood aspiration to be president or to learn magic. She took a large gulp, finishing more than half of the contents. No remorse touched her. Her back was to Scott and so any look of profound concern went unnoticed. "I already know how Seth is because we email every few months. No news, by the way. Your son is still well-adjusted, living in San Francisco, and blissfully far from you." She sat back down, drink still in hand, while her father began speaking again.

"I think you are peckish, young lady." Harold stood up and pointed at Scott. "Jim! Start your car."

"His name is Scott." Gloria hissed between sips.

Harold continued unfazed. "We are sallying forth for dinner on the town. My treat! Your appetites will be sated along with your curiosity, as we will be dining with Nika at a delightful haunt on the selvage of Edgartown proper."

Scott looked at his fiancé before getting up and fishing out his keys. Harold continued. "Oh, and Jim? Gloria? Congratulations. You make a lovely couple." He was now searching for his shorts.

Gloria had just finished sitting back down when the men began moving for the door. Her nostrils were flared and teeth grinding as she watched them. She finished off the glass and set it down on the couch arm. Get up? Sit still in protest? Protest would be too much like *him* so she got up, tipped a little from the effects of the wine on her otherwise empty stomach, and pulled her raincoat out of the luggage.

"Wait!" Harold practically yelled. Logan picked his head up and raised his ears. Harold walked over to the bong and dragged it to the couch. It made a sloshing sound as if it contained the entire ocean. From under an end table that was draped with a blue and purple scarf, Harold pulled out a large metal cooler. On the side of the cooler was a piece of masking tape with the words "vital effects" penned in marker. Out of it he pulled an excessive Ziploc bag bulging with marijuana buds. Gloria was unclear how all of it had fit inside the cooler a moment ago. Harold held the bag next to his aging face, shook it, and raised his eyebrows twice in rapid succession, Groucho style. Then in a Groucho voice, he said "A celebratory bong hit of Alaskan Thunderfuck for the newlyweds?" When Harold opened the bag, the smell took over the room.

Scott smiled like a naughty child. "My company performs random drug tests. But that is a little tempting given all of our good news."

Harold sat on the couch next to Scott. "I like the cut of your jib, Jim. 'Random' drug search is much preferred to 'guaranteed.' Be a gambling man and pull up a couch." Harold looked at his daughter and pointed to the mouth of the bong. "Gloria? Celebratory bong hit?"

Her yellow raincoat squeaked as she crossed her arms. "I'll be in the car." Logan followed her to the door.

Scott called to her. "Careful. Don't let Logan ou-"

"I know!" She slammed the door and was outside. She heard Logan whimper. "What am I doing?" she asked herself as the drizzle tapped her forehead and made her squint. It is too soon for this. Her father should not be able to get to her. It was all good news, right? She was getting married but so was he. That is doubly good. Both were moving on to new chapters in their lives, replacing Mom with a new nurturing soul. Don't do this, she thought. Be bigger than him. Go back in and smile. Wear a big, fat, dumb smile. Harold had done nothing wrong beyond his baseline of 'always wrong in every word and action.' If one accepts the way he is then the past several minutes should have been expected, and that made everything her fault. Again. Go back in, she told herself. Go back in and adorn yourself in that smile. Plus, there's more wine in there.

Gloria stepped back in and stood looking at the men on the couch. "Raining too much out there" she explained to no one. Logan walked back to his spot near the sliding door, plopped down, and joined Gloria in pondering the two humans before them.

Scott looked at Gloria and began repenting. "I should probably skip the weed and get the car st-."

"Bollocks" said Harold as he packed the bong's bowl with his thumb. "It is too late for apologies, Jim. Gloria is already mad at you despite her smile. You have already belly flopped. May as well enjoy the underwater calm for a time."

"I'm fine" Gloria said. "Go ahead and celebrate. I'll wait."

Scott appeared to see the logic in this and grabbed hold of the bong. The tube was to his mouth and Harold was waving the lighter over the Thunderfuck. Scott sucked, eyes locked with Gloria's. Gloria looked back, smile still in place. The bubbling sound of college days filled the room. It was a sound like something emanating from Frankenstein's laboratory as a monster was born. The weed glowed and his face cringed. Gloria could vicariously feel the pain in his throat. Then he was deathbed coughing. He was never going to stop coughing, it seemed, until an organ leapt from his mouth. Poor 'Jim' she thought. That coughing was an express lane to High.

Harold patted Scott on the back, maybe to say 'job well done' or 'get those coughs out' or both. He then took a more professional hit himself, exhaled the smoke and said "Let us repair to dinner in Edgartown!" He made for the door and slipped on flip flops, carrying the shorts and a t-shirt in his hand.

Scott rose from the couch slowly and began to walk toward the door, each step over-calculated. His weird simulacrum of normalcy was entertaining to Gloria. Why is he smirking, she asked herself. Something was apparently funny about his useless condition. The wine was kicking in and Gloria imagined she was momentarily on his wavelength. She smirked too.

"Let's go" he whispered to her as he opened the door. Logan tried to get out but Scott stopped him with his leg. "No, dog" he said too loudly. Gloria closed the door with Logan crying behind it. She followed Scott down the steps. He was pointing at Harold. "Your dad's naked but for flip flops." He was giggling now. "But for flip flops?" he asked himself. "Is that even the right words?"

Gloria passed him and got in the driver's seat, starting the engine.

The world was dripping, warm, and humid. Grey clouds looked to be only yards above them and they moved at a rapid clip despite the lack of wind, like they raced of their own volition, wanting desperately to get away from the island.

The car lowered noticeably when Harold got into the back seat. Gloria looked back at him, sinking into the leather seats. "Please be polite and sit on the dog's blanket."

Harold replied "Please be polite and not ask me to sit on a dog's blanket."

Best just to look forward and say nothing, she thought.

Chapter Four

On maps, Gloria always saw the island of Martha's Vineyard as a huge triangle, twenty miles wide, lying flat on its longest side. with a smaller triangle jutting out of its southwestern corner. It was within this smaller triangle, a part of the island that the Wampanoag called Aquinnah and everyone called "up island," where the car now followed narrow, winding roads. It was that time of day when headlights are optional and all colors begin their graceful collapse to a deep cobalt.

Up island is isolated and lovely, Gloria observed, especially in the rain. There is only silence, pitch pine wilds, and the weathered homes of those who wish to be left alone. No ferries dock. No towns sell wares. For a fraction of the year some tourists visit but they keep to one spectacular stretch of clay cliffs and are gone by nightfall. Up island is ringed by beaches that offer no amenities other than communion with Heaven and Earth. The inland forests were haunted with memories. Her mother and father used to take her there to walk the seldom-used trails which led to the island's history; cabins of settlers, only slightly more broken down than the homes of the living; a rock ten feet high, used long ago to demarcate borders, "Wampanoag on this side," her mother would explain. "Honkies on the other," her father would continue.

Gloria always had a feeling when up island like the end of the world could come and go – a meteor, a tidal wave, a wronged god - but this place would remain untouched. Lights would still go on at night. Fishermen would still smoke roll-your-owns on the docks. Cape Cod would burn on the horizon, but the island's alpaca farmers would continue their shearing, and its famed writers would still gather for white wine and lobster on these peaceful shores.

The Volvo was leaving all of this. It was headed for the eastern side of the island; the land of what Gloria saw as Mammon in sandals. She avoided it whenever possible. The towns of "down island" teemed with tourists looking for island authenticity among the shops. Every hour or so, a ferry arrived from the mainland, spilling out tourists into the towns like chum onto the ocean's surface, followed shortly thereafter by store merchants feeding. The ferries always seemed to Gloria to deliver more people than they collected, and by July the island was overwhelmed. Cars could barely move down Circuit Avenue. Cops were breaking up fights outside of bars before lunch. Any notion of transcendental escape was drowned out by the din of moped accidents and white kids blasting Bob Marley on their jeep radios.

There were three towns on Martha's Vineyard: Edgartown, Vineyard Haven, and Oak Bluffs. Gloria described them to her friends as follows: If they were three people, brothers perhaps, Edgartown was the brother who got straight A's in high school, played lacrosse, and got into Harvard early decision (but had a boozing problem he kept to himself). Vineyard Haven was weirdly quiet and a little religious (it was a dry town). He might snap one day and kill his entire family. Oak Bluffs was the brother who bought urine on the black market to pass a drug test. The Volvo was now on its way to the preppy Harvard student.

Gloria was gripping the wheel and looking straight ahead, making no conversation. Her father's marriage announcement was starting to bother her again, maybe because the wine buzz was turning unpleasant after its initial novelty. Scott was next to her, STX Lacrosse baseball hat pulled down low, studying his hand as if it had just sprouted from his stoned body. He chuckled and said "I am *not* okay."

Harold was in the backseat looking out the window at cyclists braving the rain. He was talking at length to no one.

"Look at the dearth of recognizable businesses! I'll tell you, the executives who struggled and succeeded to get their chain stores onto this island are the true heroes!" Harold picked his nose absentmindedly. "Do you know how hard Duke's County and its hippie aristocracy make it for a man to grow a business? Nigh well impossible. You would have a better chance opening a McDonald's in a Buddhist monastery. Islanders say they do not want these big box stores, but they do not mean it. I paraphrase a noble Wal-Mart executive-nay *warrior*-who said, 'The true measure of whether a community wants a business is how many people shop there when it opens.' And to his point, Martha's Vineyard should burn its regulations, let a Caldor open on the island, and see how many people come. Let the self-righteous prove they do not want these businesses by not shopping there!"

"Caldor's been gone for years, dad" Gloria said.

"The wrath of unions no doubt. Their heads should be on pikes!" Gomberg pressed a button, a low hum was heard, and the window lowered. He let rain hit his face. "I would bet you my last ducat you would find any one of these communists at the Grand Opening of a Wal-Mart buying yarn and uncooked beans at rock bottom prices to craft their own homemade hacky sacks."

"So hungry," Scott blurted out.

"Soon enough, Jim, you will be dining as if you were sitting at the table of the Count of Monte Cristo himself! Ah here we are, turn right."

Gloria studied the turn-offs that were her options. "After the Dairy Queen?"

"No. Turn into the Dairy Queen" Harold replied. "Here! Turn now."

Gloria did as he asked, wanting to ask for an explanation but too busy turning and parking. While her father could cop to thousands of shortcomings, fast food was not one of them. He was a gourmet of the highest order. Growing up, her house had been filled with glorious smells of garden-picked basil, vegetables being sautéed in garlic, poached eggs with béchamel sauce, and the menu went on. Why her epicurean father was requesting they turn into Dairy Queen was beyond her.

"Should I ask?" was all Gloria mustered.

"We are meeting Nika here." Harold leaned forward after saying this, head between the seats. "Remember when you were a child and you had those nesting dolls?" He chuckled and put his hand on her shoulder. "And you called each one Gloria? And the whole collection was The Glorias? That was so adorable."

Her father had remembered something from her childhood and was now nostalgic about it. For Gloria, this made the entire trip worth it. The Glorias had been very special to her. She had had them since before her memories began. Her parents told her it was a family heirloom, one of the few items that escaped the Soviet bloc, carried through checkpoints and across oceans by her great grandmother, Maida, when Maida was only a child. Whoever had painted the dolls must have been touched. They were odd, each one in a slightly different way. The largest doll was a silly but sinister black devil with tiny painted ram's horns and fire coming out of his nose. His forked tongue licking out of a menacing smile. His eyes were immense white circles save the tiniest red pinpricks of irises in their centers. He had a pointy tail painted on his rear end. If you opened him up, you would find the next largest doll. He looked much the same as the biggest one except that his mouth was closed, his eyes less bugged, his features softer, and his painted horns were gone. His tint was closer to grey. Each successive doll would continue this progression, losing threatening characteristics, gaining more pleasant ones, becoming more feminine, and moving from black to blue. At the center, small and lovely, was an angel.

As a child Gloria felt this angel was magical. Small, hidden, and humble, Gloria believed it was quietly powerful enough to control events in her life for the better. When their dog Grendel recovered from cancer, it was the littlest Gloria's doing. When thunderstorms rolled over Connecticut and lightning blew out transformers on their dead-end street, Gloria hid in her closet and held onto the littlest Gloria for protection. When the storms passed, she thanked the littlest Gloria for protecting her. But even more importantly than being her protector, the littlest Gloria was the keeper of secrets. Gloria had been too distracted by life to keep a diary. Instead, she whispered things to the angel for safekeeping. No friend could be trusted with certain facts and feelings. Only the little silent angel could be taken into her confidence. To this day, she felt that the Glorias, wherever they were–maybe in an antique store in Vermont–held her secrets in their bellies, never letting them go, never betraying the little girl who had loved them so deeply.

"I need you to keep a secret," her father continued. "Just for a little while. A big one. Just like you did with your Glorias."

Of course, Gloria thought. His sentimental moment had been all to an end that served only him.

"Let's hear it. What secret, Dad?"

"I have not told Nika yet that I was married before. And so, by extension, she also has no idea I have a daughter. So, could you please pretend to be my niece?"

Gloria had been rifling through her purse for lip balm, but felt her hand move toward the mace. It took all of her strength not to pull it out. She did not move, nor did she open her mouth. She was too unclear on too many things to respond lucidly.

"You did not tell her I am your daughter."

"I also told her you invented Red Bull."

"Why *that* detail?"

"I have no idea," Harold said. "She likes Red Bull. I thought this might impress her and make her a little less prickly."

Scott made a spitting sound as a mosquito flew into his mouth. He swatted the air with his hat. "The air is mad" he mumbled.

"Less prickly? What kind of person are you marrying?"

"Thank you for doing this."

Gloria thought for a moment. "I am not doing this."

About to turn and walk, Harold stopped and looked sternly at his daughter. "What do you mean?"

"I am not telling your fiancé that I'm your niece. You can lie all you want, but if I'm meeting her, I'm introducing myself as your daughter who did not invent Red Bull."

"Look, I plan to confess to her. Just on my own schedule."

"Schedule? What schedule? Look at you. You've never had a schedule. She will never find out."

Harold thought for a moment and then said, "Tell you what. Give me the remainder of the day. I will tell her tonight. Please.

I beg of you. You can watch me do it. Tonight, over drinks. Just please do not make me tell her here and now. It will not go well with a crowd present."

Gloria stared at her father for a long time. What was in his brain? Was it made of the same material as hers? Did it run on electricity like other brains, or did it proceed on its reckless course charged by some other element? Whatever the structure and function, she always felt like it was missing parts. Key components that generated empathy. To be sure it had other parts that replaced it, such as a capacious long term memory bank and deep understanding of politics and music. But the emotions (other than anger) and empathy. Where were they? She finally spoke. "Why haven't you told her yet?" A mosquito, thriving on the breezeless wet air and the end of the day bit her leg and she slapped it hard. "Would she have cared? You're old enough that an earlier marriage would make good sense. You're single now."

"Because of how it ended."

Gloria considered this. It was a reasonable point.

She said, "Then just tell her about Mom but not how it ended. Just say she died, which is true. And tell her all of this tonight."

Harold looked at the ground and was silent for a moment. Then he shared his verdict. "So be it. I will tell her tonight. I promise. My word is my bond. Until then, I am not introducing you as my daughter. Be prepared for that."

"Fine."

With that the conversation ended and they made their way to dinner.

The Dairy Queen was newly painted. Other than that fresh coat of whiteness, Gloria thought it looked ancient, like a spaceship arrived from the 1960's delivering food that had no business in this century. Several tourists in ponchos and rain slickers hovered near the order window or sat on wet picnic table benches, trying to enjoy ice cream and burgers in the sporadic drizzle. The mosquitoes were not helping. Speaking voices were hushed, but Gloria could imagine that many were mumbling their hopes that the Memorial Day weekend weather would improve. Gloria did not intend to check the forecast; her phone was dead and she was in no rush to charge it. Scott and Gloria had agreed to keep the phone time to a minimum and she was sticking to that.

"I'm so hungry" Scott said as they approached the order window.

"There's a surprise," Gloria responded.

"I recommend the Doily" Harold said. "That is their signature menu item. At least I believe that is its rightful name."

"What is it?" Scott asked, through a rictus born of marijuana.

"I do not know."

Scott looked around and asked, "So where's Nika?" There was no response, as Harold had disappeared. Gloria also searched the area because she did not see her father run off either. Without Harold in tow, the couple approached the window to order. Through the ordering window, a disinterested blonde-haired woman stood doodling on the back of a pad. Gloria saw that she was drawing a rather impressive likeness of a ballet dancer. The woman snapped gum in her mouth and did not register Gloria and Scott. Gloria felt her impatience grow until she finally cleared her throat. Now the young woman looked up.

"May I help you?" the woman asked in an Eastern European accent.

"Hi yes. I'd like the…hmm. What do I want?" Gloria asked no one.

Scott barged in, "While she's thinking about it, I'll have a double cheeseburger with the works and a diet soda."

Gloria then spoke up. "I'd like a plain cheeseburger, please."

"Plain?" The woman looked at her with half-moon eyelids and a very slow chewing of her gum.

"Yes, please. Nothing on it."

"So, no cheese. "

"No. Cheese."

"No cheese?"

Gloria paused and took a deep breath. "No. I want a cheeseburger. With cheese, but nothing else on it. No lettuce or tomato or ketchup or pickles. Just cheese. Burger. Bun. That's-" She stopped speaking. Out of the corner of her eye, she saw her father crawling on all fours along the wet cement in front of the Dairy Queen. He was smiling. Gloria was about to ask what he was doing, when he made the "shhh" gesture with his finger in front of his lips. Gloria continued. "Just a cheeseburger, please."

"Plain" the woman confirmed.

Gloria was very distracted by her father's behavior. But she responded. "Huh? Yes. And what's the smallest size of soda you have?"

"Small."

"I understand but can I see the cup?"

At that moment, Harold nudged Gloria aside, rose up with all of his might, stuck his head through the window and yelled "Bwaaaaaahhhhhh!" at the Dairy Queen employee. The unsuspecting woman screamed while Harold laughed maniacally. She brought her hand with the drawing pencil up and jabbed it into the aggressor's temple. Harold ceased laughing, howled in pain and reeled back, sending the top of his head into the top of the ordering window. This stopped his howl and sent him staggering back across the wet grass, the pencil holding fast, lodged under layers of skin and flopping around with his movements. The lead finally lost its purchase and the pencil fell to the ground. Harold sat down next to it. He was holding the back of his head with both hands. A dot of blood appeared on his temple where the pencil had been.

The woman disappeared momentarily. She then reappeared outside, marching up to Harold and speaking loudly in broken English, "You are motherfucker! You fat motherfucker! I ought to murder you!"

"I am sorry" Harold said quietly, dazed. "It was a joke."

"It was joke telling me you have never been married before?"

Harold looked up with large eyes.

A man wearing an apron, no older than twenty with a large blonde afro and acne, came out of the Dairy Queen. "Is this man bothering you, Nika?"

She did not look back at him. "Go back inside, Todd."

"Okay," Todd said as he turned and disappeared into the building.

Harold was squinting through the pain when he spoke. "Who told you I was married before?"

"Prissy told me! I was outside burning your mail like you ask me to. Prissy go by in stupid running clothes even though she walk. She smile like she gives a shit about me and say how sad it is that 'woman of house' is no longer alive. The house is falling apart since she is gone Prissy says. That is how I find out about you and historical whore."

61

Gloria snapped "Watch what you call my mother!"

"Your mother? Mother! So, you have child too! How many?"

"Two" Harold mumbled.

"Two" Nika echoed, turning to look at Gloria. "And I am sure you did not invent Red Bull."

"No. I'm an event organizer."

"Ugh," Nika said, exasperated. "That is very *boring*."

"You work at a Dairy Queen!"

"I did not claim to make Red Bull!"

Gloria looked around, eyes wide. "Neither did I!"

Tourists in ponchos snapped photos. Gloria walked over to her father and helped him up. He was dripping rainwater and blood. She looked at Nika. "I don't know you, but you make one hell of a first impression. My Dad's not perfect, but that doesn't mean you can stab him. Get a grip!"

"Thank you for advice, daughter of historical whore."

Nika stormed off to a nearby blue sedan. She slammed the door while getting in. She backed out and sped off into the descending darkness.

The three of them ate in silence at a wet picnic table. Fearless seagulls roamed among their feet looking for dropped fries.

"We really don't have to eat here," Scott observed. "Nika was the only person tying us to this place. Anywhere else you guys want to go?"

Gloria was already finished eating. She looked at her dead phone and said absentmindedly "You ate about a thousand burgers. So why the insight about going somewhere else?"

Scott shrugged his shoulders. "Making conversation, I guess. Put your phone away please."

Gloria was not happy about the request but knew Scott was right. She put the phone in her purse and looked around. She swatted at a mosquito that bit her leg right where her shorts met her thigh. The smell of ketchup was making her sick. She wanted this moment to be over and for tomorrow to start. She and Scott would leave Logan with her father and traipse off to Nantucket for the day. It was amazing how she already needed a vacation from her father. She was reeling from the events that had just transpired. Even more than that, she was reeling from Nika's youth. Gloria would be surprised if the girl who had just stabbed her father was a day past twenty-five. The fact that her father lusted after young women and the fact that this woman was after her father's money was all very distasteful. Had her father not been holding an ice-filled napkin to the back of his head, she would have taken him to task about it.

Harold spoke up. "What is it you do for a living, Jim?"

"Here we go," thought Gloria. She was repulsed by Nika. Now it was time for Dad to be repulsed right back.

Scott seemed tired. "I work for Lockheed Martin."

"In what capacity?"

"I'm chief designer in their defense arm."

"You design weapons."

Scott bit into a French fry and wiped a dollop of ketchup off his lip. "Yes."

"I used to know a gentleman named Forrest Bartley who was in their employ in their New York office. Looks like Gregory Peck with hydrocephalus."

"Still there! Project manager. Tall guy."

"Tall? That is what your keen eye picks up? How about the capacious head? With that height and head he looks like the Seattle Needle."

Scott laughed and Harold smiled.

Gloria looked on, deeply disappointed. She cut into their laughter. "Dad. How do you feel about the fact that Scott supports the U.S. military in their efforts to secure the world?"

"Eh," Harold replied. "He works for a private business which makes him a hero. That the business profits off of the U.S. government? Money is going into the economy. It is all good news. You ever eat at the Oyster Bar?"

Scott lit up. "Yeah! How couldn't I? It was in the basement under our offices."

"Exquisite fare," Harold reminisced.

"Did you work near there, sir?"

"'Sir?' Sir! I like that! Did you hear that, Gloria? Now that is respect. You chose well, Gloria. Yes, Jim, I did work near there. In the eighties for a spell. Turning a profit trading the life insurance policies of people dying from AIDS. Before you hate me, know that I failed at it. People stopped dying and my business went tits up. I lost everything."

Gloria said, "You can't be mad at the young psychopath who only succeeds in killing four out of eight puppies."

"I was not killing puppies. These terminally ill people were willfully selling their insurance policies. They had no beneficiaries. I merely provided a service for them."

"Sorry. I shouldn't have compared you to a psychopath. I should have compared you to Ché Guevara."

"Oh balls!" Harold exclaimed as he grabbed the baseball hat off of Scott's head and secured it on his own. He placed it low and looked down at his fries so that his face was hidden from view.

Scott asked "What are you doing, Mr. Gomberg?"

Gloria was about to ask the same thing when a voice from nearby said "Heyyyyyyy!" She looked over her shoulder to see a familiar face from her home turf. A tall, slender woman with long red hair approached. Gloria said, "Oh my gosh! Holly!" She got up and gently shook the hand of her friend.

"Oh, come on," Holly said. "Hugs!" The two women laughed and embraced. Gloria kept her arm around Holly and turned to the two men at the table. "Dad. Scott. This is Holly Alexander, plastic surgeon extraordinaire."

Harold did not look up, but Scott rose to shake her hand. "Hi. Pleasure." he said. "So you know Gloria because of all the great work you've done on her?"

Holly laughed politely. "Nonsense. Gloria will never need a day of my help."

Gloria said "Holly's basically my boss. C'mon. You've heard me talk about her, Scott."

"Oh that Holly!" Scott said. "Sure I've heard of you. All good stuff, of course." Holly and Gloria laughed again, but Gloria was only thinking about the conversation that would inevitably have to transpire between her boss and her father.

Gloria looked over at her father, who was still hunched over. "Dad, Holly here and the Association of Plastic Surgeons hired me to run the annual convention. Line up the hotel, organize the dinners, set up the meetings, presentations, evening entertainment, things like that."

Holly broke in. "Gloria's too humble. She also helps us plan other events all over the place."

A child walked up and grabbed Holly's hand. Then another smaller child did the same thing on the other hand. Holly looked over both shoulders before finding who she was looking for. A young man with thick black hair and spectacles sauntered up and settled in behind Holly.

"I didn't know where you went to, Mommy!" the older one said.

"You ended that with a stranded preposition, sweetheart!" She rubbed the boy's blond head sympathetically. "Gloria and family, I'd like you to meet my husband, Kyle. Kyle, this is Gloria Gomberg. She does all of the event planning for our association."

Kyle held up his hand and said, "Hello." Scott responded with a polite wave. Gloria could not understand why Harold stared at his fries as if trying to decipher the Talmud.

Holly continued. "And these little guys are Gunner and Maddy." Gunner and Maddy hid behind their mother and looked up at their father for some kind of reassurance."

Gloria said, "Hi guys! It's okay. I don't bite!" She could not stand kids, but she was proud of her ability to make it look like she was just cool around them.

Holly gave out a delicate little laugh and said, "We just came out here to take a break from being inside all afternoon and get the kids some ice cream, but this weather. Right?"

"I know" Gloria said. "I hope it gets better before Monday. We need at least one good day."

Holly looked at her, concerned. "Well, that's unlikely. Didn't you hear the news?"

"No."

Kyle suddenly spoke up from behind his wife. "Oh man. Fifty percent chance we're gonna get hammered by this big old-"

Holly smacked her husband's stomach lightly with the back of her hand which stopped him from speaking. "What?" Kyle asked, somewhat annoyed. But Holly was staring at something. At Harold. She cocked her head to get a better view of the aging man in the red STX Lacrosse baseball hat.

Then Holly stood up straight and said "Well, well, well. Look who we have here." When Harold did not look up, Holly reached across the picnic table and tapped the brim of Harold's hat. He looked up and scanned the new arrivals. His eyes were wide. Holly continued, "If it isn't the naked philosopher."

Harold looked around, betraying a man wrongly accused.

Kyle was silent. He stared at Harold for a moment. There was no anger in the stare, only curiosity. He then peacefully took the children by the hand and guided them back to the car. The older child, Gunner, said, "I thought we were getting ice cream" to which Kyle responded, "Somewhere else, buddy" in a hushed tone. He opened the back door to a massive white SUV and began placing the crying Gunner and the oblivious Maddy into their car seats.

Holly had not moved from her position. She hissed, "You really screwed up our day, you know that?" Harold still said nothing. "Kyle and I have been fighting for hours. Our kids have been in tears. That's why we took them for ice cream in this weather. No one's talking to anyone now. I hope you got the quiet time you wanted, just you and the beach."

Gloria asked "Wait. You know each other?" She had no idea what was going on.

Holly pointed at Harold and said, "Ask Penistotle here if we know each other."

Harold gave out a chortle and said, "Penistotle! *Le mot juste*! A play on the words 'penis' and 'Aristotle.' That is rich. I would have preferred Cockrates but so be it." Holly went to speak but Harold continued. "That is truly a shame you and your husband fought today. But I fail to see how your family's communication problems are my fault. If you had a psychologically healthy dynamic, you would be able to overcome the trials of seeing an old naked man at the beach.

Gloria finally understood and broke in. "Again? You did it again, Dad? You terrorized another family at the beach? Last time it was Kevin and whoever. Now Holly and Kyle? *You did this again?*"

Harold continued as if he did not hear his daughter. "There are worse threats in this world than naked people on the beach believe me. What will you do when government operatives swing through your living room windows and steal your guns?" Harold looked past Holly and Kyle. "I like your car. Ford, right? What model?"

Holly seemed puzzled by all of this but especially the last part. She looked back and then said "What? You like our-? Explorer, I think. What does that have to do with anything?"

Harold said, "Nothing I suppose. I like that you are bold enough to drive a large car in today's world. The Jewish media has convinced everyone that they like small cars."

Scott spoke up. "Aren't you Jewish, Mr. Gomberg?"

Holly said "Oh no, he's not. We learned that at the beach today. He kept spouting off that he follows no religion. He actually said a lot more." She turned to Harold. "You're a real jerk. You know that?"

For the second time that day-that hour in fact-Gloria found herself snapping at a woman for the sake of her father. "Watch what you call him. He's my father. Who the hell do you think you are?"

Holly looked away from the large old man sitting at the picnic table and set her eyes on Gloria.

"Someone you should probably speak a little nicer to."

Gloria thought. Then she thought a little longer. Finally, she heard herself say, "You ended that with a stranded preposition." She smirked as she said this and she heard Harold laugh. Joy shot through her. This was followed promptly by regret as Holly walked away without another word. Her red hair stuck to her wet, blue poncho as she moved toward the passenger side of the white SUV.

Harold yelled behind her. "Penistotle?"

There was no response. Holly was already inside the monstrous SUV. The car's lights came on and then Gloria's career drove off into the building night.

Behind Gloria, Harold said, "Did she say an Explorer? I need to remember that. I want one of those."

Gloria knew she was mad at her father once again but she could not reach it. She was too deep into the sadness that was settling in. "I miss my mom," she thought. "I miss my mom. I miss my mom so badly." She felt a loneliness and a panic like a child dropped off at sleepaway camp. Her mom was not coming back. She was stuck here. Stuck on this planet with her father. This does not feel like home, she thought. Not with Dad. I want my mom to come back. Of course, she said none of this out loud. She just swatted a mosquito on her shin and scrunched up her shoulders against the weather.

The rain had picked up. Scott finally spoke. "Maybe we should go home," he said, clearly sobering up a little. Gloria put up no fight, although she questioned his use of the word 'home.'

The windshield wipers on a low setting performed a funeral march. Harold, his pants off again, looked out of the backseat window, at what Gloria was unsure. An occasional front porch light was all that broke up the darkness. They could be on their way up island or they could be somewhere in outer space. Harold asked, "What kind of music are you into, Jim?"

Clearly comfortable with his new name, Scott responded "Big Phish fan. A Phish Head as they call us."

"Who's 'they'?"

"The media."

"What kind of music do they perform?"

"Sort of a jazz rock fusion."

Harold let out a wince that was audible from the front seat. "Those words have no business together. That is like eating a risotto lint fusion."

Scott bristled a little. "Wait a minute," he looked back from the passenger side, his hat falling off in the process. "You need to hear them. They are pretty talented musicians. You probably know Steely Dan. They're another band I love." He began singing. *"Any major dude with half a heart surely would tell you my friend."* He held his hand on his chest. *"Any minor world that breaks apart falls together again. When the demon is at your door..."* He stopped singing, likely because he did not know the words from there. He spoke again. "They're kind of like-"

"Do not utter the dildo-inspired phrase Steely Dan or sing their goofy music in this car, even if it is your car and I am in it. They and your Fish Heads use their talent for evil. You should listen to Miles. Or Ellington. Or Coltrane. Ornette. Jazz without the infusion of garbage. The myth that rock music is music at all is simply nonsense on stilts. It is music born of neglect. Generated in cotton fields by people who would have preferred to be making other music but could not because the slave masters did not provide them with the resources to do so."

Still looking into the backseat, Scott said, "I hope I'm not overstepping any boundaries but that theory seems, well, confused. Oh, Mr. Gomberg, you forgot to buckle your seat belt."

Harold looked down at his naked torso. "Forgot? You mean 'willfully refused,'" he replied. "I never wear a seat belt. That goblin Ralph Nader force fed those to the auto industry and I will be damned- "

Gloria hit the brakes jerking everyone forward, including her. Her dad slammed into the back of Scott's seat. He moaned and massaged the bruise on the back of his head, and then did the same to the wound on his temple.

"Just put the goddamn seatbelt on and shut up!" Gloria yelled into the rearview mirror.

Harold looked at her for a moment and then did as she requested.

When they pulled into Harold's driveway, they saw one small light coming from the steps up to the door. It was Nika, smoking a cigarette, waiting for them in the rain. The blue Camry she had driven was parked under the stilts of the house. Harold hopped out immediately. As he opened and closed the door, Logan's bark could be heard from on high. Scott and Gloria watched from the car as Harold walk to the young woman. Nika stood up when he approached. The two of them, framed by the headlights, spoke to each other. There were no arms flailing in argument, no pencils used as weapons, and their lips barely moved. Gloria was amazed by Nika's age and beauty. What on earth was the girl doing with her father? Going after the money from her mother's side of the family? Gloria doubted much of that was left. Nika put up her hand to block the glare from the Volvo's headlights. Gloria turned them off. In the western sky, one insubstantial crack of dim orange light shone through the clouds. But even that one bit of luminescence was enough for Gloria to see Nika and her father hugging.

She would never eat again. But she would definitely drink.

Her eyes focused on a roof shingle resting on the driveway dirt next to Harold's rusted-out bicycle. She scratched furiously at the mosquito bite on her shin and woke up Scott who had passed out next to her.

"Whuh?" he asked in a daze.

"We're here."

She had failed at her goal of surprising her father with her wedding announcement. He had even checkmated her with his counter-announcement. She was also no closer to her goal of pissing him off with her choice of a mate (Steely Dan references excluded). And she was nowhere near completing her goal of solving the murder of the younger Harold Gomberg. This distant stranger who called himself Dad was more distant and stranger than ever.

Chapter Five

Gloria was showering, soaping herself with one hand, holding a glass of wine in the other. She needed to get the events of the day off her skin before she could make polite small talk. Did other people plan their chit chat, she wondered? She would never, *ever*, go into a social situation without having some talking points ready. With Nika, she planned to ask about place of origin, reasons for coming to the United States, and where she met Harold. Just maybe, Gloria would offer up some anecdotes about herself that would establish trust. Gloria loved sharing. That part would be easy. For example, in college at the University of Vermont, she had played bass in a power pop band called The Cheap Seats. She had been terrible and got kicked out by her best friends. Such a self-deprecating story was sure to bring Nika's guard down. Finally, Nika would give some honest answers as to why she was with Harold.

She walked into the guest room in her towel and opened her travel bag. Before digging in to find her clothing, she took a moment and looked around the room, which may not have been used since the last time she had been here. The queen bed's light blanket and floral sheets were tucked in with hospital corners, something her father would never have done and she suspected was also not a quality of Nika's. Only she herself was capable of such precision. A layer of dust rested atop everything, from the windowsill to the 1980's bedside clock. The only detail of the room that had changed since her last visit was the lack of family photos. Missing from the top of the chest of drawers was the framed eight-by-ten of Gloria's mother in her wedding dress, her eyes looking directly into the camera, and therefore, into the present day. Also missing was the photo of Gloria and Seth as children, sunburned and laughing, waiting in line for the Flying Horses carousel. A forgotten third child, an older girl with brown curly hair, had been in the photo as well, blurred and looking away from the camera. Gloria had fooled Seth for years that that girl in the photo was their long-lost sister Beatrice, older than Gloria by two years and crazy as the day is long. Dad wanted to keep her but Mom was afraid of her rage and sent her to an orphanage. This inevitably made Seth cry, and he would run to his mom and dad begging for the return of his oldest, misunderstood sibling.

Where were the photos now? Harold had obviously hidden them from Nika, but Gloria would have loved to track them down. Gloria's thoughts on the matter ceased when the jazz on the turntable in the living room stopped long enough for Gloria to hear Harold say, "I have not seen a movie since nineteen ninety-one."

Scott loved movies and was most certainly trying to convince the old man to see one later in the weekend.

"I believe it was that vomit bubble *Prince of Tides*. Almost made it to the closing credits, but did not." Gloria heard the bong gurgling after that.

The next song kicked in and the conversation disappeared again. She changed into flannel pajama bottoms, pulled her greying hair back into a ponytail, and donned one of Scott's white t-shirts. Before she opened the door to join the others, another sound rose above the music. It was the laughter of her father and Nika. Curious, she thought. What was Scott up to?

Her short walk into the main room was uneven thanks to the steady wine intake. She had to grab hold of the fridge for a moment to gather her composure. Her grip on the half-full glass was never compromised.

Gloria took in the scene. Scott held the bong in his hand. Smoke emanated from his nostrils. He was practically a puddle on the couch, his head in the cushions, using the "vital effects" container as a footrest. But he spoke loudly from his sloth. The others were sitting across from him, hanging on his every word.

"So this kid Sam was my nemesis, man" he slurred. "He made high school a living hell for me."

Harold inquired, "So he did more than sq-" He had to stop he was laughing so hard. "Squirt mayonnaise packets on you when you walked by?"

"Oh yeah. So then, sophomore year I think, me and Sam were put on a science project together, so he declares a truce and we got along. But I could tell he was dying to mess with me. But he stayed cool. Then along comes Halloween and I'm dressed up like a guy from the seventies, you know polyester patterned shirt, gold necklace, bell bottoms. It was like nineteen-eighty-four, so why did I think that was funny? It was practically still the seventies. Anyway, I decide I want chest hair to add to the costume. I grab a marker, walk over to Sam and say, 'Dude draw chest hair on me.' He does it and I walk down the hall at school showing off my chest to the girls, the teachers, everyone. Then I go into the bathroom and see that Sam hadn't drawn chest hair on me. He'd written 'I am a dick.'"

Nika spit out her beer. Harold was chortling. Gloria had heard this story ten times.

Harold turned to Gloria and said, "I love this man! At what Vienna salon or thinkers' round table did you find him?"

"I picked him up at a bar in Ditmas Park. I was drunk."

"Oof. You are not as clever a storyteller as your fiancé." Harold laughed anew at his own words.

Harold stood and began dancing to the music, buck naked and alone, the Band-Aid on his temple coming off and flapping as he hopped to the beat. The music stopped, another began, and Harold pointed to the stereo speakers, lecturing Scott over the music. "Yes! Yes! Music! Is it not heart-boggling? Minutes ago I put the needle on the record in a silent room. Suddenly another entity had arrived, swimming from the speakers. Sinuous and enchanting. Not individual instruments but a single entity, punching through the ether, filling the room, and rewiring our brains. Dammit does that beat everything!"

"That was a very spiritual statement," Scott commented. "Are you a religious man, sir?"

Harold went back to dancing as if not being addressed. "No," he responded tersely, vainly trying to reapply the Band-Aid to his temple while his legs continued to waltz.

Gloria sat down on the couch next to Scott. Nika was in the ripped vinyl Lay-Z-Boy and Gloria spotted her pack of menthol cigarettes on the armrest. Gloria hated menthols but any cigarettes would go well with cheap white wine.

"Can I bother you for one?" she asked Nika as she timidly pointed to the pack.

Nika's eyes opened and she looked at the cigarettes. "Help yourself," she replied and then closed her eyes again.

"Thank you so much." The cigarette was in her mouth in an instant and Nika's nondescript green lighter was put to work. Gloria was pleased because, she convinced herself, the little request of asking to share her cigarettes was a method of bringing Nika closer. It was not a nicotine craving that drove the request, although satiating the craving was a side benefit. Her act

76

was subtle Machiavellian maneuvering. It was social nanotechnology.

"Shed clothing. Shed government. Shed god." Harold was saying as he danced, his bare buttocks shaking with each footfall. "Those are the words I live by, Jim."

"Don't forget 'shed family,'" Gloria said as she exhaled smoke.

Harold did not stop dancing as he said, "Zing noted! Well executed, Glor." He unexpectedly stepped outside onto the deck.

Gloria was hit with a wave of guilt that had managed to wend its way through her drunken haze. She was convinced she had drawn blood, but now came the inevitable urge to apologize. It was not in her nature to hurt people; at least, that was her belief *after* she hurt people. She got up and walked outside, leaving Scott and Nika to bob their heads in unison to Duke Ellington.

Her father was not moping, licking his wounds after the 'shed family' comment. He was urinating off the side of the deck and blissfully whistling along with the music coming from inside. Seagrass was just visible in the light emanating from the house, but water in the atmosphere obscured the distant ocean waves.

"She's young, Dad" Gloria said.

"Yes!" responded Harold enthusiastically.

"How old?"

"Twentyyyyyy," he thought about it as he spoke. "Five. Twenty-five."

"You know that I'm forty-seven, right?"

"So?"

"So your daughter is almost twice her age."

Still facing away from her, he looked over his shoulder. "What does your age have to do with anything? I find her beautiful and smart and, as the kids say, cool."

"They don't say that."

"Does the farmer consult the age of his family when deciding when to harvest the corn?"

"That analogy is disturbing. She's not corn to be harvested. And anyway, I think your priorities are messed up."

Harold turned to her. "What priorities do you mean?"

The glass of wine in her hand screamed for her attention, and so she swallowed it down hard before speaking. "A man your age is only with a woman her age for one thing. Do I need to spell it out?"

"That must have worked well for you in your events planning job."

"What must have worked for me?"

"Omniscience. The ability to see the intentions of others. It must make any vocation simple. And I am sure it will help you find a new job as well. Erase all other items from your curriculum vitae and replace them with 'Omniscience.'"

"Fine dad. You're with Nika for the deep talks."

The two of them returned inside together. Scott was looking around with eyes bulging as if the marijuana had just delivered him to a destination he had not intended to visit. "I'm going to bed," he said to Gloria, kissing her on the lips and standing up very slowly.

"Not yet" Gloria responded. Scott grunted loudly. She held Scott's hand. "Dad, Scott and I want to know if we could go to Nantucket tomorrow for the day and leave Logan with you."

Harold did not stop dancing and said, "Follow your bliss, young lovers."

Clapping seemed to Gloria like an odd response to Harold's approval, but she was inebriated and could not help herself.

Scott's eyes were closed but he was standing. "Mr. Gomberg," he said, "Are you sure you haven't confused 'libertarian' with 'libertine?'"

Harold stopped dancing. He stared down the young man and then spoke with excessive enunciation. "What exactly do you mean by that, sir?"

Scott's head was down and he was rocking slightly. "Well, I mean you're naked and talking about following bliss and you smoke a lot of weed and you're dating a young girl..."

"Woman," Nika interrupted, eyes fixed on Scott.

Harold crossed the room slowly and came so close to Scott that their feet touched. If Harold had intended to intimidate Scott, he had failed because Scott had no idea Harold was even in front of him. Eyes still closed, Scott turned and walked into the kitchen area where earlier Harold had baked cauliflower with olive oil, salt, and pepper. Scott ate them like they were from a candy store. The others watched while he picked and picked from the ceramic bowl on the counter until all of them were gone. "Good night," he said to everyone and walked to the threshold of the guest room.

"Just one moment." Harold called out to him. Scott turned to face him but was smiling with his eyes closed. He was still chewing on cauliflower. Harold proceeded. "My nudity has nothing to do with sexuality. In fact, it is quite the opposite. When perverts call up women in the middle of the night, what is the first question they inevitably ask?"

Scott asked, "Do you have any juice?"

Harold replied "No. They ask 'What are you wearing?' You see? The most immediate question that will rile the loins of a sexual goblin is a description of a woman's sartorial preferences. Men and women alike have been dressing themselves in their sexual identity for years. Not I, sir. Nudity liberates me from such overly neurotic kabuki."

"Do you have any juice?" Scott asked again.

Harold replied, "Top shelf of the fridge door. Another thing. Do you know what my wife did for a living?"

"No I do not," Nika said loudly from across the room, trying to be heard over the music.

Harold continued. "She was a voice actor. She voiced radio commercials. Television commercials. Cartoons. You name it. I *heard* her before I *met* her, and it was her voice that did me in. What she wore or did not wear was irrelevant. The sound of her voice could turn rivers, land clouds, or peel the crust from the Earth. Whatever she needed it to do. The sound of her. Oh, the sound of her." He paused and was gone for a moment, looking somewhere nondescript beyond Scott's shoulder. Then he returned. "I am no libertine, sir. Some might even call me a prude."

"Nude prude!" Nika blurted. Then she laughed at her own joke and took another drag of her menthol.

Harold continued. "Nudity frees me from sexuality, but that is only part of it. My nudity is a flag."

"It is good flag because it does not come close to touching ground." Nika added.

"It is a flag that yells 'Don't tread on me.' I have shed my cotton shackles, and all other shackles now follow… religion, government, everything. When people see me in my comprehensiveness, they will understand."

"I told you," Nika said through exhaled smoke, "They will see naked old man. Unless you tattoo that bullshit onto your belly, no one will know."

Harold ignored her and continued speaking to Scott. "But I will forgive you this one transgression. Go to bed and let us make peace in the morning."

Scott was drinking his juice on the way to the guest bedroom. He gave the thumbs up and closed the door behind him.

Harold turned to Gloria, who was making every effort to control her facial expressions, hiding the fact she was internally celebrating the rift.

"I like him," Harold said, removing Duke Ellington from the turntable and replacing it with Stan Getz. The needle contacted the exceptionally scratchy record and music again held sway. "He seems nice and intelligent."

Gloria was back to disgusted. She changed the subject. "So, Nika, where are you originally from?" She had trouble enunciating this due to her wine buzz. She also had trouble making eye contact with her conversational partner.

Nika answered, "Town called Perm. Near Urals. You have heard of Tchaikovsky? He is from Perm. My father worked in factory there."

"What kind of factory?"

"Russia builds many of weapons in that part of country, far from border, deep inside, to keep factories safe from attack. My father always told me since I was little girl that he made bicycles." Nika took a drag, stubbed out her cigarette, and exhaled. "For years I did not know what my father made in factory, but I was pretty sure it did not have a bell on it. It turn out to be particle accelerator. My father is one of only people on

81

planet to be struck by particle accelerator beam in the face and live. My father is hard person. There is no bullshit in him. He raise a hard person in me. Not even laser can kill us!"

"And what brought you to the United States?" Gloria asked.

"Camp counselor. Young women from Russia can get jobs in America working as camp counselors. I took one on Martha's Vineyard working with special needs children, until head counselor touched my breast saying he had 'special needs.' I punched him in throat and his –what is called – windpipe collapsed. I took him to hospital myself. Now he has special needs."

"That's terrible," Gloria said as cigarette smoke caused her to squint. So now what?"

"Now I am marrying your father." Nika looked over at Harold and a sinister smile crossed her face. "Look, Harold. Our daughter is all growing up. Was it yesterday she was little girl?"

Gloria took this in stride. She had to. The annoying imp was her only source of cigarettes. She laughed instead. Gently taking hold of Nika's arm, Gloria said, "Join me out on the deck." Without looking over at her father, she addressed him. "Dad, I'm stealing your Nika for a minute. We're gonna go talk girl talk."

Harold, who was reaching into the "vital effects" container again, simply said "Have at it."

Gloria got up, pulling ever so slightly on Nika's arm as she did so. With great reluctance, the young woman rose and followed Gloria into the evening, wet and stagnant.

She had planned on getting out there and going right into a delightful anecdote, but Gloria could not control herself. When they were out of earshot of her father, Gloria asked, "Why?"

"Why. Why what?" Nika asked.

"Why are you with my father?"

"Because when he makes love, he does it with urgency as if Death itself is knocking at bedroom door."

Gloria covered her ears. "Stop stop stop! Jesus Christ."

Nika laughed and wiped drizzle from her head. "I joke. Why do you care why I am with your father? It is not for you to care about."

"It is every bit my concern. Look, if it's money you want, I don't know what he's told you, but I'm pretty sure there's little of it left. He has some from my mother but as far as I know he isn't making any more."

"I don't give a fuck about money."

"Then what? You're marrying him so you can stay in the States?"

"No. I stay in the States so I can I marry him."

Gloria was not sure what to say. It probably would not be a good time to ask for a cigarette but she wanted one badly.

Nika looked at Gloria and asked "Have you ever heard of Bechdel test?"

"No."

Nika took out a cigarette, put it in her mouth but did not light it. "Look it up," she mumbled. "If we were in movie, we would have just failed it. I blame you. Congratulations."

When the two women returned to the main room, there was a man sitting where Nika had been. Harold was paying him no mind, selecting records from a high shelf. The man was looking down, rummaging through a purple backpack. Gloria stared at the top of his entirely bald, tanned head. He wore a doctor's coat and appeared to be in his late forties. Even without seeing his face, this man gave off the air of someone who had been to a place none of the others had been.

"Hello, handsome," Nika said to him.

The man looked up, exposing wireframe glasses and bushy black eyebrows. "Hey," he said, standing up to hug the young woman before him. He did not acknowledge Gloria and sat back down to resume his search through the backpack.

"Hi," Gloria said with great enthusiasm. There was no response. She continued, "I'm Gloria Gomberg." Nothing. "Harold's daughter."

Finally, a "Hey" but it was followed by "you got a flashlight, Harold? Oh never mind." He pulled a sandwich bag out of the backpack. It was full of a dark brown clay.

Harold looked over and smiled. "Capital!" he blurted. As he walked over to inspect the bag, he said "Gloria, I'd like you to meet Amos Adams. Friend. Island doctor. Weed dealer. And now branching out into hash!" Harold grabbed the plastic bag and squeezed the contents as if that move could gauge its quality. Perhaps it could for all Gloria knew.

"Nice to meet you" Gloria said even though it was not nice at all.

Adams put up his hand as a form of salutation but was more focused on pulling a pipe out of his pocket.

"Are you a government hater like my father?"

"I'm Wampanoag," he said. "You tell me what I think of the federal government." Amos looked at Harold.

Harold corrected him. "Half Wampanoag."

Amos retaliated. "That's a white man's distinction." He packed the pipe with precision and gentle movements. "You see the new façade they put on the movie theater? Lotta money spent to make something look bad."

"Agreed," Harold said. "Peach color! Like this is Miami."

"Plus they finished the work right before a huge storm. That's unfortunate." Amos took a drag off of a joint he had just rolled.

"What storm?" Harold asked.

Before Amos could answer Harold's question, Gloria stepped in. "What type of medicine do you pract-"

Then a third conversation was proposed by Nika. "Tell Gloria how you men met. I love this story."

Harold smiled at this request and launched in. "I was drinking at the Black Goose Grill in Oak Bluffs a few years back when this guy comes in. He struts in like a big deal and I did not cotton to that at all."

"Do you hear that, Amos?" Nika asks. "You are big deal."

Harold continued. "The bartender, you know Alex, leans over and tells me this bald guy drinking some imported IPA in a sleeveless fleece is the new doctor on the island. I sidle over and offer to buy the new gentleman a cocktail. 'Hail new fellow well met,' I say to him.' 'I'm not new' he says back. Well, he was new to me I tell him. Then I put my hand on his bald head and say to Alex 'Another beer for Chemo here.'"

Gloria's face contorts as if she smelled something foul. "That's a terrible thing to call someone." She slapped her father's arm in a way she would do only if she were drunk.

"It gets worse," Amos said, now listening with a slight grin on his face.

"This is the best," Nika said.

Harold continued. "So I keep working him over. I had a beard at the time you might recall and I offered to shave it off and glue it to his head. I told him he might fit in better. Amos says again – this time with a little anger in his voice – probably because I called him Chemo – he says 'I'm not new. I grew up in the Wampanoag tribe and only left to go to medical school. I just got back.' And by the way, he has not made eye contact with me yet. And I say to Alex, 'Where's that drink for Chemo?' and then I turn back to Amos and I say, 'Actually, given your heritage, I am going to call you Chemosabe.' With that he finally looked at me, lifted himself out of his chair," Harold raised his shoulders and arms, suggesting a monstrous form rising, "reaching his full height of six foot five, glared down into my eyes, smiled, and-"

Nika interrupted "-and pulled Harold's fucking beard out. I love that story!"

Gloria did not smile.

Harold continued. "Not the whole beard, mind you, but a sizable chunk! So much for the Hippocratic Oath. Needless to say, I never called him Chemosabe again. And I shaved off my beard. Would you deny any of this, Amos?"

"No," Amos said as he pressed the hash down into the pipe.

Harold had some realization that made his eyes widen. "Oh, Gloria! That reminds me. Amos never, ever, ever, lies. Ever!"

"No!" Gloria slurred. "That is so, so interesting. Is that, like, part of Wampanoag culture?"

Amos looked at her in a way that concerned Gloria. He was smiling, but it was a smile that seemed to signal a deeper yen for aggression. He said, "I love white liberal crypto-racism. It's always swaddled in false respect. No, it is not part of Wampanoag culture. It's part of Amos Andrews culture. I cheated on my wife repeatedly, lying to her day after day about still being faithful to her. When she finally left me, I swore I would never lie again. And I haven't."

"Try him out," Harold said.

Gloria had stopped drinking for enough time to be tired. Despite exhaustion and disliking this man who sold drugs to her father, the buzz won out and she decided to play along.

"Did you ever cheat on a test?" Gloria asked.

"No."

She rolled her eyes. "Well this is no fun. Are you just going to expose that you're a goody-goody?"

"No."

Harold stepped in. "What is the worst place you've ever slept?"

"In a warehouse. In my underwear. Covered in mud. I had crossed an inlet drunk at low tide and passed out in the first structure I could find."

"What is your favorite song?"

"'Hollywood Nights' by Bob Seger."

"Jesus," Harold responded. "Maybe the truth is not an ideal goal. Have you ever been arrested?"

"Yes." Amos was taking a drag from his pipe while he did this.

Harold continued his line of questioning. "For what?"

"Got caught trying to pass a fake ID when I was a kid. Was in the jail cell in Edgartown for the night waiting for my dad to go my bail."

"'Go my bail.' Who are you Johnny Cash?"

"No."

"That was a rhetorical question. Did you ever try to fondle an anesthetized patient?"

"Was that a rhetorical question too?" Amos asked.

"No."

"Then no."

Gloria barged in. "Does my dad annoy you?"

87

"Yes. Pretty regularly."

Harold laughed at this. "But am I your favorite customer?"

"Yup."

"And do I play a mean game of poker?"

"Yup."

"And chess?"

"Yup."

"Do I prepare the meanest gravlax outside of Scandinavia?"

"Yup."

"What do I owe you for the hash?"

"On the house for last week's gravlax."

Harold smiled. "A gentleman and a scholar. And a doctor. And a dealer."

The buzz won out yet again and Gloria asked Amos, "Do you find me attractive?" She heard the words come out of her mouth and knew she had had too much to drink.

There was silence for a moment and then Nika laughed heartily and said, "You prostitute!"

"Just testing his limits," Gloria slurred, unfazed by the insult.

Amos looked directly at her. "I thought we were done playing this game. But if you must know, yes."

"What about me?"

"You don't dye your hair and keep it long. It's bold and sexy. Plus, you have amazing eyes."

Gloria looked away in embarrassment. Her eyes were amazing, she knew. She would have basked in the moment more but she also felt herself falling asleep standing up.

Harold ran to Nika and held her closely, asking in a caricatured, throaty female voice, "Do you find *me* attractive, lover?"

Nika responded, "Your chest does not exist and your ass is like white sheet hanging from clothesline."

Harold recoiled. "That is why I am marrying you, Nika. You are a female Amos!"

At that moment, Scott came barreling out of the guest bedroom with a look of terror on his face. His eyes were bloodshot and his pupils were dilated. Sweat was visible on his forehead. His hands were flapping up and down, as if he was trying to push down the air in front of him. Logan the dog, asleep this whole time, raised up and barked at his master.

"Mom! Mom? Where are you?" Scott cried.

"Whoa," Harold whispered.

"What the fuck?" Nika asked.

Scott continued, looking around desperately. "Mom? I don't see you."

Gloria walked over to him and touched his face gently with her hand. He startled and looked at her. "It's okay," Gloria said. "Let's go back to bed. You're having a bad dream."

"I what?"

"You're okay."

"Mom?"

"No."

Logan stopped barking.

Gloria turned Scott around and began guiding him as best she could in her condition. He seemed to calm down and soon he was walking on his own back to the bedroom. Gloria turned to the others in the room.

She said, "He has these pretty regularly. I'm sure the weed didn't help."

Harold looked confused. He said, "I did not know."

"It's okay, Dad. Not your fault. I'm gonna turn in. Good night."

Harold put his hand halfway up in a lazy salutation. The bandage on his head finally fell off. Amos and Nika just looked on, unblinking. Gloria turned and walked into the guestroom with Scott.

She brushed her teeth, took four aspirin with a large glass of water, and slipped under the sheets next to Scott. Logan jumped up onto the bed and situated himself at Gloria's feet like he always did. Gloria was repulsed by her own stink. Cigarettes and wine seemed to suffuse from every pore. Burrowing her face into Scott's hair and neck helped mask her own funk. But then Scott mumbled "You stink" into his pillow and so she turned over.

She did stink. The evidence was all around her.

That night, Gloria dreamed that the ocean outside rose and took the house off of its stilts. Now floating far from shore in their makeshift boat, she was filled with panic. The only comfort was that she was not alone in the floating house. Harold, Logan, Gloria's mother, Bob Seger, and Barbra Streisand also looked out the window for land. Bob Seger was singing "Turn the Page" while staring at the mountainous swells that threatened to overturn and pulverize the shelter around them. Then the storm subsided and the sun came out. The horizon outside was flat in all directions. Stable earth was nowhere to be found.

Friday

Chapter Six

The day of the first disaster dawned magnificently. A red sunrise cast its light on the bed and woke Gloria from her fitful sleep. Scott was gone, out for an early run, no doubt, but Logan had taken his place next to her. She put her hands through the dog's coat and basked in the absence of an alarm. Her phone remained in her bag as planned. Connections with the outside world – email, texts, news, social media – were not going to disrupt this weekend and especially not this heavenly moment.

When the peace had run its course and her mind became too active, Gloria rose slowly with much stretching and yawning. Her head did not hurt. Last night's aspirin and water seemed to have worked. Logan hopped out of bed with her.

When she walked into the main room she was greeted by the smell of coffee and stale smoke, and the sight of Amos sleeping in the exact same spot he had been in last night. He was still in a sitting position with his head back, eyes closed, and deep snores sporadically coming from his head. Gloria could hear his phone or pager buzzing away in his pocket. Just some kid's appendix erupting, she thought.

She poured herself some coffee and walked out onto the deck. The ocean was exceptionally turbulent, but otherwise the day was idyllic. A warm breeze played with her hair and seagulls flew low over the sea grass. She could see a speck far to the east that was likely Scott. Waving would not work at this distance. Much closer, she saw Dick, her father's neighbor, moving slowly down the beach with his metal detector, sweeping the sand in front of him. He looked down at the equipment's readings. When he did look up for a moment, perhaps to get his bearings, their eyes met and Gloria waved. Dick waved back, but with little enthusiasm. What did she expect? She was the daughter of the enemy.

Unlike yesterday, Gloria felt full of optimism and excitement. The sparkling weather paired with the pending trip to Nantucket was enough to lift her spirits. Even though she was mortified each time her mind returned to the questions she had asked Amos, she had the excuse of having been drunk.

What truly surprised her was the fact that she had lost her hard-won sobriety yet remorse did not plague her. The only explanation she could think of was that when faced with her father, alcohol was the only option. She simply had no choice in the matter.

Gloria showered and got dressed for the day. Her eyes glanced one time at the bureau top where the family pictures were still absent, and then she moved to the main room to pack a lunch for the day. Scott returned, kissed her with his sweaty face and got washed up to go.

"Dad," Gloria whispered into her father's room. The shades were drawn. He was face down on the bed, nude in the darkness, Nika snoring next to him wearing an expansive white t-shirt that read "New Orleans Jazz Fest 2005."

"Dad," she whispered again.

"Ungh," Harold said into the pillow.

"We're leaving. We'll be back tonight. Please remember to feed and walk Logan. And please, please, please remember to put Logan on his leash before you walk him."

"Ungh," Harold said again.

The small Hy-Line cruise ship rolled with the brutal churning of the sea. The sun beat down and a light breeze blew, but it was hard to appreciate these delights when struggling for balance. After a time, Gloria and Scott gave up and took a seat inside, among the cushioned passenger seats. Gloria hated the inside seats. Sitting in them felt like traveling by bus.

Despite the turbulent rocking, the two of them chatted, read David Sedaris to each other, and laughed enough to disturb others around them. If the captain were to turn the boat around now, Gloria would have had few regrets. She was truly experiencing a moment of joy. It was not even the kind of self-aware joy one might have. There was no thought like "we are having a moment of joy." It was experienced pre-consciously and fully.

About halfway through the journey, Scott rose to buy an iced coffee at the snack bar. Upon his return to the seats, the ship pitched hard and he almost fell over. About a quarter of his iced coffee wound up on the floor. Scott uttered an intense "dang it" and viewed his clothing for any sign of staining. There was none. A ship employee with a bushy mustache strode by at that moment, his walkie-talkie blaring indecipherable nonsense.

"Excuse me," Scott asked.

The seaman stopped and silenced his radio.

"Is this normal? These waves?"

Gloria was not sure why Scott had asked that question as she could have answered it for him, and she was pretty sure he could have answered it for himself. No, it was not normal.

"Beatrice," was all the man said.

"I'm sorry. What?" Scott asked.

Before the man could answer, the ship pitched again. Scott stumbled, slipped in the puddle of iced coffee, and went down fast. He hit the ground hard, the remainder of his coffee erupting overhead before drenching him. "Ooh jeez," the seaman said. A crowd gathered around Scott but many of them quickly dispersed because no one could stay standing due to the sea's chop. Gloria and the seaman tried to help him up, but Scott winced on the way to his feet. He complained that his neck hurt terribly. He could not move it. The remaining bystanders helped lower him into a seat as slowly as possible.

"What's your name?" Scott asked the Hy-Line employee.

"Lance," the man replied.

"I think I'm gonna need an ambulance in Nantucket, Lance."

The ferry employee wasted no time. He was on his walkie-talkie speaking to distant, static-voiced people who would prepare medical services for Scott.

Gloria could not hold her fiancé to comfort him because even the slightest touch caused him to grit his teeth and groan. Instead she simply sat next to him and whispered, "It's okay" repeatedly. Deep down, she had no idea if the situation was 'okay,' but what else was there to say? Scott explained to her that he had jerked his neck upward when he fell to avoid hitting his head on the floor. He had made an instinctual, utilitarian decision: Submit to a neck injury to avoid a head injury.

Gloria was not listening to him. She was drowning in her own disappointment about the disintegration of the day's plans. Of course it was selfish, she thought, but the pain of that thought was real to her. Moments earlier, she had thought an early return home would have left her with few regrets. Now she knew that was a self-inflicted lie.

Upon making landfall, Scott was escorted off the boat by a host of kindly tourists and ship employees. EMT workers took over on the dock and placed him in the ambulance. Gloria walked beside the escorts, feeling disdain toward the gawkers on line to board the ship. She knew in her gut that they were innocent, but she wanted each of these winter-pale mouth-breathers dead.

As they rode in the ambulance the short distance to the Nantucket Cottage Hospital, Gloria had a strong urge to post her disappointment on social media, but refrained, deciding to keep her promise to Scott and stay off the phone throughout the weekend. The vacation seemed less glorious than before, but it was still a vacation and it was not over.

Doctor Marcantonio was about ten years younger than Scott and Gloria, squat with an aggressively full head of black hair. He was pale for a man who lived on an island getaway. The doctor explained that in response to the fall, Scott's neck had "Hulked out." Reflexes kicked in, adrenaline spurted, and Scott pulled his neck with unusual power. In short, Scott had whiplash. He was to rest at the hospital a bit longer while they affixed him with a neck brace that he was to wear for three weeks.

"Hey," the doctor said with a smile, "At least your head didn't hit the floor. You would've been out like a light. Maybe dead." A few minutes later, Gloria saw Dr. Marcantonio outside of the window, vaping and staring at women's rear ends as they passed.

Gloria was no longer sad. She dug into her optimism reserves, went out shopping, and returned with pizza and wine. "May as well take advantage of being off the wagon," she exclaimed as she entered the room. Scott was displeased.

"C'mon. You slipped last night, but it's time to get back on the wagon."

"When we go home, I swear," she replied.

He was stuck in bed and clearly had no control over the situation, so he went with it.

They ate pizza and slowly loosened up. She got him laughing ("It hurts!" he complained at the slightest chortle), and he had her howling with his flat delivery brought on by injury. After a long, satisfying conversation about everything and nothing, they grew quiet, held hands, and watched the wall-mounted TV. The remote did not work so they tolerated *Days of Our Lives*.

Gloria basked in the moment. She was having quality time with Scott on Nantucket. That was all she had wanted from the excursion. She looked at Scott watching the television and thought about the many variations of love. In college, she had been deeply in love with a DJ at the school's radio station named Phil Bergeron. Phil was a gaunt malcontent with unkempt red hair that looked like a grease fire. He had the kind of skinny build that concerned mothers who thought he was on drugs. He smelled of clove cigarettes at eight in the morning on his way to class. Phil and Gloria had spent every waking hour together. He sang in a band called Collect All Four (there were three people in the group), and whenever they played at one of the downtown clubs soaked in stale beer and sutured with band stickers, Gloria was up front singing along, even skipping gigs with her own short-lived band to be there. That was part of the reason the band was short-lived. Phil and Gloria's relationship was mostly fueled by alcohol. But it did not matter. Regardless of whether she was throwing a French textbook at his head or making out with him in the back of a Safe Rides car, she loved him deeply. The quality of that love was different from what she had now. When Phil was not near her, her stomach hurt like she was hungry. When they were on the outs, she felt like she could not function in public. She would smoke cigarettes in her dorm room, drink cans of Coors Light, and read back issues of *People*. And when he finally cheated on Gloria while back home in Jericho, Vermont for the summer, she died for at least a year. She stayed in bed and only got up to put on a hairnet and work at the deli. The hairnet was perfect because it desexualized her, which made sense to Gloria in light of her recent soul-death. A corpse should not be attractive to anyone. That was her first run-in with love.

Now she was going through her second run-in, and she hardly recognized it. Scott's physical absence or presence did not wrench her stomach. He did not control her spirit like the moon on the tides. And this was good, Gloria explained to herself. This is the new love. Older, sober, more mature. Phil was a boy; Scott is a man. And the love she felt for him was refined and mature.

Gloria looked at Scott, looking at the television in silence, and knew she had chosen the right man.

The quiet was broken by Scott. "What did he do?" he asked.

"What did who do?"

"Your dad. What did he do for a living?"

"I've never told you that?"

"No. From your descriptions, he's been the way I saw him this weekend his entire life. All I got from him was one snippet about trading insurance policies or something."

"The better question is what didn't he do for a living. Mom's money gave him too much freedom to change his mind, which he did every five minutes." Gloria ate a bite of cold pepperoni pizza before continuing. A long strand of dried out cheese hung down her chin. "And even before meeting Mom, he wasn't able to decide. In the first year out of college, he was a poet, then a lyricist, then a shoe salesman, then a car salesman. The real world just slapped the hippie right out of him." She took

Scott's slice, cut off a piece, and served it to him. "Some friend of his from Princeton, a guy who had been a lot more successful, got Dad a job at some ad agency in the city. Dad did copy. That was the longest he stayed at a job, I think. Like seventeen years. While we were all growing up. He met Mom at that firm."

"She worked there?"

"Sort of. She was a voice talent who was selected to read his copy for a shampoo ad. 'I fell in love with her voice.' Remember him saying that last night? He married her almost instantly. I was born a year later."

"So that was sixty-eight he married her?"

"Right. But then the shit started going down with him while I was in high school. He started descending into the lower circles of hell. Must have been hot because it was also around then he started taking his clothes off." She tore off another bite of pizza. "He became a radio consultant, which seems to me like a total betrayal for a man who has loved music deeply since childhood. That lasted about, I want to say, two years? Then, get this. He was sick of reporting to someone else so he decided to go into business for himself. He took a chunk of my mom's money and bought a bunch of shit houses in the worst part of South Norwalk. He rented them out but barely lifted a finger to make repairs. Total slum lord. He made some money but I guess it wasn't enough."

Scott was fading. Gloria knew his drowsiness had nothing to do with the lunch of heavy pizza, nor with the meds. It was caused by her speaking *at* him as opposed to *with* him. She continued speaking regardless. "I have no idea what happened while I was at college, but my dad was starting to crash and burn. Taking progressively more desperate, unsavory jobs. I think the cops brought him home once for hanging out naked at the beach.

Then that asshole friend of his from college came back on the scene. He was making a mint doing truly evil work. That insurance thing. He was an investor who bought life insurance policies from people dying of AIDS. They would then sell the policies at a profit to people who had families and needed them."

Scott's eyes were closed. She continued.

"Dad took a job with this ghoul's firm and pulled in a lot of money for a while. Mom called me every day, really worried about him. She felt he was going off of his rocker. I always liked talking with Mom so we would be on for hours, trying to figure him out. He had not been this sociopathic weirdo when I was a kid. Why was he like this now? Mom was always so honest with me. She scoured her brain for reasons and came up short. I was minoring in psychology at school, so I had a bunch of explanations, but none of them made perfect sense."

Scott's eyes were still closed and now his mouth was slightly open, his mind now undoubtedly blending her voice with his dream world.

"Anyway, people stopped dying of AIDS and the firm hemorrhaged money. They closed their doors. Dad was at home all day, every day, taking up his new hobby of becoming a libertarian asshole, answering the door for cops visiting for public indecency complaints, and generally driving Mom crazy." Gloria looked up at *The Days of Our Lives* where a woman was nervously aiming a gun at another woman's face. "That was when Dad made his last career change and hatched the plans for his cemetery."

Scott's eyes opened and he looked at her with his eyes only, being sure to keep his neck motionless. "His cemetery?" he asked.

Gloria remembered the moment she learned about the cemetery. It was easy to remember because it was the same moment her mother died. Other than the hospice nurse with a beautiful Caribbean accent, Gloria had been alone by her mother's side in her bedroom in Norwalk. Dad was nowhere to be found since the separation, and Seth was still traveling to be there. Rachel Gomberg had been silent for days since the stroke-induced embolism had hit, and she was slipping away in the same peaceful manner. Gloria was holding her mother's hand at three-twenty in the afternoon when the nurse explained that she was gone.

Roughly thirty seconds after the nurse's gentle words, her mother literally rose from the dead. She opened her eyes and sat bolt upright in bed, gasping and nearly crushing her daughter's hand. Gloria screamed. The nurse screamed.

Rachel Gomberg's eyes were wide. She took in deep, rasping breaths. Gloria had seen her mother sleepwalk and she was giving off that vibe now in whatever transitory world she inhabited.

"Not the cemetery," she pleaded with Gloria.

"What? What mom?" Gloria cried. She had heard her mother loud and clear but wanted to hear her speak again, maybe for the last time, no matter how pained her words sounded. The request could only be interpreted as a request not to die; not to be interred.

"Not that cemetery!" she croaked.

"*That* cemetery?" Gloria thought in a panic. The interpretation of her mom's last request now shifted.

The nurse said nothing. She simply looked on with her mouth agape.

Her mother's head dropped back down to the pillow, eyes wide open and unblinking.

The cicadas outside could be heard through the window and nothing else existed at that moment but that sound. Gloria let go of her mother's hand, stood, and walked directly over to the hospice nurse and hugged her.

Hours later, paperwork and call to her brother complete, Gloria had raced to her father's temporary condo situation in Stamford. She caught him as he was carrying a bag of groceries through the indoor garage, shirtless. She knocked the groceries out of his hands, and hit his bare chest over and over with her open hands, slapping sounds echoing through the cinderblock space.

"Where were you?" she cried.

"What are you-"

"I called you over and over."

"I disconnected my phone. I don't use it anymore."

"Mom's dead."

Harold sat down in the middle of the garage, surrounded by produce, hamburger meat, and two broken wine bottles. There was no sound for a time other than a family of pigeons cooing among the concrete crossbeams. Father and daughter looked at the floor and suffered independently.

When they had gathered the strength to move, Gloria helped pick up the scattered groceries and they moved up to his apartment. The place was a mess. It smelled of dirty laundry and bong water. Her father was naked within seconds of crossing the threshold and grabbing a baggie of weed from the back of a cupboard otherwise full of baking supplies. Gloria wasted no time finding a bottle of red wine and pouring two glasses.

Without being asked, Harold offered, "I said my goodbyes to her, you know. Earlier. In my own way. Trust me."

"I don't care." Gloria replied. "I needed you there with me. It was very hard alone. Seth's not here yet. You weren't there. I was alone."

"I am sure you did great."

"I was not in a dance contest, Dad. I was watching my mother die. I needed you there."

"There was no way I could have known. I have purged my phones. I could not take the nagging anymore."

When Gloria realized that no apology was forthcoming, she changed the subject.

"Dad, Mom did a weird thing at the end. She kind of, well, she came back to life for a minute. It was like she had to get something urgent off her chest and fought off death for a second to make sure she did. She sat up. The hospice lady nearly passed out. And Mom looked at me with the biggest eyes I had ever seen on her and she said, 'Not that cemetery.' Do you have any idea what she meant?"

Harold looked disappointed. "Yes. I am working on a business venture. It is truly ingenious but clearly it went over your mother's head. I planned to tell you about it when it was a done deal. Of course the local government is putting up roadblocks left and right, but it will be done."

Gloria did not like the sound of this. She pulled a cigarette out of her pocket.

Harold continued. "Cemeteries are mostly wasted space above ground. Grass and stone. Nothing more. Meanwhile, another problem exists. You have lost all connection with your loved one who is now below the ground. This does not have to be the case."

"Coffins above ground? It's called a mausoleum. It's been done," Gloria said, nauseated by the idea.

"Better. More poetic. More lovely." He stood up and began pacing the room. "A vegetable garden, each plot planted by the loved ones of the deceased. The plot soil now produces food that they can enjoy, thereby re-establishing a connection between living and dead."

Gloria was overwhelmed, not necessarily because it was a good idea, but because the still-fresh loss of her mother made her desperate to believe that a connection with the dead could be maintained. She started to cry.

Harold was patting her on the back then, saying, "It will be okay" like a robot trying to simulate human warmth. At the moment of physical contact with her father, Gloria began to realize the nauseating problem with the cemetery idea. She looked over her shoulder at her father with wet, bloodshot eyes.

"That is revolting," she said.

"You have seen me naked eight million times."

"The cemetery."

"What? Why? It is elegant, and it is going to put your brother's four sons through college, about ten times over. I envision a franchise!"

"Dad, who is going to eat food planted in a garden that has a rotting body under it?"

"It is not just any body. It is your friend or family member."

"I don't care whose body it is. They're all made of the same materials and I'm sure they pollute in the same way."

"I am so glad to hear that my daughter has the same point of view as the Norwalk Planning and Zoning Committee."

"It's good to know the Norwalk Planning and Zoning Committee is doing their job."

They stared each other down.

"I did say my goodbyes, Gloria. I really did."

With that she gulped the remainder of her wine, put out the cigarette, stood and walked to the door. Her throat burned from crying.

Before she left, she turned to him and said, "I would hug you. I need one. And I have to believe that you need one too. But it's very awkward with you naked."

No offer to put clothes on arrived. Harold had moved on to rolling a joint. She walked out the door and cried openly in the hallway for the loss of both of her parents.

Gloria looked at Scott, who was now very awake and rapt. "That was his last job, if you want to call it that. The fall from decent family man was complete. It's been seventeen years since he first hatched that scheme, and he's still waiting for Norwalk to grant him the land."

"I don't know. I see something interesting in the cemetery idea."

Gloria was about to lace into Scott when Dr. Marcantonio entered the room, stinking from a late lunch that had involved an improbable amount of garlic. He said that Scott was good to leave, but first he told them about the proper care and maintenance of Scott's neck; choice of pain relievers, how to wash it, and which activities to avoid. Scott groaned at the news that the brace would have to stay on for three weeks.

"Take it off earlier if you want," Dr. Marcantonio said. "It's for your comfort. Your head won't fall off."

After the wheelchair ride out of the hospital, but before a quick taxi ride to the ship, the two vacationers decided that they had to at least share a bowl of New England clam chowder. Gloria eased Scott across the street and into a booth at a local fried seafood place. She spooned soup into his mouth and they enjoyed themselves thoroughly. Scott kept begging Gloria not to make him laugh as she imitated a mother feeding her baby; the old 'Here comes the airplane for a landing' gag.

The boat ride back to Martha's Vineyard was even more hazardous than the earlier ride out. They did not budge from their seats the whole way, and Gloria accepted help from others getting Scott on and off. A seasick woman in a yellow cable sweater and blue jeans vomited in her own lap. Clouds were piling up again as they pulled into the harbor at Oak Bluffs. They seemed darker than the previous day, and they moved across the sky from east to west with startling momentum.

They got a taxi in Oak Bluffs and arrived at Harold's house at sunset, or what would have been sunset had the sky been clear. Everything was a dark orange and nothing moved. Seagulls had no comment on the matter. Gloria heard her father's ancient Camry clicking, which it did for almost an hour after running. She also noticed that he had not turned the lights on in the house yet. The fool was lumbering around in the dark.

It took what seemed like ten minutes to get Scott from the taxi to the top of her father's outer staircase. "I feel like we're Brad and Janet right now walking up to the castle."

"Who?" Scott asked, clearly struggling through the pain.

"*Rocky Horror*? Never mind."

107

Gloria walked in first, fully prepared to deflect the excited Logan from jumping on his master. But the bounding did not come. Harold sat in the dim room petting Logan on the couch. Nika was in the kitchen area cutting onions and melting butter in a skillet. No music was playing. Harold was breathing heavily, but smiling.

"Hello?" Gloria said.

"Hey," Harold replied. Gloria found this an unusually informal salutation from her father.

"I see you've made friends with Logan," Gloria added. They had had pets growing up, but Harold had never shown any kindness toward them. They had been almost entirely ignored, and when forced to walk their dog, Otto, Harold would never pick up the poop. He would simply walk in front of the houses of neighbors he detested, which included pretty much everyone, and wait for the dog to dispense karma.

Scott entered the room, slowly, carefully, holding the wall as he moved. Harold was on the brink of asking what had happened, and Gloria was on the brink of saying, 'I would have called to tell you but you have no phone' when Logan began growling. The dog raised up on his front legs. He bared his teeth. Drool dangled from his lower jaw. He was looking directly at Scott. The growling was apparently loud enough for Nika to hear it over the sizzle of the sliced onions she had just thrown in the skillet because she stopped what she was doing and looked for the source of the sound.

Scott looked back at his dog. It was not fear that registered in his eyes. It was confusion. "Logan? Why-"

The Rottweiler jumped from his place next to Harold and was across the room in what seemed like less than a second, fully extending his body to lift himself into the air and knock his

108

master to the floor. Scott let out a howl, perhaps from the pain of his neck being forced into motion or from teeth snapping closed on his flesh. Gloria could not see the dog's head from where she stood. She ran to another location for a clearer view but was sure not to move any closer to the conflict. Harold was also skirting the perimeter.

The dog was struggling with something. The neck brace. He was trying to snap his mouth shut on Scott's throat but the brace would not permit it. He moved to one of Scott's arms and his teeth sunk in. Scott screamed fully, the sound of it modified by saliva bubbles popping in the back of his mouth. The first specks of blood appeared on the floor. Where the dog was biting and snapping his head back and forth, Gloria caught glimpses of exposed bone.

For the briefest moment, Gloria locked eyes with the dog. His features—pupils dilated, teeth bared, nostrils opening and closing—all sang to her in harmony the words "I have never been more alive." Gloria saw many other things in those eyes, all of which she wished she did not. Worst of these was partnership.

Scott was bringing his free hand down on the dog's neck to no avail. The Gombergs, father and daughter, simply looked on as the dog released his grasp on the arm and made for the neck again. When he found that his teeth slid harmlessly off of the plastic over and over again, the dog swiveled his head around and caught Scott's punching hand in his mouth. Scott screamed again.

"What are you doing?" Scott asked the air in a cracking voice. It did not seem to Gloria that the question was aimed at the dog, but rather at her. And Gloria did not have an answer.

No more than twenty seconds had passed since Logan had leapt off of the sofa. Perhaps realizing that the Gombergs were of no use, it was Nika who finally acted. She ran from the kitchen area, wielding the sizzling pan of onions. She yelled something terse in Russian, checked Gloria out of the way with her shoulder, and brought the smoking skillet down hard on the dog's haunches.

Logan cried and ran top speed out of the door that had been left open after the couple's entry.

Scott emitted a drawn-out, pained "Owwww." When he ran out of breath, he started again. And again. It was the only sound in the room save the drizzle that had started again outside the open front door.

Only then did Gloria approach. She got down on one knee and held his cheek. "Take it easy. Deep breaths. I'm going to find my phone and call 9-1-1." She then turned to Nika. "Close the door. I don't want Logan coming back in here."

Scott mumbled something through lips that bled from a self-inflicted bite upon hitting the floor. Gloria leaned in to hear him better.

"What was that, sweetheart?" she asked.

Scott whispered, "That wasn't Logan."

Chapter Seven

Arriving at the hospital for the second time that day had been more unpleasant than the first because Harold was involved, and he had walked in naked except for a fleece vest.

"You can't come in here like that," the elderly, balding nurse at the front desk had said.

Harold had bristled. "This is a hospital. Your patients and corpses all wear Victorian garb?"

"When they're in the waiting room, yes," she replied. "Put on some pants *now*." Harold grumbled something about local government funding and slipped out to the parking lot to grab a pair of Bermuda shorts he always kept in his Camry for just such an occasion.

Now they sat in silence and Gloria took in her surroundings. The hospital seemed smaller than the one on Nantucket, but more nicely appointed. It smelled of freshly-cut spring flowers and bleach. The paintings on the wall were not the generic type found in most medical establishments. Local artists had clearly been commissioned to provide warmth to an otherwise practical space. Watercolors of lighthouses hung side by side with charcoals of ferry boats long out of service. It was Friday and the room was busy. Gloria, Harold, and Nika were sitting across from a fretting mother and a teenage boy holding a bag of ice to his eye. The boy was unfazed and playing a game on his phone with the hand not holding the ice. A man sitting away from the others in a darkened corner of the room had a camouflage backpack on backwards so it covered his chest and stomach. He looked inebriated. No other discernible ailment was visible. He burped under his breath every minute or so.

Gloria turned to her father. "So. Any thoughts?"

Harold looked up from his dog-eared copy of Hayek's *Road to Serfdom* and reviewed the room. "Yes. Look at how pristine this facility is. The water fountain works. Not one fluorescent light is flickering. Can you imagine what kind of fetid waste-hole this would be if our healthcare system were run by the state? That boy right there would enter here with one sore eye and leave with the selfsame sore eye plus a case of pleurisy." This was said in easy hearing of the boy's mother, who looked across at the large, excessively tan old man with a look of deep consternation. The boy did not react. Harold was back in his book.

"Yes, but magazines are old," Nika complained. "I am going outside for smoke. If I read one more *Good Housekeeping* from two thousand thirteen I am going to blow up this place and its nice light and water fountain." She moved through the sliding doors listlessly, her cigarette already lit before she had completely left the premises.

Gloria persisted. "Anything else? Maybe a thought not about the quality of the hospital? Maybe about the events of the day? About why a strange dog that looked kind of like Logan—but was female and aggressive—went psychotic and mauled my fiancé?"

The book was closed and reading glasses removed. Harold scratched his chest through the coffee-stained vest. "I will tell you, but you are going to overreact."

I should probably sit on my hands before he speaks, Gloria thought. I may strangle him otherwise.

The day had apparently started out idyllic. The stoned doctor Adams woke up, wiped the drool from his chin, and raced out of the house around ten. Harold and Nika put the leash on Logan and took him out for a stroll along the blasting surf. It was then that Harold questioned the leash. 'Why,' he asked Nika, 'should this dog be held back? Let him roam. Let him be. He knows who feeds him so where is he going to go?'

Nika urged him not to, but Harold had now crossed the mental Rubicon and could not be dissuaded. He detached the leash from Logan's collar and Logan responded instantly. Legs in motion blurred and kicked up sand. Within a minute, the dog was so far in the distance that Harold and Nika could not see him. No attempt was made to chase him as Logan's clip was easily four times that of a healthy sprinting man. Harold and Nika were not healthy people.

They stood in silence for a while then, waiting for Logan to return. Thirty minutes they waited before Harold said, "Well, shit."

They drove to the tiny Chilmark police station and asked whether any word had come in of a Rottweiler sprinting down the beach from the direction of Aquinnah. No luck. Harold then dropped Nika off at work and drove to the animal shelter that was only yards away from the Dairy Queen. No sign of Logan there.

At that point, Harold would later explain to his daughter at the hospital, he changed strategies. Finding Logan was no longer the goal. The goal was now to find Logan's replacement.

He drove to see Alex Parker, the bearded, barrel-stomached bartender at the Black Goose. Alex was the kind of guy who knew everyone and everything about the Cape and the islands, and he told Harold that the nearest shelter off the island was on the mainland, in Falmouth, about forty minutes from the Woods Hole dock. Not twenty minutes later, Harold had boarded a ferry boat on foot. The trip to Cape Cod is much shorter than the one to Nantucket, forty-five minutes all told. Upon arrival, Harold hopped in a cab and was off to Falmouth.

At the Falmouth Friends of Dogs, Harold had found a specimen that looked exactly like Logan. At least Harold was pretty sure it did. It was a Rottweiler at least, with black fur and perhaps a few shocks of white. The dog was quiet, unlike the beasts barking relentless jeremiads in the neighboring cages. Harold borrowed a shelter volunteer's cell phone and asked Nika to describe Logan to him (he had never paid much attention). Her description had been close enough for Harold's purposes and he asked to take the dog.

"This dog had a rough life," the volunteer had explained. "Someone smacked her around until she got a chance to escape. We got her from a kill shelter in Brunswick, Maine. She may respond to certain people aggressively. Anyone who looks like her former owner."

"How much?" Harold had asked.

On the way out of the shelter, they passed a tall, middle-aged man in blue button-down shirt, crisp khakis, and docksiders. The replacement dog became enraged, snapping her leash taught, issuing a growl and bark from the netherworld, and leaping at the stranger's neck. It took all of Harold's strength to stay the animal from killing the stranger who, in hindsight, had a passing resemblance to his future son-in-law.

With new pet in tow, Harold returned to the island with just enough time to pick up Nika from her half-day of work, pull a few bong hits on the couch alongside the new Logan, and settle into the couch while Nika prepared dinner for themselves and their guests.

Gloria had lost interest in the story after her father had confessed to looking for a replacement dog. She was elsewhere now, taking mental inventory, organizing data, weighing variables, and drafting conclusions. The outcome of her analysis was a surprise even to her. She was not in love with Scott Simon.

That fact had originally crept in when she was watching a dog tear him apart. Why had she stayed back? Why had she feared damage to her own flesh over his? This thought had allowed others to flood in while she sat in the waiting room, and Gloria concluded that she only loved him if one defined love as an act of vengeance.

She rose from her seat in the waiting room and walked away from Harold without excusing herself. Nika had returned from outside, stinking of fresh smoke, and almost bumped into Gloria who was passing her with a purpose. She exited the ER building and walked over to the wing that housed in-patient guests.

Scott was in a room with two beds. He slept in one, the other was empty. His arms were both bandaged and raised; he looked as if he were walking waist deep in frigid water. The bandages needed to be changed as blotches of blood were appearing near his wrists. He had a self-inflicted black eye. In the ambulance, Scott had explained that he had punched himself in the face while trying to punch the back of the dog's head. His neck brace was still on. He snored like a drunk.

It was dark outside now and the overhead fluorescents were off. Only under-cabinet lighting and machinery readouts provided visibility. She sat next to her betrothed and listened to him breathe for a few minutes. Then she spoke.

"Scott?" she whispered.

He continued to snore.

Louder now. "Scott."

Nothing.

She gently touched his bandaged arm and said in a louder voice, "Scott."

"Mom-owwwww," Scott tried to sit up in his dream state and just as quickly gave up and winced.

"Hey," Gloria was back to whispering now.

Scott looked at the ceiling with one eye as he had no other choice. When his voice came, it was hoarse from sleep and screaming.

"I'll assume that's you," he said.

"Yeah," she said. "It's me."

"You talk to the doctor yet?"

"Not since we arrived."

"He said I need X-rays and may need surgery for my neck."

"I am so sorry, Scott."

"But they can't get me to the mainland for the work because of the weather."

"I want to call off the marriage."

Scott was silent. He looked at the ceiling as before.

She continued. "This isn't right. It's not feeling right to me."

He spoke slowly, each word isolated and enunciated. "What. Do. You. Mean?"

"I'm not sure what I mean. It's hard to explain because I'm having trouble explaining it to myself." She paused. "How about this: Have you ever bought an album just to be cool and you don't even really like it but it will impress people that you bought it?"

"So you were just marrying me because I'm cool?"

"No. You're not cool. At all. What I mean is, I think I was marrying you specifically to piss off my dad. And it didn't work. He likes you. I was marrying a concept, not a person."

"He likes me? How did you figure that out? Did the fact that he unleashed a Rottweiler on me give it away?"

"That was an accident. He likes you a lot. I can tell. But we need to end this. I was dragging you into marriage for the wrong reasons."

Scott chuckled a humorless chuckle. "I've been making weapons my whole adult life. Here you were using me as one."

"One that didn't go off. My dad's unscathed. What did you tell me those were called? The ones that don't go off?"

"I'm a squib load."

"You're a squib load." She stood up and kissed him on the head. "I can stick around the next few days and keep you company if you'd like."

Gloria had expected Scott to be sad when she told him. She thought he might even cry. Instead, the one eyebrow that worked furrowed. He gritted his teeth. He turned his head toward her with great difficulty, squelched the gasps of pain trying to escape his mouth. His look was one she had never seen. It was a face of profound disgust and disappointment.

"Don't bother. Your company is not wanted. Or needed. My dad's trying to fly in before the weather turns too grim."

"What weather? What are you talking about?"

"Hurricane Beatrice. You and I avoided our phones too long. Didn't check the news. Didn't know a Category Five hurricane was spinning its way toward us."

She probably should have worried about herself at that moment; about her safety and the safety of her ex-fiancé. But her first thought was about the dogs, Logan and the fake Logan. She hoped they were both okay. Where would they hide when this Hurricane Beatrice made landfall?

She began walking out, but Scott kept speaking. "All those reasons you gave for breaking this off are bullshit. That you were in love with a concept not a person. That your dad liked me. They're not the real reasons."

"Oh really? What are my reasons then?"

"Your past is too screwed up to think about creating a future. You're not over losing your mom and your dad is the hydraulic force behind every one of your decisions and actions. Saying the fault is mine and that I failed to accomplish your mission of pissing off your dad is absurd. It's like if Don Quixote blamed a warped lance for his failure to defeat non-existent monsters."

Gloria made to exit again, but first she said, tearlessly, "I'm sorry."

Scott said to the ceiling, "I hope this storm takes you, your fat father, and that Soviet witch to the bottom of the sea."

"Goodbye, Scott. Someday you'll realize I was right to do this."

"No, I won't."

Doctor Amos Adams passed her as he entered the room.

"Hey Gloria," he said. "Nice meeting you last night."

"You've got to be kidding me." Scott practically yelled into the air, recognizing the voice. "What happened to the last person who was taking care of me?"

"Shift change," Amos said.

"No way I'm being seen by you. You're gonna saw off my nose by mistake. Get me another doctor."

Adams said, "Relax. You're in good hands."

"Wait. You always tell the truth, right?"

"Yes."

"Are you high right now?"

"Um. No."

Gloria closed the door behind her, but not before hearing Scott say, "This is a mistake, Gloria Gomberg."

"How is our favorite Lockheed Martin employee faring?" Harold asked as his daughter re-entered the waiting room. "I wonder if the damage his weapons inflict can hold a candle to an old-fashioned dog. Oh, Amos is here by the way. His shift just started. Where are you going?"

Gloria continued to walk out of the sliding hospital doors, not saying a word and not even giving her father so much as a glance. The night air's temperature felt no different than what she had left indoors. But it was dead. Not even a whisper of air. The only difference was the smell, pungent with the tide that churned up the seafloor a half mile away. In a parking lot devoid of anyone, she slipped into her father's unlocked car and took the keys out of the glove compartment. The stink of food—pepperoni, peppers, olives—was enhanced by the stagnant wet weather. After punching the dashboard and hurting her hand, she drove off through the evening's mist.

This is a mistake, Gloria Gomberg.

The words rattled through her skull. She couldn't make out if they were in Scott's voice or her own.

Regardless, the body count had begun.

119

Chapter Eight

Gloria had heard a nice story about her parents as younger people. She had no idea what made her think of it while lugging the metal "vital effects" cooler outside into the pending storm.

"I was at my desk at the ad agency, doing my usual drudgery as Wordsworth-turned-robot," Harold often said, "and I heard this voice say, 'Excuse me.' Now tell me. Have you ever a heard a voice before looking at the face uttering it, and you can already tell you are going to spend the rest of your life with it? I suppose not, but that is what happened. I looked up and there she was. Red hair like a Serengeti brush fire. Brown eyes one thousand generations old. The elders of the Old Testament staring at me through those eyes. And she spoke some more, something about 'Where's the coffee maker,' and her voice made everything else in the room go blurry with irrelevance."

She was there to audition as a voice talent for radio spots. Company leadership liked Harold, and so he had some say regarding who they chose, and sure enough he did not hesitate to pull strings. Rachel began work with the company one day after auditioning, and it was not long before she and Harold were spending time together outside of work. They went to bars in Greenwich Village, fed pigeons in Washington Square Park, and once pretended to be the worst buskers in the city, placing a baseball hat on the Union Square subway platform and singing off key for an hour. Rachel told Gloria many years later that Harold would read his old poetry and lyrics to her and she liked them but mostly found them adorably silly, the words of a grown child. Nonetheless, she sang them back to him in her deep, throaty voice and he was lost.

Despite having some influence at the office because of his charisma, Harold was the youngest employee; twenty-two, almost twenty-three at this point and he was a bachelor living in the city. The problem was that Rachel was two years his junior and still living with her mother and father in Connecticut. Having conservative parents, Rachel was expected to come home every night until she got married and moved out. She could be out late, but needed to come home. This left Harold and Rachel frustrated, wanting to spend their nights out in the city and their early mornings together in bed. At the time, Harold had enough common sense and decency to respect the wishes of Rachel's parents and so he would walk her to Grand Central Station every night and put her on the last train to Connecticut.

Unable to contain his passion any longer, Harold decided to take a chance. Well after midnight, he drove bleary-eyed to Norwalk from the Upper West Side of Manhattan. Parking his dented tan Volkswagen Beetle down the road, he walked to the back of the palatial Victorian home of Ezra and Doris Goodwin, retail clothing store magnates. Harold knew which room was Rachel's because he had been to the house once before for dinner (Ezra and Doris had not taken to the young man who had grown up poor in New Haven). He also knew there was a roof just under Rachel's window, and if he could just get up there, he could rap on the glass, wake Rachel, and get invited in.

Harold had climbing experience, having summited the Shawangunks in upstate New York during his college days. That skill allowed him to climb up the sills, trellises, and other footholds. When he knocked gently on the window, waking the lady of his life, Rachel was upset, but her love won the day, and she let Harold in. They stared at each for a time and then kissed. Years later, Rachel would recall to her daughter that she had loved Harold more at that moment than ever before. She knew he was the one and wanted to spend the rest of her life with him.

The evening ended poorly. In addition to some unneeded climbing rope, Harold had brought a bottle of champagne and plastic cups in a backpack. In an unfortunate plan to calm his nerves before his daring ascent, he had decided to take several sips of the champagne on the drive to Connecticut, resealing the bottle upon parking the car. With all of his meticulous planning, he had not counted on the amount of shaking and shimmying involved in scaling the side of a house. As he pulled the bottle out of his backpack, the cork popped prematurely, hitting him in the mouth. Two teeth from his upper jaw dislodged and flew in multiple directions along with champagne foam. The incurable romantic yelled in anguish, waking Rachel's parents and necessitating a hasty exit.

The open window, teeth, blood, and puddle of champagne left no doubt in the minds of the parents what had transpired. Rachel's father called Harold the next day, telling him to either marry his daughter or go away. The young man was not quite ready, and neither was Rachel, so on the next late-night visit, Rachel took the risk and snuck out of the house. They met on the corner of her darkened road and drove to the local reservoir with a six-pack of beer. Deep in the woods on that perfect early summer night, cicadas keening over the brevity of their lives, Harold and Rachel escaped from everything. They huddled on a blanket inside some graffitied concrete remnant of the industrial age. And within that strange chapel, stubbly with twisted rebar and pocked with rain-damp divots, Harold and Rachel created their daughter.

Ezra Goodwin was waiting up when Rachel walked through the front door at sunrise. Harold and Rachel were married three months later.

Now that same daughter was struggling to walk upright. The fifty-four-quart metal cooler in her arms was heavy despite only holding marijuana. The contraband was so tightly packed it gave the container density. As she shuffled awkwardly across the room, Gloria cursed under her breath. The cooler felt like it had been built to survive a nuclear winter, all stainless steel and minimal ergonomic consideration. The two handles that flipped up on the sides pressed uncomfortably into her fingers. She put the whole thing down with a thud to open the sliding door onto the deck and then she picked it up again. As she stepped onto the porch, she felt a breeze. It came as a relief after days of stagnant air. The gentle gust was warm, having traveled across the southern oceans. It was hard to imagine the beastly weather that was spinning a path toward her in the dark at that very moment. She looked up into the humid emptiness of the sky and saw nothing but black. From below, the raging surf sounded as if it were only feet away.

And it was. The approaching storm had stirred up a tide that was disturbingly high. In the light generated from the living room, she could see below foamy salt water after each wave crash. Whenever it reappeared out of the dark, she witnessed the ocean nearly touch one of the stilts upon which the house rested.

The air had become a slightly more anemic version of the ocean. It smelled of the deep. Microbeads of water, illuminated by the light from the house, moved in unison this way and that through the atmosphere. They clung to every surface, from Gloria's now kinky, wild hair to the porch chairs to the metal cooler.

She was slightly unnerved by the ocean's approach but she was not deterred from her mission. After she had lugged the cooler down the ocean-side steps, she opened her father's unlocked storage shed and rifled through shredded beach chairs, umbrellas, empty gasoline containers, Wiffle Ball equipment, and unexplainable items like a laser disc of *The Gumball Rally*. It was not long before Gloria found what she was looking for. In the corner, resting against the wall behind an ancient fireplace grate was a shovel, big and heavy.

Could she have just thrown the container into the ocean? Perhaps, but then she would not have the leverage of knowing its whereabouts and how to retrieve it. Yes, she thought, better to bury it somewhere in the seagrass.

Gloria was smoking a cigarette and sipping white wine on the couch, trying to feel dry, when Nika came through the door. The young woman threw down her handbag and flung her arms up in the air.

"You know you abandoned us, hussy? You stole your father's car and left us there. We had to take taxi!" She looked around and spotted the overturned skillet and food lodged in the pile carpet. "And thank you for picking up onions I dropped all over floor saving your fiancé."

"He's not my fiancé anymore."

"That is not interesting for me. Oh, and thank you for asking before taking cigarette also. Take whole magnificent carton and smoke them now." Nika walked over to her pack of menthols, pulled one out, and lit it. She sat next to Gloria on the couch and exhaled copious amounts of smoke. Her mind seemed to have moved on.

"Where's my dad?" Gloria asked.

"Outside, looking to see if dog is around."

"Which dog?"

"Any one. I am getting Red Bull from fridge. Do you want?"

"No."

Harold barged in at that time and he was already naked. Throwing the t-shirt and shorts in his hand at Gloria (and missing), he bellowed at her, "Have you been eating roofing cement?"

"What are you talking about?"

"You stole our car!"

"I was angry. That bullshit you pulled with the dogs was beyond, Dad. Just utterly beyond."

"That does not give you the right to take my car."

"Why are you so obsessed with this? You got a cab home."

"I cannot afford a cab."

"Since when?"

Ignoring Gloria's query, Harold posed his own. "When are you going back to pick up Scott?"

"I'm not. He's not my fiancé anymore."

Harold made a dismissive gesture with his hand and walked away. "You are better off. That little man was an unintentional flute squeak in the music of the spheres. Where is my pot?" He was searching under the end table for the cooler and then he was searching everywhere. His movements became aggressive. He was setting things aside, and then he was tossing them. "Where

125

is my container? I never, ever place it anywhere other than under the end table. Gloria Gomberg, this is your doing! Where is it?"

"I buried it. Outside. In the sand."

Now in the kitchen, Harold stopped looking, folded his arms, and stood staring at his daughter. "Do you want to tell me why? And where?"

Gloria said, "No and no. Actually, yes to the first question. I buried it because you're going to start growing up. I'm sick of figuring out who to be in life by looking at my father and doing the exact opposite. It's like you've laid out a negative blueprint for me to follow." She mimicked unrolling a large scroll and laying it on a table. She then aped her father's voice. 'Now look sharp! See the white lines on the blue background? Avoid the white lines and build something in the blue. That is how you make a life.'"

"I am not wasting any time with this interrogation. That surf is coming up quickly and I cannot watch several weeks of paychecks get washed away." He walked out onto the deck and disappeared into the wind and darkness.

The two women smoked cigarettes looking in the same direction at an empty room. The moist sea air added an adhesive quality to everything, and Gloria stuck fast to the couch.

Nika rose and began sifting through the records leaning against the foot locker coffee table. She pulled out *Safe as Milk* by Captain Beefheart, the only non-jazz artist Harold Gomberg appreciated, and put it on the turntable. "Sho 'nuff and Yes I Do" began to play, all bluesy guitar and scratchy voice, accompanied by forty years of pops and skips.

"Two of us live in this house," Nika said. "We both work. I am at Dairy Queen and your father delivers pizza for Island Pizza in Vineyard Haven. Taxis and buried marijuana are not in our budget. And your father cares about car because if anything happens to it, he cannot deliver pizza. We do not afford this."

Gloria Gomberg put her cigarette out in her wine. She stared at Nika. Broken English words had entered her ears and she could extract the meaning, but she was damned if she could place that understanding into her existing model of the world. The man who had raised her was delivering pizzas.

Moments later, Gloria was outside, squinting against sand thrown in her face by the wind. She could not see her father. Vision out in the wet night was ten feet at best. After scanning the seagrass with complete futility, she made her way to the beach. Despite having witnessed it earlier, she did not expect the waves to meet her so far inland. She gasped at the sound of the approaching foam and the feel of cold water on her bare feet made her yell. She heard her father not far off yell, "Balls!" He had undoubtedly just experienced the same shock.

"Dad?" she asked the night.

There was no response.

"I'm sorry about the car. And the cooler! I didn't know!" She was yelling to be heard over the ocean. "I know where the cooler is. I'll get it for you. It's closer to the house than that."

Again, no response. She shook her head in defeat and walked back toward the light of the house. The idea of her father delivering pizza made her nauseous. And hungry for pizza. It was elitist and snobby, she knew, to consider her father "above that," but her heart went out to him. In hindsight, it made perfect sense that he had blown through Mom's money. He lived in one of the wealthiest counties in all of Massachusetts where the taxes were undoubtedly outrageous, smoked a lot of expensive weed, and except for Dairy Queen, ate only gourmet ingredients. The man was a fiduciary black hole. She pictured him now, driving

127

naked to make deliveries, donning the clothes he kept in the back of the Camry to walk the pizzas to people's front doors. Occasionally taking a detour to sit on the beach and smoke a joint. This was her father now.

The house was only a few steps away when a gust of wind kicked up sand and blew it into her eyes. She winced and went down on one knee. Blinking repeatedly and covering her face with an arm seemed to help and the grains worked themselves out ever so slowly. While she waited for her vision to clear, the focus of her mind's eye became exquisite. This dark beach, so hostile now, had been the location of much of her childhood happiness and she saw it vividly. She saw vacations here with her family. Her brother Seth was running along this stretch in the summer sun, her chasing close behind, trying to spank him with a Frisbee, him trying to laugh and sprint at the same time. The world had not yet introduced a thousand different distractions, and so that single Frisbee kept them entertained all day. It was a tool for spanking, a flying saucer, a shovel for building sand castles, a wave maker, and of course, a Frisbee. Mom bobbed in the daunting ocean surf and Dad read a book about Teddy Roosevelt. The beach was busy with fellow summer visitors, but it was the nineteen-seventies, before the onslaught, and they were "up island," so the volume was sufferable. It was certainly the case that only two months hence, on the other side of the Earth, helicopters were being shoved off the sides of battleships to make room for fleeing American civilians and soldiers; and it was true that the country's own children had recently bombed its State Department; and sure, the federal government was collapsing in a firestorm of scandal. But there on that beach, with suntan lotion unevenly applied by counter-culture parents, and

128

cans of ginger ale waiting for them in icy coolers, the world was a splendid, magical, and safe place.

When high school came, the family trips to the Vineyard became more problematic for Gloria. Her parents were clearly not getting along, hissing weaponized jibes at each other over gin and tonics mixed with only enough tonic to hide in the surface tension; but even when they were getting along, Gloria was starting to resent their quirkiness. She had reached that age when you realize your parents are not infallible tour guides of Life, but instead fellow tourists who have just been there a little longer. Mom, despite her grace, could be overly theatrical and attempt to inject drama into every moment. Each walk to catch a ringing telephone elicited a sigh of exhaustion. Each of Seth's skinned knees sent her into a panic. A tough day at work recording a voiceover for some dishwashing detergent could cause her to exclaim, "My life is an endless nightmare." Her father was quite the opposite, never speaking his feelings (other than anger) and lacking any of his wife's grace. He was loud, clumsy, rude at times, and getting worse by the day. His politics were swinging to the right even though they had traditionally been a liberal household. Harold could go on for hours about "the impotence of that sanctimonious peanut-farmer-in-chief." Gloria saw these two people as grown children. Worst of all, they seemed proud of their everyday defiance. They reveled in being "off." They reveled in listening to atonal 20th Century composers like Berg while their neighbors listened to The Eagles; in shopping at the Salvation Army; in embracing organic produce before other people knew what that meant; in rejecting compact discs; in playing chess by lamp light; as Dad put it, they proved they were alive by being "non-standard issue."

Gloria responded to her parents in the only way that made sense: She rebelled against rebellion. Throughout high school, she dressed immaculately. Any stray hairs or dry scalp were obsessively picked from her wool sweaters before she left for school in the morning. She studied late into the night, excelling in algebra, and she flossed twice a day. The only kids she hung out with were the well-adjusted sort who played by the rules of etiquette and field hockey. Any dates were with straight-A students who were on the varsity lacrosse team. Her efforts had the desired effect: Harold and Rachel found their daughter maddening. And she loved that.

Granted, when she got to college, alcohol came into her life. And without her parents around she exhaled and slacked and stopped flossing so much. She drank a lot. And she met Phil who broke her heart.

But oh, goodness, she thought, before the anger of high school and the confusion of college, she had once run happily on these shores. How odd to be in that same place now, losing her father in the darkness.

Once she had made it back into the house, she used the bathroom, sat down with some more pinot, and winced at the memory of jettisoning Scott, of decreasing her military operation's footprint. But she fell asleep shortly after the wincing and so no change of heart or act of redemption could come of it.

She was dreaming that she was missing a foot when Nika's voice awakened her. The young woman was standing in front of the sink, arms akimbo, asking the kitchen window, "What the fuck is this now?" Flashing lights outside illuminated her profile.

Gloria rubbed her eyes, still wrestling with the logic of her dream, trying to grasp why she was missing a foot, but now also parsing the scene of a Russian girl in a huge man's white t-shirt asking questions of a window displaying a light show. Once reason returned, she stood on her two solid feet and dragged herself to the kitchen.

"Police," Nika said.

The red and blue lights were diffused by water in the air, making the entire night look psychedelic. Occasional human silhouettes darted in front of the car. Whatever was happening, it was happening over in Dick and Prissy's driveway.

"I am sure Prissy is upset. Flipping her cow. Did I use that correctly?"

"I'm not sure what it is you used."

"We are going," Nika said taking Gloria's hand.

Gloria did not fight her on this. "Let me get some shoes on."

Nika continued pulling. "Shoes? Who needs?" Off they went, down the front steps, into the sandy driveway, and out to the blacktop of Moshup Trail. The wind was strong. It would drop off to nothing and then snap like a whip, tearing at their skin with an aggression that made them close their eyes.

Halfway between the two houses, they heard the first voices between gusts. They were raised in anger. One was hard for Gloria to make out. The other was very, very recognizable. Gloria ran ahead of Nika, but could only pick up so much speed due to gravel stinging her bare feet. She splashed through cold puddles and more than once suffered a scrubby pine branch slapping her in the face.

As she ran up the muddy driveway, she began to understand the scene. Her father was in handcuffs, flanked by two officers, both shorter than him. The police car idled behind them, lights

131

spinning, exhaust emanating from the tailpipe and immediately being caught up in the weather. Her father was naked except for a white towel that read "Prissy" in a rounded, red cursive. He was yelling at Dick, who was looking unprepared for company in his boxer shorts, untied bathrobe, and docksiders. His glasses were fogged and his hair was flapping everywhere.

Harold exclaimed, "Leave it to you, a disgraced neocon, to call in the lapdogs of the Leviathan to do your dirty work!"

Dick rebutted. "What's politics got do with this, you baboon? You were breaking and entering!"

"Oh please, Dick. All your lights were off-"

"That doesn't mean you can break in!"

"Your lights were off so I thought you were on the mainland."

"And again that doesn't mean you can break in. What's more it's two in the morning! That's another reason people sometimes have their lights off. And the Saab's right there! Of course we were here."

"I cannot be expected to know how many cars you own."

"You poor thing, being expected to know how many cars I own before trespassing on my property. Maybe *I* should be arrested for my insensitivity!"

The older of the two police officers said, "Guys, you need to talk about this later." He gestured to the sky. "We got other things to deal with."

They moved to place Harold in the police car but Harold pushed back. He said, "Come on, Dick. This is overkill. Can we just talk this out?"

"No. You were breaking into my house and I want you behind bars."

132

Harold snapped, "The globe still bleeds from your inept neocon crusades!"

Dick retorted, "I was a McCain man in two thousand. Don't blame W's actions on me!"

"Regardless, you and all of your old-money bow-tie wearing ice-people are wingnuts in the military industrial complex. You should be ashamed of yourselves."

"We invited you into the local party meetings, Harold. You could have joined us. You could have changed us from within; that was your opportunity to convert us. Not when I'm having you arrested for breaking into my house."

"I was not breaking into your house for land's sake. I was breaking into your storage shed."

"Dad!" Gloria broke in. The police had only given the two approaching women a brief glance before. Now they focused on them.

Harold said, "Ah Gloria. These are Officers Chris Kensler and Brian White. Officers, this is my daughter Gloria."

"Hi guys."

"Ma'am," they both mumbled.

"What happened?" Gloria asked her father.

"I was merely trying to get into Dick's shed-"

"Breaking the lock more specifically," Dick added.

Harold continued "I was trying to get to your metal detector. Just to borrow it."

"Metal detecting in the middle of the night?" Dick stated and asked at the same time.

"That's my fault, Dick" Gloria said. "I had a fight with my dad and to get back at him I-"

Gloria noticed her father's eyes had grown large. He was looking at her and shaking his head very slowly. She realized that mention of the cooler was probably a bad idea given its contents. What to say, now that she had paused but was on the spot to say something? She changed the subject.

"Do you guys really need to leave the car idling like that? That's gonna be the death of all of us."

Everyone went silent and looked at her. Finally, Officer Kensler said "Global warming is the least of your issues right now."

She continued. "I'm serious! Did you ever think that this weather we're having is a direct result of people doing what you're doing right now?"

Officer Kensler looked at Officer White as if he might have the answer. Then he turned back to Gloria and said, "Not really."

Harold spoke up. "My daughter is clearly trying to distract us from my activities, bless her heart. The truth is that she was mad at me for making so much noise when she was trying to sleep. I am a night owl as you know, Dick, and I was walking around playing records. To get back at me she locked me out of the house."

Dick laughed. "So instead of breaking back into his own house he breaks into mine. Folderol. Up until now, you've just been an annoying neighbor. Now it's criminal. I'm going to bed. See you around the beach, Harold. I hope your Al Gore wood nymph of a daughter goes your bail."

"You can't leave until we take down some information, Dick," Officer Kensler said.

"Ah guys!" Dick moaned. "Can't we deal with this tomorrow?"

"Sorry. No."

Dick swore while clutching his bathrobe to close it more. At the same time, Officer White guided Harold into the car.

"Officer White," Nika said.

White stopped walking to the driver's seat and fumbling to find his car keys to listen to Nika, his eyes flagrantly moving between her face and her wet shirt. "Yo," he said in a manner that communicated a forced kind of casual.

"Can I drive with my fiancé to station?"

Officer White rolled his eyes and said, "Not supposed to, Nika." He looked at her chest again. "Just don't tell anyone." He winked.

"You are hero," she said. "For thin blue line you are very big and strong." She squeezed his bicep and stepped past Gloria.

White helped Harold into the car while Nika slid in on the other side. Officer Kensler asked Dick questions for at least ten minutes, Gloria watching the whole affair silently while the wind blew her hair across her face, The officer then joined joined his partner and the others in the car. Dick struggled to keep his robe from flying off in the wind as he made his way up the stairs to his front door.

"Goodnight," Gloria yelled after him.

Not getting her sarcasm, Dick lifted his hand exhaustedly and went inside.

Gloria turned to the police car. Her eyes were blinded by the spinning red lights and the sand spitting into her face.

A voice that was clearly Nika's said to her from the open squad car door, "Come to courthouse in Edgartown and bring money."

"Sure."

Before Nika could close her door, the engine of the squad car went into spasm, coughing and stopping and starting.

"Shit!" Officer Kensler yelled, looking down at his feet. Gloria stuck her head in the door. The engine kept sputtering and then made noise no more.

"What is it?" Officer White asked.

"We're out of gas," Officer Kensler replied.

"Ahhhh shit."

"You're goddamn right 'ahhhh shit.' If I recall, you were gonna fill it up."

"Things got nuts tonight."

"Directing traffic at the church play? I don't think you know what 'nuts' means."

"What can I say? Sorry."

Officer Kensler sighed and looked back at his civilian passengers. "Hate to ask this, but can you give us a ride to the station?"

Nika and Harold looked behind themselves at first, then back at Officer Kensler. Nika asked, "What are you fucking kidding me?"

"Sorry no."

"Why don't you call other cops?"

"Time and resources. This storm is building by the second. We need to get Harold back and start attending to other issues pronto. We'll get the car later."

"We don't care when the fuck you get car. It is in Dick's driveway and does not affect us."

Officer Kensler looked at Officer White and said, "Fair point. So can you give us that ride?"

The four passengers got out and began to walk down the street to Harold's house.

Harold asked, "Could you help me out, Brian?"

"Whadya need?" Officer White asked.

"My towel is coming loose and I cannot easily fasten it because my hands are cuffed."

"I'd rather not. Have your lady friend do it."

"I'll do it," Gloria said.

"Thank you," Harold said.

The others moved ahead and this gave Gloria the time she needed to catch up with her father.

As she tightened the towel, rolling the top over, making sure not to look down, she spoke. "I had no idea you were delivering pizzas, Dad. You should have told me! I could have helped. I could have sent money or found you a place to live in the city or…or…I don't know. But I wish you would have told me."

"Why would I? It is just a job I have."

"Yeah, but it's not a job I would expect you to have."

"Life does not always take the trajectory you expect. Besides, it is temporary. Until the cemetery gets approved."

Gloria held back. Now was not the time to remind him that the cemetery idea was bonkers and was never to be approved. Whatever kept him going was fine by her.

"Okay, Dad. I understand."

"Let's go, folks," said Officer Kensler to the two stragglers.

Gloria continued. "I'm so sorry about tonight. I didn't expect things to end in an arrest. I was pissed and so I hid the cooler."

"Ah, don't worry about it."

"No, really. It was a shitty thing to do."

"You do not need to worry about it, young lady," he said as he patted her hair. "I threw your phone into the ocean."

"What?"

"You left it on the counter. When I went out to find my cooler, I took your phone with me. It has a new home in the briny main!" He started walking again. Gloria did not follow. She simply watched him begin his walk down the driveway. "I was able to make it skip!" he called back. "In this weather no less!"

Officer Kensler protected Harold's head as he guided the toweled man into the backseat of his own car. Gloria wondered if she had enough time to run at her father and punch him in the gut before they closed the door. She concluded that she did not.

She waited before bailing him out. She took her sweet time. She had a few glasses of wine. She smoked Nika's cigarettes. She even went out on the deck and let the wind whip her hair everywhere. Who was going to bother her? Gloria had no phone. The house had no phone. The tide had come up and now waves broke over the dunes and pooled in the driveway, so it was unlikely anyone would drive up. She wasn't even sure where's Scott's car keys were. The world was as distant as it would ever be. It was clearly time to get drunk.

After three glasses of wine, her monomania kicked into high gear. She cursed her father's name. All Gloria wanted in that moment was for the man to admit that he had gone nuts, grown distant, failed her as a parent, and then go down on his knees and ask for forgiveness. None of this was forthcoming, she knew, but she would enjoy dreaming about it when she passed out, which she did directly.

Saturday

Chapter Nine

Her father had walked around the house naked since before Gloria was a conscious human being. She witnessed it through her formative years but did not notice or care. To her, it was an ever-present and therefore uninteresting fact of the universe. It was fine. Things did not truly enter the realm of the odd until nineteen eighty-six, when Harold began venturing *outside* without dressing himself.

The "unveiling" had occurred one spring day in Gloria's junior year of high school. She had come home after chemistry class on a Friday with two of her friends in tow—Tina and Nicole. Tina Knox was arguably the most popular girl at school and that mattered to Gloria back then. She had a crush on Tina, wanted to be her, and felt total pride when hanging out with her. Was Tina nice to Gloria? Did she say interesting things? That was unclear and irrelevant. Being Tina Knox made the things she said nice and interesting. All that mattered was the way she laughed so joyfully, searched the sky in a pensive way when thinking, sang aloud to songs without fear of her peers, and seemed to know everything about everything that mattered. Sometimes at night while falling asleep, Gloria imagined running away with Tina, just the two of them on the road, living off diner food, camping under the desert sky, and chatting about everything and nothing all night. She would have Tina's company all to herself, and Gloria would be the happiest person on Earth. For now, it was good enough that Tina had started coming over to her house. This was only the second time it had happened in the past month. They were becoming friends, which fulfilled a goal Gloria had had since the eighth grade.

It was the end of the school year and the afternoon was hot. The girls had been in classrooms with no air conditioning all day and so decided to lounge by Gloria's pool, drinking tall glasses of blue Kool Aid, sunning themselves, and dipping their toes into the still frigid water. They were listening to the classic rock station on Gloria's portable radio. Bruce Springsteen sang about how he was on fire. He delivered this message calmly and slowly; in a manner that was not at all suggestive of someone on fire. Gloria explained to Nicole that that was what made the song so special. Nicole didn't seem to care and turned the conversation to summer jobs and then to their classmate Ruth who was smoking cigarettes at sixteen. Gloria and her friends would have nothing to do with that. They agreed that when Ruth was diagnosed with lung cancer someday, they would not feel badly for her.

Having just returned from a friend's house, Gloria's brother, Seth, walked by, lugging his backpack and carrying a book of Bernard Kliban cat comics in his hand. He said 'hello' politely when the girls greeted him.

"Oh my god are you wearing cologne you little freak?" Gloria asked.

"No, you bitch!" Seth retorted.

"You shouldn't call girls that," Tina said in a very calm tone. Seth was in middle school but he knew who Tina was and, like other eighth grade boys, he was enamored with her.

"Fine," he said. "Then she's a douche."

The girls laughed.

"Get out of here, nerd," Gloria yelled at him as she threw the empty bottle of suntan lotion at him. Gloria felt justified in calling him a nerd. He certainly was one. He was so nerdy that he was writing fan fiction before it was a documented thing. *Star Wars* fan fiction was not nerdy enough for him. He was writing George Lucas fan fiction. He actually wrote short stories about the director's day-to-day dealings at Skywalker Ranch. What a little freak. Seth ran into the house smiling about his verbal victory.

Tina then held court for a time, telling the other girls about an R-rated movie her way-older boyfriend had taken her to the night before. It was called *Blue Velvet* and it was totally weird and disgusting. After saying she could not even talk about it, she went through every graphic detail while the other girls took turns wincing. Gloria was rapt, basking in the experience of this idyllic young woman regaling her with the details of a film that exposed the dark, unspoken landscape of the American suburbs.

It was then that Harold strolled out of the house and into the yard wearing nothing but a pair of beat up running shoes and carrying a can of gasoline.

"Ladies," he said rather formally. That was his only acknowledgement of their existence. There was neither an apology for his appearance nor any ashamed explanation. He simply broke into a whistle and walked into the garage.

Gloria scrambled for something to say, to Tina in particular. Nicole's opinion was less important. Tina's mouth was agape and she was clearly on the brink of insane laughter. Instead she just whispered, "Oh. My. God!" Nothing came to Gloria's mind. What explanation was there? Should she claim he had dementia? Maybe he did.

"I am so sorry. He hasn't been himself lately," was all she could think to say. And that was true. He had been acting strangely—even for him—the past several weeks. Angry. Staring at the floor. Terse words had been flying between her parents lately. She had heard the words through the walls at night, muffled but quite clear in their message.

It had been around that time that Gloria heard the thing her dad had said about life being like a trip across the country. "*At times life feels like a trip across America eastward. When you are in the middle of the trip there is so much road ahead, but all the beauty is behind you. There is nothing but flat land and straight interstate. The charge of the mountains and canyons is not even in the rearview mirror anymore. All that waits for you is the eternal mundane.*" The deep sadness of that statement had been met with complete indifference by her mother. The woman had not responded at all. She had just walked out of the room, leaving him to his melancholy.

Before Tina and the other girls could say something to Gloria like "Don't worry about it," Harold returned to the yard pushing the lawnmower and whistling the same tune. When he squatted down to fill the tank, too much of his hindquarters became exposed and Gloria suggested that they all go inside. The other girls met her request with enthusiasm. As they collected their towels, lotions, drinks, and radio, the raucous sound of the mower filled the air.

They had moved into the living room and were playing Trivial Pursuit without keeping score, taking turns reading out questions and seeing who could answer quickest. Gloria slowly brought her head back into the moment and forgot about the show her father had just put on. She answered correctly almost every question posed to her except for the ones from the sports category. Nicole made up fake questions and answers, not letting on to her friends. When she confessed, the girls went into a somewhat exaggerated rage and then laughed uncontrollably.

Through the windows, from out in the backyard, they heard howls of pain over the muffled lawnmower wail. The three of them moved to the window to see what was happening, but the scene was unclear. Harold was dancing frantically, as though celebrating a daughter's wedding that was not happening. The dance was alpine, Teutonic, involving spinning and a slapping of legs and feet. It took Nicole's cry of "Oh shit" and a squinting of her own eyes before Gloria saw the wasps erratically orbiting her father's body. He was, for the moment, a sweaty sun attracting vengeful planets. Harold swatted at his groin and screamed, and then his buttocks, and then the back of his head. Finally, the whole solar system leaned forward and ran headlong into the frigid pool.

To his credit, Harold stayed below the surface for some time. Gloria frantically opened the window and yelled "Dad!" through the screen. She heard no response. Where was her mother? Why was she not coming in from the kitchen? She had told Gloria that she had no recording sessions scheduled for the day. So why was the other adult in the house, who theoretically knew what to do in these types of situations, not coming? Again, she would have to be the parent of the house. Dad had stopped being a parent years ago and her mother had never been one. A friend, but not a mother. Gloria summoned up her nerve and bolted through the back door, arriving at the pool's edge.

Harold came up at that moment and gasped for breath. A few wasps lingered but showed no signs of regrouping for a subsequent attack. Gloria was on her knees and she put out her hand. "Swim over here, Dad, and I'll help you out." He completely ignored her offer, pulling himself out of the other side of the pool in one smooth action.

"Is he okay?" Tina called from inside. Gloria looked back but said nothing.

"Great Scott!" Harold yelled as he stormed across the yard, red welts already appearing across the sweeping expanse of his flabby body. He was on some mission about which Gloria had no insight. A long string of curses rolled over his swollen lower lip. In the past, his outbursts had skated the poetic, but now the words were base. Primal. Enraged.

He disappeared into the garage, the filthy rant still audible through the garage walls despite the mower still running. Gloria turned off the machine and went inside. Her heart sank when she saw that her two guests had their clothing back on over their swimsuits and their backpacks over their shoulders.

"We should go, Glor," Tina said gently.

"No, it's okay. He's fine. You can stay."

"Seriously, your dad deserves some privacy."

Tina was right, Gloria knew. He needed his privacy. Why was he the only one who seemed to miss the fact that he needed more privacy? He needed it so much. He needed several years of privacy, preferably in a room with only a few very specific guests who could administer the proper amounts of Thorazine.

"Okay. Are you guys doing anything tonight?" Gloria asked.

The two girls looked at each other. "Not sure" they said in a kind of lazy round.

Gloria showed them out, certain that she would never see them outside of school again (To their credit, Tina and Nicole remained Gloria's dear friends for decades). She went to get a refill of Kool Aid from a pitcher in the fridge. It was then she saw her mother, washing breakfast dishes left in the kitchen sink. She was singing to herself, bobbing her peppermint head of red and white streaked hair, and she was bouncing her body a little to music that was not playing. Seth sat at the breakfast table, eating a slice of pound cake and thumbing through his cat book.

It was unusual for Gloria to see her mother in her bathrobe in the middle of the afternoon. The woman was usually out and about all day, as frenetic as a hummingbird, working in the garden or hosting a reading group or having dinner with newscasters after a recording session at the local network. She was politically active in town and had even considered a run for town council. She was Auntie Mame made flesh, a powerful, wealthy woman consumed with living life to its fullest. Why was she dressed for nothing at three in the afternoon?

"Mom?" Gloria had asked.

Her mother did not hear her over the running water.

Gloria moved closer and said "Mom!" a little louder.

Her mother did not jump at all. She just turned, her hair covering half of her face, and she smiled deeply at her daughter.

It was then that Gloria realized her mother was very drunk.

"Mom?"

"Hey, sweetie. How are *you*?"

"Did you hear Dad?"

"No. Whadyou mean?"

Seth looked up at Gloria and then pointed to their mother. He made the universal "crazy" gesture next to his head, swirling his finger and then pointing at the robed woman at the sink.

Gloria continued. "He was screaming in the backyard. He ran over a wasps' nest with the lawnmower." Gloria noticed a glass of blue Kool Aid and a bottle of gin next to the sink.

"Is he okay now?" her mother asked.

"I'm not sure. You know what? He's fine. Never mind. He has it under control."

"Okay, sweets. Let me know if I can do anything." She went back to washing the dishes.

Drunk in the afternoon. By herself. This was a day of firsts for both of her parents, Gloria thought. She went to the fridge, saw that the blue-stained pitcher on the top shelf was empty, and poured herself a glass of water instead. She went to the living room window, which was still open and admitting the cries of goldfinches and orioles nesting in the ancient maples ringing their property. Sipping her water, she watched as her father poured gasoline into a hole in the yard. An occasional wasp flew out and darted around the grass seemingly without destination. Gloria caught occasional whiffs of the gas on the breeze, mixing with the scent of freshly cut grass and roses in bloom.

"Take this, scoundrels," Harold hissed as he lit a match. His left eye was completely swollen shut and the left corner of his mouth was drooping. The hand that held the match shook, maybe due to rage, or pain, or fear or a mix of all three. He moved this trembling hand down to the mouth of the hole. An audible "whump" reached Gloria's ears and a small fireball rose from the earth. Harold had pulled his hand away but stared at it with great surprise, because flames rose from it as well. "Great Scott!" he yelled again, flapping the hand around manically.

"Wudz all that racket?" Rachel Gomberg slurred loudly from the kitchen, finally noticing that things were amiss.

"I'm on fire!" Harold yelled as he ran to the pool. Gloria felt that her father delivered the line with half the subtlety of Bruce Springsteen but with twice the sincerity. Harold submerged his hand and cursed up at the sky, demanding an explanation from no one.

That night, a group of rather loud high school girls sat on the playground swings three blocks from Gloria's house. They were taking turns sipping from a bottle of Smirnoff and practically screaming about how their biology teacher was a total pervert who stank of blue cheese. Every other word out of their mouths was the sort that a youth swallows in front of parents. One of the girls was by the see-saw squatting and urinating. Two others were so drunk they were holding onto each other for balance and laughing in each other's faces.

Gloria approached them alone and cautiously. She went straight to the girl who was clearly the ringleader, rocking on a swing in the center of the others. She was a mousy child with outsized feathered hair and too much lipstick. She wore torn jeans and a faded denim jacket, and she peered suspiciously at Gloria through layers of eyeliner.

"Gloria," the girl said.

"Ruth," Gloria said.

The other girls were quiet.

Gloria spoke without hesitation. She could not be bothered with fear. She feared her family's dissolution, not the tough front put on by mere kids. "Word has it you have cigarettes."

"Yeah. So?"

"I want one."

It was a day of firsts not just for her parents, but for Gloria as well.

Chapter Ten

On the day of the second disaster, she woke to the wind screaming, rain splashing on the sliding doors, and grey light streaming into the room. Her head pounded and she was nauseous. She searched for Scott before remembering he was gone. Gloria needed him right now. His calm. His gentleness. His frustrating habit of making a decision and sticking with it, disregarding any proposal of course-correction.

Nothing could be done about it. She had closed the Scott door, and she had no phone to re-open it.

The night had passed and she knew she had to get her father out of jail. After brushing her teeth, she grabbed Scott's car keys and threw on what appeared to be Nika's poncho. As she opened the door and the wind screamed, she worried about Logan, the dog. Where was he? Would he be okay? And what about that other one, Logan's doppelganger? Dogs were not cats; survival in bad weather was a long shot.

Her mind was taken away from that concern quickly when she saw Scott's car. It was sitting in the middle of a pond, the waterline far above the wheel wells. The tide had receded but each time the waves broke, they still rolled ominously over select low points in the dunes and filled the new driveway pond. One did not need to be a mechanic to know that the Volvo was no longer an option. A moment of panic gripped her. Was she going to die here? Would the house collapse and be dragged out to sea? She had no idea what the hurricane held in store. This might be the height of it or just the spinning teeth of its outer bands. The ocean may have passed by its worst tides or all of the low-lying southern shores of the island might be submerged within the next six hours.

In the distance, through the pelting sand, she saw Dick and Prissy getting into the abandoned police car. Gloria wasted no time. In the dumbest of biathlons, she waded through the pond and sprinted down the road to the neighbor's house. When she arrived at the police car, she was soaked and terribly winded. The poncho flapped up over her face relentlessly. She looked around and noticed that her fancy neighbors' BMW was in the same predicament as Scott's car.

Dick had apparently removed two sets of body armor, a pair of bolt cutters, and a defibrillator from the trunk of the squad car and placed them carefully on top of a white towel by the side of the driveway. He now replaced those items in the trunk with his tennis racket and a black garment bag. He looked at Gloria.

"Well, well, well," he said loudly over the wind. "Look who it is."

Prissy stuck her head out of the passenger seat and got out to greet the unexpected company. The woman was tall, easily six feet, without an ounce of fat on her. She wore runner's black tights, black sneakers, and a black track jacket. She had to be twenty years Gloria's senior but was far better maintained. Her shoulder-length dyed blonde hair had been perfectly assembled this morning but now it blew in every direction. It did not matter what the day held in store, she had applied a sufficient, but not overdone, amount of lipstick and eyeliner. The truth was, Gloria thought the woman looked breathtaking. Then as friendly as a favorite aunt, Prissy squealed, "Gloria! What a nice surprise." The words rolled over her tongue and teeth in a manner betraying Prissy's Locust Valley heritage. There were no hard edges, each consonant smoothed like seastone. And Gloria

151

marveled at the words Prissy chose. The old woman's ability to adhere to etiquette regardless of circumstance usually fascinated Gloria but right now it was stomach-churning.

Then Gloria heard herself respond and realized she was the same type of human. "Well, hi there, Mrs. Hoyt."

"Oh please. Call me Prissy!"

No thank you, Gloria thought. "How's your daughter? Casey?" she continued over the din of the storm. "Last I remember she was at Lehigh studying anthropology."

"What a memory you have. Case is all grown up. A mom herself. She's living in St. Louis with her-"

"Priss," Dick said with frustration. "Can you please help me with some of this stuff?"

Prissy looked both ways as if she was going to share an earth-shattering secret. She urged Gloria to come closer and then said with a loud whisper that could be heard over the wind, "We're planning our getaway from this nastiness. With a police car! Officer Kensler practically begged us to drive it. He left the keys in the ignition! Isn't this fuhhhhhn?" She said this through a conspiratorial grin while playfully slapping Gloria's wrist.

"It is!" Gloria responded with a smile, repressing her hangover and a profound panic about leaving her father in jail overnight. "But isn't this car out of gas?" Gloria asked.

"Well," Dick yelled as he placed a suitcase into the backseat, "I returned your father's favor. I broke into *his* storage shed and took a gallon of gas."

"Fair enough," Gloria replied. "Look, can I ask a favor?"

"What is it, sweetheart?" Prissy asked. "Oh silly me. Look at your car over there. You need a ride."

"Yes, thank you. To town."

"Hop in the back," Prissy said as nice as can be. "There should be a little room."

They drove down island, swerving to avoid fallen branches and a downed telephone pole. The area screamed abandonment, but then again it always did feel empty outside of the summer season. The morning was monochrome. White sky and grey earth. How could there be such a thing as sun? Gloria wondered. When things looked like this, it was hard to imagine them ever changing. Prissy had handed Dick a lowball glass full of clear liquid with a lime twist floating atop, poured herself a glass, and now both were sipping away.

"Gin and tonic, dear?" Prissy offered her own drink to Gloria through a large slot in the Plexiglas divider between the front and back seats of the police car.

Gloria thought she might vomit at the thought, but kindly said, "No thank you."

Prissy pulled the drink back and continued to talk through the slot. "Sorry about the business last night." She whispered to Gloria in a way that Dick could obviously hear. "He has a tendency to overreact."

"You were the one who told me to go outside and see what the problem was," Dick snapped. He nodded his head slowly and said, "My mother said never marry a Cornforth."

Prissy laughed. "Oh poo. Now what were we talking about? Oh, right, so Case is in St. Louis with her husband. Nice man she married. Paul Dunn. Of the New Canaan Dunn's? Decent, handsome man. Anyhoozles, she's working for a non-profit. Some hippy dippy situation focusing on food safety." Prissy made air quotes when she mentioned 'food safety.' Gloria knew to keep her opinion to herself and continued to listen politely.

153

"They're demanding all food be labeled as organic or, what is it, Dick?"

"Genetically modified," Dick said, chewing his ice.

"Right. Genetically modified."

"And what does her husband do?" Gloria asked.

Prissy swallowed her gin and tonic and said, "He's legal counsel for Monsanto. Turn right here, Dick."

Dick rolled his eyes. "I know the way to the ferry dock, Priss."

"Oh, of course you do. How could I have forgotten?" She looked back at Gloria and winked. "It's the same direction as the package store."

They drove for what seemed to Gloria too long to sustain small talk. Nonetheless, Prissy prattled on about the dreadful weather and Case in St. Louis and the Clement family that lived on the other side of them on Moshup Trail and the son the Clements had to throw into military school after constant arrests for shoplifting, all the while Dick gulping down his drink and negotiating debris in the road. Prissy's phone began to play a techno ringtone that clearly came as the phone's default. "Oh that's Case now checking in on us. One moment, Gloria."

Gloria could not believe she was momentarily jealous of the relationship between the Hoyts and their daughter. "So, Mr. Hoyt," she said. "Are you concerned at all about stealing a squad car?"

"Not in the least, young lady. I donate heavily to the force on this island. They consider me a friend. Plus, they have enough on their plate right now." He flicked on the police radio and it crackled to life with what seemed like a nonstop barrage of desperate queries and no responses. Gloria understood almost none of it as it was a palimpsest of numerical codes and cop

154

terminology. It sounded awful. Like no one was in control of the situation. Like the world was rolling off of its plinth. Dick switched it off. "Bedlam," he continued. "This car is the least of their worries."

Prissy was not so much talking with her daughter as talking at her.

"Is someone picking you up on the mainland?" Dick asked Gloria.

"Oh, I'm not getting on the ferry. I'm going to pick up my dad at the jail."

"He's at the jail?" Dick laughed. "You left him there all night? Golly gee you must dislike him as much as I do. Sorry, but we're going to the ferry, hon."

She did not like him calling her 'hon' one bit and may have punched him in the back of the head if the Plexiglas was not in the way.

Prissy took her head away from the phone. "Oh silly us. We never asked where you were going. You said 'town' and we just assumed the ferry. We can take you over to the courthouse, right dear?"

Dick responded with a sigh. "I guess we can. Look." He pointed out to a spot beyond the windshield. They had reached the edge of the land and a wooden gate blocked off the ferry loading dock. Nobody was around for Dick to chew out.

"Blast it," Dick said. "Ask Case to look at the internet? Ask her if there's any word about ferry service or any other damn thing on this island. I'm not staying here. I'll charter a goddamn tanker if it's the only way off this rock." He nervously flicked the headlights on and off.

Prissy did as Dick asked, and then things were blessedly silent for a moment. Gloria watched the ocean rage. An occasional wave would hit the Oak Bluffs sea wall just right, or wrong, and send water twenty feet into the air. The splash would start in one location and then continue down the stone barrier into the distance until it was beyond Gloria's sight. A liquid fireworks display. There were no seagulls. At times the wind would blow against the car so hard she felt the whole thing shift slightly.

Prissy held her hand over the phone. "Ferry service is canceled because of the storm. It's stalled over the northeast." She went back to listening and then back to her hand over the phone. "They're asking everyone to take shelter at the high school gym."

"Stellar," Dick said. "Looking forward to a glorious day eating cheese sandwiches on cots with the rabble." He put the car back into drive and eased out onto Seaview Avenue. Driving rain on the car's windows presented the town park as a green bubbling abstraction. The gingerbread houses beyond the park appeared and disappeared with each wind gust, a silent film with too many beats between frames.

Prissy slapped Dick harmlessly. "Cheer up, sourpus. It'll be an adventure."

Gloria was with Dick on this one. "You know what?" she said. "I'll take that gin and tonic, please."

"Refill me, too," Dick said, holding out his glass.

"Now that's the spirit!" Prissy said, pulling an impressive thermos up from between her legs. The effort made her groan and briefly expose her age. "It's an impromptu party!" She turned on the radio, maybe hoping for a song to fit the mood, but was greeted by Nanci Griffith's "Love at the Five and Dime."

They drove toward the high school. Gloria felt she had spent sufficient time with her unexpected company and was pretty much caught up on their lives; there was no question her car-mates felt the same, with Prissy now staring silently out the window and Dick humming along to the radio, clearly not familiar with the song. Gloria sipped her delicious drink and watched the ocean roil. She was shocked to see windsurfers skipping along the surface. Were they suicidal? This tide was nothing to provoke. The earth had lost some age-old dominance and the sea was simply pulling away from it. There were a few spots where the water had jumped onto land and was crossing the road. For a drunk, Dick deftly swerved and recalibrated, safely directing the car to the spot where the road finally turned inland. He looked in the rearview mirror at Gloria. "Listen, hon," he said. "You may be able to help us. And the police. I was just going to ditch the car at the ferry. Then at the school. But why don't you drop us at the school and then continue to the jail? You can deliver the car right to the police's door. No one's going to be upset. They'll thank you."

Gloria saw the logic in this but was nervous about driving the thing.

"Don't worry. We'll call the station and let them know you're coming. It's fine."

She thought a beat more and said, "That'll work great. Thanks, Mr. Hoyt."

"So I hate to pry," Prissy said, "but since we have a bit longer, I have to ask, what's your situation?"

Gloria, who one moment earlier had been re-evaluating the Hoyts and considering scratching them from her personal shit list, raised her defenses.

"What do you mean?" she asked.

"Oh you know, darling. A man. Is there anyone in your sites?"

Was the military analogy purposeful? Did they know about Scott? Did they intend to draw blood? Probably not, but Gloria's stomach turned. She saw no need to lie to them so she decided on full disclosure.

"No," she said.

"Hm. And why not?"

"I believe that someone not in a relationship should be free from having to explain 'why not' and those in relationships should be required to answer 'why?'"

Prissy raised an eyebrow and spoke. "I was not trying to be insulting, dear. I was merely trying to make conversation."

"I'm sorry." Again with the apologies, she thought. "I didn't mean to be defensive. It's just that I broke off an engagement literally yesterday."

"Ohhhh." Prissy put her hand to her mouth. "I'm the one who should be sorry. My prying is relentless. You had every right to snap at me. I am terribly, terribly sorry."

Guilt washed over Gloria like a tsunami. Making others feel guilty was her greatest source of guilt. "No no no," she exclaimed. "It's totally okay. You didn't know."

"Still," Prissy said. "I'm sorry."

Silence enveloped the car for a time and then Prissy said. "And you're right. The onus is on people like me to explain why we're in a relationship."

"No no. It's not." Gloria said. "You're in love and that's a good enough reason."

"I suppose so. That wasn't the case with your man?"

"Scott? No. It's not like my heart beats faster when he's nearby."

Prissy nearly spit up her drink. Dick laughed out loud. After she had swallowed, Prissy said, "Are you kidding? What does a racing heart have to do with love? A racing heart is something that happens on a rollercoaster. Can you imagine spending your entire life on a rollercoaster? You'd be whoopsing for eternity! Do you respect him?"

"I think so," Gloria said.

"Is he nice to you?"

"Sure."

"Does he respect you?"

"A lot."

"Does he bite his fork when he eats?"

"No."

"I'd say you've found a wonderful man."

Gloria considered this, then said, "But I dated him to get back at my father."

Prissy gestured toward her husband like a game show model displaying a new car. "Meet Dick Hoyt."

"What do you mean?"

"Cornforths do not marry Hoyts. And that's why I did."

Perhaps I've misjudged these people, Gloria thought. After all, her father had broken into *their* storage area and scared them. It made sense that Dick had him arrested. Rule of law had to be obeyed. Was Dick so wrong to protect his wife who had been scared witless by an intruder in the night? Come to think of it, Prissy looked like she should have been protecting Dick. And speaking of Prissy, Gloria was amazed at how delightful the woman was being on this drive. Past interactions had been so cold. Then again, Harold had also been present in every instance, so that would explain a few things.

Prissy lovingly combed her husband's hair with her fingers, looked out at the grey world and said, "Well, Dicky my sweet, once again our vacation has been ruined by the Jews."

Dick was swerving quite a bit now, even though this stretch of road had no debris on it. Gloria looked at the front seat passenger while her brain continued to process what she had just heard. It took her some time to summon words, but all that came were "Who did you say ruined your vacation?"

"Oh no one," Prissy said. "It's just a theory I heard about the weather. You know I really miss your mother. She and I were good friends. We got along famously." Prissy had not put on her seatbelt and was turned completely around for the discussion. "What an elegant woman Rachel was."

All of the hour-long talks on the phone between Gloria and her mother. All of their late-night gab-fests on the couch in the darkened Norwalk living room. All of the dirt the Gomberg women dished while lying on their backs by the shore under the Aquinnah sun. After all of that, Gloria had absolutely no idea that Prissy Hoyt and Rachel Gomberg had anything other than a neighborly relationship.

"You spent time with my mother?" she asked.

"Oh of course! We lived a stone's throw from each other. I mean, sure, your father and Mr. Sweetheart over here didn't mix, but it never stopped Rachel and me from having an iced tea in the afternoons."

"What did you talk about?"

Prissy waved her hand dismissively. "Oh this and that." One of her eyes blinked slower than the other and her tongue seemed to be losing precision. "She certainly had a lot to get off her back."

"Oh?" Gloria sat forward slightly. "Like what? Stuff about my dad?"

"Now now. I'm not saying a word."

Gloria was having none of this arch behavior. Especially from a weird anti semite. "Oh come on, Mrs. Hoyt," she said with a grin. "She's long gone and I was a friend to her in addition to being her daughter. I'm sure she wouldn't mind if you shared some tidbits."

"Young lady. What kind of friend would I be if I shared those tidbits. I will take those things to my grave w-"

The lovely, drunk woman stopped talking and opened her mouth wide. Her eyes bulged and fixed on nothing. After a moment, one of her hands went to her throat and the other grabbed Dick's shoulder.

"Ow! Careful, I'm driving!" Dick said, not taking his eyes off the road.

"Mrs. Hoyt?" Gloria asked.

There was no response. Both of Prissy's hands were now on her own jugular. Her face was turning white and her eyes were watering. She began shaking her head frantically but still no noise came from her mouth. It was then that Gloria understood fully. "She's choking!" Gloria yelled.

Dick looked over and then began guiding the car to the side of the road, but there was no shoulder and a truck was behind them. Prissy was thrusting her back against the dashboard, her head pressing against the sun visor. Her legs locked and her now purple face was pressed up against the ceiling. Hands still clutched windpipe, trying vainly to remove the lodged entity.

It was then that Gloria unfastened her seatbelt, leaned forward, put her arm through the slot all the way to her armpit, and awkwardly punched the struggling woman in the stomach with the extent of her fear and rage. This action was met with a lime wedge hitting the Plexiglas, projected expeditiously from Prissy's throat. Gloria looked at the fruit chunk sliding down the

161

divider, and then up again at the gruesome vision before her, an uncontained dervish of coughing, gasping, and drooling.

Only then was Dick able to pull to the side. He went to touch his wife's shoulder, doing so like he was reaching for a hot kettle, with rapid, wary test touches before grabbing a true hold. "Priss? You okay?"

Prissy gently removed her husband's hand, turned herself around, and applied her seatbelt with the calm of a Buddhist monk. Wiping her mouth, she cleared her throat and looked forward into the storm.

Dick exhaled deeply and went to pull the car back out into traffic.

As the school entrance appeared through the sheets of rain, Prissy said to the windshield, "The friendship was a two-way street, you know? I was able to tell your mother things that no one on the island had known. About our short separation. About how I was almost an Olympic swimmer before my bout with cancer. About the loss of our son..." Her voice broke and she stopped talking for a moment. Dick reached over and put his arm on her shoulder again.

Prissy managed to collect herself faster than anyone Gloria had ever seen. The aging beauty wiped one eye and said in a bubbly voice. "But that's neither here nor there." Her attention shifted to a sign they were approaching that read 'Martha's Vineyard High School.' "Isn't this the school right here, Dick?" she asked.

"What gave it away," Dick asked.

They parked behind the gym next to a line of buses, where a group of Asian tourists retrieved luggage from the many vehicles' bottom compartments. The Hoyts got out of the squad car, mixing in with the group, and Gloria slipped into the driver's seat. As was the apparent nature of their marriage, Dick carried four large bags over his shoulders while Prissy carried a tennis racket. Prissy looked down and spoke to Gloria through the open squad car window. "Safe travels, dear, and best of luck with your father. He sure is a handful! Oh, and reconsider your boyfriend. He seems like a doll." Then she loudly cleared a lime rind from her throat and walked off to the school.

The engine of the Crown Victoria gently hummed beneath her. She required more noise or she was afraid she would fall asleep at the wheel. What better solution than to turn on the scanner? She tried a few knobs before she found the volume. The chaotic chatter returned, none of it making sense, and audio Tower of Babel. An eleven forty-one on Circuit Avenue. Someone required a ten thirty-five. Far from snapping her to attention, the police chatter hypnotized her. She felt her head bob down, caught herself, and her heart jumped.

More extreme measures would be required. She looked for the siren and found a box beside her right thigh that left no mystery. Above several knobs it read 'HIGH POWER SIREN' in all caps. Turning the knob until it reached its first detent, the world became a blaring trumpet. Too much, she thought. The noise itself did not pose the problem. It was the attention she was certainly drawing to herself. The idea was embarrassing. She turned off the siren and drove on, hoping the momentary excitement would keep her up long enough to get to Edgartown.

She drove no faster than ten miles per hour. The defog was set high but it failed to clear the windshield. She never knew what temperature the air should be when defogging, and she suspected she was making the problem worse. She began clearing the windshield with her hand. While continually doing this motion, all she could think about was her mother and the mysterious summits she had held with Prissy. Cancer, child death. It sounded like those talks went *deep*. Harold's shapeshifting and dalliances were almost certainly discussed. What Gloria would have given to hear even a moment of those exchanges. But she never would, thanks to Prissy, the ultimate gossip, deciding now to be Gandhi and take the high ground. The murder of her father would have to go unsolved for yet another day. And here she was, driving a squad car, unable to work on a murder case.

Through the madness on the scanner, one message rose above the others by employing words she understood. "We got a ten ninety-one. I mean..." The officer's voice paused. "Well." Static. "It's a ten ninety-one but not sure if it's a ninety-one A or what." Static. "Two dogs. Called in from South Beach. Folks say black rottweilers. Caught in the surf. I'd say V type. One of them bit someone. Over."

The urgency of everything came to her now. She switched the siren back on and stepped hard on the gas. The Crown Victoria blasted into the nothingness ahead.

Chapter Eleven

The day's light was anemic and strangely hued for early afternoon. Everything appeared moss-covered, dark green and wet. The sky no longer arched above the world but collapsed and bled into everything beneath. The wind moved across the island and made an urgent effort to run through objects in its path. Where it could not run through, it ricocheted and amplified, becoming more eager to demolish. Tree branches, litter, and power lines rested atop homes and cars alike. Plastic garbage lids and magnolia petals blew across town streets. The ocean ringing Martha's Vineyard strived to encroach and reclaim. Jetties constructed of gargantuan boulders crumbled. Moored sailboats congregated where the sea's vortices dictated and ran aground in once peaceful inlets. The center of the hurricane had not even arrived.

Inside the Black Goose Grill in Oak Bluffs, Gloria, Harold, and Nika sat around a wooden table, celebrating Harold's new freedom from jail, which he referred to as "the belly of the beast." He and Nika were terrifically intoxicated, whispering into one another's ears and laughing heartily. They had been there all day, from noon to now, the world outside darkening with the unseen sunset. Gloria was sober. Being responsible for driving her father's pizza delivery car had her nervous about ordering anything stronger than a ginger ale. When she had bailed her father out several hours earlier, Nika napping on a bench all night in the courthouse, Harold had demanded they go to the Black Goose for his celebration. Feeling guilty for coming to his rescue so long after his incarceration, Gloria agreed and chauffeured. Any urgency Gloria had felt in the squad car - to contact Scott, to find the dogs, to get off this island - now went unsatisfied. This bar is Purgatory, she thought. But there's no Virgil to guide me through.

Harold was wearing a Hawaiian shirt, cargo pants, and flip flops, all several sizes too small, leant to him by police officers at the jail. The mattress in the prison had been washed with some type of detergent that caused his skin to break out in a rash. Red blotches covered the left side of his face and his left arm. Sticking out of his shirt pocket was the toothbrush and small tube of toothpaste the jail had provided him.

The memory of Prissy's brief emotional unwinding was occupying Gloria. Losing a son. What an unimaginable bane. She thought of her brother and the love her parents felt toward him. Seth had always been a little shit to Gloria, admittedly because she acted as his personal dictator, but to everyone else, he was a lamb. Making birthday cards for family and friends by hand, actually listening to people when they spoke. His mother hugged him whenever possible. She bragged about her little bookworm to everyone at work, at the synagogue, and in the kitchen when neighbors visited. Harold only spent time with Seth when he needed someone to spot him on a ladder. But he would mess up the boy's hair at times and say, "You are a fine fellow." If Rachel and Harold had lost their son, the devastation would have been unimaginable. Harold would have been even more far gone than he was now.

Gloria's mind was also consumed by Prissy's editorial regarding marriage. Had Gloria made a mistake dismissing Scott? Was he good enough? No, she told herself. He was not. Maybe Priscilla Cornforth could settle for Richard Hoyt, but she was not Priscilla Cornforth.

166

Populating the bar that day were the resistant and the foolish; men and women who wanted nothing to do with taking refuge and cowering from the storm in a school gym. Gloria was familiar with this crowd after years of coming to the island. They had all seen storms come before and were not about to hide now. Most of the patrons were older people, caked in salt, leathery, drunk, and belligerent. These were a potent sampling of "year-rounders," people who could not stand the tourists yet depended on their money to stay afloat. Two silver-haired, red-faced men played pool and smoked despite state law. Alex, the bartender, who had been serving Harold for many years, was not interested in enforcing such restrictions today. The jukebox played the Allman Brothers' "Melissa." Gloria could tell the music was starting to get to her father. Between smiles aimed at Nika, he would suddenly frown and look at the jukebox. Gloria did not like drunk Harold. Stoned Harold was obnoxious and chatty, but at least somewhat poetic. Drunk Harold, a much rarer event, was only the former two. His moods would swing hither and yon depending on which stimulus was winning out for his attention at that moment.

He shouted at Alex the bartender, "Play Dizzy Gillespie you philistine!"

Nika added, "Play philistine you Dizzy Gillespie!"

"Low-born curs! The lot of you. Where is my drink?" Harold asked no one.

"It is in your hand," Nika pointed out to him.

Gloria said for the third time that day, "I really think we should drive over to the school. We don't know how bad this is going to get."

"I miss kvass," Nika said.

"Kvass?" Gloria asked.

"Yes. Kvass. Wonderful drink in Russia. I miss sitting with father and drinking kvass in front of television." She sighed. "He would yell at Spartak Moscow football match. I see him." Nika closed her eyes and smiled. "He is wearing track jacket covered in cigarette burns. Mother is telling him to be quiet." She opened her eyes again. "What I don't miss is winter there. Or also spring. Roads are rivers of water and litter when filthy snow melts. No. I do not miss Perm. I do not miss Russia. But I miss my mother and father."

"I never asked," Gloria said.

Nika opened her eyes.

"Why you dislike me this much, bitch? What did I do to you? I am good to your father."

"You're an infant. Are you even allowed to be in here? Not only are you young enough to be my dad's daughter, you're young enough to be *my* daughter."

"If I was your daughter I ask could I sleep in bed with you and when you fall asleep I will punch you in face!"

"Not before I abandon you at a supermarket."

No one spoke. An occasional gust of wind would scream over the music and the bar window would vibrate erratically. The wooden floor could be felt to shake as well. Gloria looked down to see if her eyes could detect any sign of the wood splitting. The floor held. While she was looking down there, she tried to take mental inventory of her situation. She had been surprised to hear herself snap at Nika, thinking she had made peace with the girl. Gloria felt that if her two drunk companions would just agree to leave the bar, perhaps she would stop feeling so belligerent toward them. She had to try a new tack, something other than antagonizing her future stepmother. Perhaps being nice would

168

make them bored, antsy, and willing to leave. Time to apologize yet again to yet another person.

Gloria spoke. "I'm sorry. You're right, Nika. I apologize. There's no reason for me to snap at you. Tell me more about Perm."

Nika sipped from the Red Bull and Smirnoff she was drinking. After swallowing, she said, "Perm is small city. That is all I have to say about this question. Your father and I. We are going to get married at the house, you know? On the deck." She put her arms around Harold's neck. "Amos is also justice of peace and will make the wedding be true."

"Dad, are you going to- Dad!" Harold, who had been falling asleep sitting up, jumped to attention when he heard Gloria yell his name. "Dad, are you going to meet Nika's parents?"

"Of course!" Harold said, furiously scratching the rash on his face. "On any given night I get an order for ten thousand pizzas and I pull in one thousand dollars in tips. Mere weeks after accepting the position at Island Pizza I owned a fleet of alabaster planes, each more breathtaking than the last. It is with those I intend to fly you, Seth, your aunts, uncles, and a cast of hundreds to Perm to meet my parents-in-law. We will then hold the wedding in Red Square where Lenin's ghost will be the ring bearer."

Nika spoke. "My parents would not like him. Mother would only speak Russian and every word would be mean thing about him. If my father was sober he would say nothing. If he was drunk, he would punch. No, Harold is not meeting my parents."

Gloria was thrilled to see Nika yawn.

Harold spoke through closed eyes and bobbing head. "We plan to get married at the house."

"Nika told me that already."

"Amos can officiate weddings. Wait, I should rephrase. It will be at the house if we still have the house."

"What do you mean?"

"The taxes!" Harold blurted. "The state thirsts for taxes. And back taxes. And for what, I ask? To pay police officers who will arrest me for practicing my religion. In fact, I should try to get a tax break for being a religious organization."

"What religion?"

"Shed clothing. Shed government. Shed god."

"That is not a religion, Dad."

"Bollocks. I say my mantra aloud the moment sunlight lands on the duvet in the morning."

"He does this," Nika added.

"I say it when I take my afternoon jaunt along the briny sea. I say it as I exhale Purple Trainwreck from my patriotic lungs. I sing it while I boil the jars for apricot preserves. There are few times, in fact, when I am not uttering or thinking this prayer. This *namshub*. This dictum!"

Nika said, "I am needlepointing sampler that says his words."

"Small Town" by John Cougar Mellencamp came on the jukebox and someone at the bar whooped.

Gloria was trying to keep the conversation light but had to dig. "You're clearly a Libertarian. So why don't you join the Libertarian party? Get involved. Go to meetings."

Harold looked at Gloria through drooping eyelids. "The head of the Massachusetts Libertarian Party is a functional pedophile with small teeth."

"Well, you don't need to hang out with whoever *that* is. You just need to align with him-"

"Her," Harold stepped in.

"Fine. Her. You just need to work locally to make a difference."

"I choose to change the world by example."

"That's the lazy person's answer."

"I see no lazy person here. I cook for myself. I deliver pizzas. I roll my own joints. Show me this lazy person."

"Fine. Don't join the party. How about a group of local nudists? That takes little effort and you clearly share things in common with them."

"The naturists? Please. Their reasons for being naked differ from mine. They are obsessed with fruity notions like communing with nature and bringing about equality by exposing their teats and dingles. Equality? From being naked? I suspect the opposite would occur. And besides, I would never join any club that would have my member as a member."

Nika barged in. "He uses same joke every time. I don't get it."

"You should know it, my dear!" Harold said. "It's Marx!"

Gloria rolled her eyes. "Groucho. Not Karl. It's one bad joke after another with you. Please," Gloria begged, looking outside at the storm, "Let's go before we can't leave anymore."

Harold persisted. "Why do you want me to join some larger group? Why can't I just exist as an individual, with my lady friend at my side?" He put his hand gently on Nika's shoulder. "Proselytizing to strangers when the mood strikes me?"

"Because you need a family if not your own. Or maybe you need your own. Move to New York," she suggested.

Harold snickered. "New York? No, thank you. I am not a gender-fluid Native American. No one in New York wants what I am selling."

"Well, it's not like anyone here does. And what was that supposed to mean? 'Gender-fluid Native American?'"

"Does it need explanation? Everyone in that ferkakta city must be exactly the same in their uniqueness. Except white men who need to go away. So why should I go against their requests? They want us out. 'All winners' heads belong on pykes! Hang the bankers! Garrote the honkies!' I tell you it is fascism wearing ironic facial hair. They would happily burn 'Fahrenheit 451' because it only celebrates male authors and they would refuse to see the irony as they roasted locally-sourced cane sugar marshmallows over it."

"I think you're trying to say that I live in a world that is too politically correct for you. Like women and minorities are too sensitive to white men's actions and words. Well, there's a reason for political correctness, Dad. It exists because white men dominated the world for far too long, and the political correctness which you find so annoying exists as a way of saying 'never again.' It's not just annoying word policing. We must stay vigilant and we need to overreact. Do you realize that you've never known suffering? For example, you've hit the fricking gender jackpot, Dad. You're the winner due to no skill on your part."

"Rubbish. How am I the winner just due to my gender?"

"Nika is completely silenced by your bluster. She can't get a word in edgewise. I don't doubt for a second she's as smart as you, but she's physically smaller and her vocal chords aren't as loud. And we as women have been taught since we were kids to allow men to talk over us. You're heard more than us. You hit the gender jackpot."

"And that is the line of argument you will use to execute all men, all guilty of being born men. Trust me. You will be next before the firing squad. For being white. It is a slippery slope, made slippery from innocent blood."

Gloria gave out a groan. "Man, it must be uncomfortable for you goose-stepping naked."

"No harder than it is for you goose-stepping while keeping a hacky sack airborne. Look. I am happy, young lady. Why move? I have Nika, an occasional bong hit with Amos, my easy-as-pie job, my books, my music, the ocean."

Gloria desperately wanted to say 'Move because I want my father back,' but it would not come out. Armor works both ways, she thought. It can protect but it can trap. Instead, she said "You should move because there's no way you're *not* going to be evicted. A person can't pay property taxes on beachfront property with delivery tips."

"Who says I am paying?"

"Then even worse than eviction, you're going to be arrested."

"Fear not! When the cemetery comes through, I will have a lurid amount of money that will take care of-"

"Again with the disgusting garden cemetery! You're the only person on this planet who clings to a cemetery for life! You're like Ishmael clinging to the coffin when the Pequod sank!"

"Hey!" Nika yelled. "I'm reading that, bitch! Let me tell you how Percy Jackson ends and see your pain!"

"It's never going to happen, Dad," Gloria said. "The cemetery is not a good idea."

"It will," Harold responded. "There is a non-profit requirement for cemeteries in Connecticut, and for the past decade I have been using a phalanx of lawyers to challenge it."

"By 'phalanx of lawyers' do you mean family friend and freeloader Jerry Rosenblum?"

"Precisely."

"Isn't he like ninety? He was gumming his food in the nineteen seventies."

"He is at the height of his powers."

Gloria picked up a salted peanut from a bowl in the middle of their table and held it up. "Food growing in a cemetery? C'mon, Dad. There are sanitary codes that need to be respected. And I'm not talking about the bodies. I'm talking about you."

"I am unsanitary! Capital joke! To use the parlance of the children, 'crackle!'"

"I think you mean 'snap,'" Gloria offered.

Harold's face grew dark in an instant. "But unlike your joke, there is nothing funny about my cemetery plans. I will make it happen. Nay, I *must* make it happen. I need the money. You try boiling your empty leather wallet for nourishment."

"You never did that," Nika added.

"Check with me in one month."

Enough of this, Gloria thought. The dogs are probably dead. I need to make peace with Scott despite ending it. And I need to get off this fucking island.

Lights in the bar flickered and drunkards cheered. When the room was again properly lit, Gloria happened to be looking down at her hands. She had one of those moments that hit her every couple of years. In these moments, she stepped out of her life and took inventory from some much higher plane. It was a plane unaffected by the crucible of the present with its tensions and hurts and biases. She considered this unique perspective to be the one that was the consistent Gloria across time. The 'Bigger Gloria.' The Gloria who right now was no different than the

Gloria at thirteen or the one at thirty-six or the one she would be at eighty-one. And this Bigger Gloria—of all times and places—now looked at her hands and was amazed at how wrinkles were deepening and bones were rising to the surface. It said, quite calmly, 'Our hands are becoming the rugged terrain of the West. Our body is aging.' To whom did this voice speak? To the forty-seven-year-old smaller Gloria trapped in this bar? Had she become the nesting dolls of her youth? The ones she called The Glorias? She was not sure, but she knew that all present Glorias wanted to leave.

The Bigger Gloria disappeared as quickly as she had arrived. Gloria proper peripherally noticed that while her Algonquin round table had been going on with her father and Nika, Alex the bartender had been chatting up one slouching man at the far end of the bar. The mysterious person had been wearing the hood of his rain poncho up over his head the entire time. At this moment, he pulled it down and Gloria saw that it was Kyle, the man she had met at the Dairy Queen. The husband of her ex-manager. The man her father had harassed on the beach.

"Dad," Gloria said. "Look."

Harold wheeled around and took a moment to figure out what his daughter found interesting. When he finally did identify the man, he yelled over John Cougar Mellencamp, "Kyle, you are a fellow pawn in the government's chess match! Come and join us!"

Kyle was startled by the yell but then turned his head and focused his eyes. He got up enthusiastically and made hand gestures at his drink on the bar as if he could not decide whether to leave it or bring it with him. Grabbing the nearly empty IPA, he walked over. The serpentine trail he chose suggested that he too was inebriated.

Harold patted the empty seat next to him and Kyle nearly fell into it.

"This guy!" Kyle slurred, and then he kissed Harold on the cheek.

"Sloppy!" Harold explained. "I like this you, Kyle. Can we get you another drink?"

Kyle made a stop signal with his hand and said into his own chest, "Totally good, bro! Don't need any more. That guy Alex hooked me up so super-good." He looked over at Gloria and hiccupped. "You are so fired, dude. My wife is like 'she's *outta here*.'" Kyle imitated an umpire making the call. "I told her to chill but she was like 'nope.'"

"Where's she now?" Gloria asked.

Kyle took the last swig of his beer, "Left me." He did the umpire impression again. "Outta here! That's why I'm getting' my drinky on. Do you guys have a cigar?"

Gloria said, "No. Why did she leave you?"

"Long story, bro. Ask Alex over there. I just gave him the whole spiel."

"It's *shpiel*," Gloria corrected him.

"Whatevs, bro!"

Kyle got up, stumbled, and upon catching himself started playing air guitar to John Cougar Mellencamp. He did not know the words and mumbled along to it.

"Stop that!" Harold bellowed. "This song is insufferable. The singer is a liar. He knows nothing of small towns. He is a Los Angeles robot bragging about a few hints of rust."

Harold made an awkward grab to pull Kyle back into his seat but his reach was problematic. Kyle's poncho tore off and the man was now naked. Kyle reflexively grabbed the poncho from Harold and covered his groin.

"Great Scott!" Harold yelled.

The lights in the room flickered for a moment. Intoxicated screams interspersed with laughter. Someone stood up to cheer but moved too quickly, slammed their knee into the table, and sent their mug to the floor where it shattered. Alex was not amused and yelled for everyone to "chill out."

The lights came back on and Kyle had his poncho on backwards. Harold stared at him in amazement.

"And here I thought you were a man with a closet literally exploding with khakis. But no. You are a freedom fighter like me!"

"Dad. He's a yuppie prick. That's it. His wife fired me today."

"I'm...I don't know. I might...No. You don't know me," he whined in a new timbre. "Neither do I. I was just-" He turned to Harold and touched the large man's nose with his index finger. He began another thought. "I went to look for you-" but the words were stopped by tears, and then he rose and opened the front door of the bar. Wind shot into the room. Napkins, coasters, and long hair came alive. Flyers for local bands and dance lessons blew off a cork board near the entrance and swarmed around Kyle before assaulting the rest of the patrons.

"Shut the fucking door!" Alex yelled.

To Gloria's amazement, Kyle closed the door as asked, but did so from the outside.

Alex stormed over to their table. "You let him leave?" he asked. "In this weather? Do you know how drunk he is? I totally fucking overserved that dude."

"He didn't ask," Gloria said. "He just got up and left."

Alex went to look out the window, but dark had settled in. He came back and, turning his Patriots cap backward, took a seat between Harold and Nika. The man was exhausted. "Anyone want to buy a bar?" he asked. Nika rubbed Alex's back for comfort. "I feel bad for that dude," he added. "I hope he's okay out there. Maybe he'll come back."

"Why do you feel badly for him?" Harold asked. "The man is a fraternity brother who is past his expiration date. And why did you set him up with free drinks?"

Alex looked up and scowled at Harold.

"Who the fuck are you, Harold, puffing your life away up there at Four-Twenty Weed Lane?"

"I beg your pardon."

"No, I beg yours. You don't know that dude. You should be thanking him for being the first person to listen to your bullshit."

"I do not follow. What are you going on about?"

Alex took a deep breath and began. "Kyle's his name."

"I am aware. He is my nemesis."

"Wrong, dude. He's your first follower. He's Archbishop in the Church of the Naked Weirdo. You didn't see him walk in here before because you were sloppy already, but he's been here since like three in the afternoon, sipping drinks and talking my balls off. You wanna know what he told me?"

Kyle sat on the couch in his Lehigh t-shirt and running shorts, eating an avocado with a spoon and washing it down with an imported beer. The Sox were playing the Yanks on television, but it was a Yanks blowout and he switched it off. He could not focus on anything but the events from earlier that day. Even the noise from his children—yelling and marching like mad

178

miniature soldiers around the slate laminate floors of the rental house—did not distract him. He stared out the double-paned window at the drizzle and took another swig of his IPA.

Nudity. Why did that fat douche recommend nudity as the first step toward happiness? And why did Fatso think he was somehow blessed with the only happiness in the world? Kyle looked around the well-appointed great room of the house. *This is happiness*, he thought. He went to take another sip of his beer but it was empty. A quick walk to the fridge and he discovered that they were completely out of beer.

"Shit," he said out loud.

"Daddy made a swear!" Gunner yelled.

"Sorry," he said back to his son, loudly enough that Holly might hear from the bathroom. Scarier than a rebuke from Holly was the lack of response. Then he remembered, she was mad at him.

Very mad. She had told him not to engage with the naked stranger but he had gone ahead and done it. Then he had left his kids behind to engage, and when they almost got pulled away by the tide he had blamed his wife for the moment of neglect. That had been too much for her to stand. She was pissed.

This is not happiness, a voice said in his head. Was it the voice of that old fat guy? It did not sound like him. It was not deep, stentorian and threatening like the storm brewing outside. It sounded more like his own voice, saying the things that guy might have said. You're looking around at the minarets and arabesques of happiness, but inside the ornamentation, there is nothing. It went beyond being out of beer. He was starting to think maybe he was not happy. Then his chubby kids ran by, Gunner in his underwear and Maddy in her diaper, and they did not register their father's existence.

179

He walked to the bathroom and knocked gently on the door.

"Come in," Holly said. Her tone was quite calm.

The bathroom was bright and humid, the mirrors completely steamed. It was a jungle of hard angles and porcelain. Kyle immediately broke into a sweat and he felt his hair curl.

Before he could ask about any extra reserves of beer they might have, Holly had begun to speak from the tub. She did so slowly. "I know we fought today, and it was one of our worst. But I understand you were just looking out for the kids and I appreciate that. Maybe we can just talk about how you express anger? It wasn't really fair of you to blame me for the kids being alone by the water."

Kyle was hearing the words but not processing them. Something else was overwhelming all of his thoughts and sensations. His wife spoke through a mask; a mask of yogurt, honey, and mashed banana. On her eyes were two slices of cucumber. Her body was hidden beneath mountain chains of bubbles. The sight filled Kyle with an unspeakable horror. His wife looked dead. She looked prepared for some ancient burial, already partially in the ground.

This is not happiness, the voice said again. *You're alone. Holly's gone.*

"Kyle? Honey? Are you okay?" she asked.

He walked out without answering.

"I'm being as civil as I can" he heard her say from the tub. "Do we need to go back into therapy? I hear Dr. Abbey's white noise machine beckoning us. Hello?"

His kids were playing some game in which Maddy was a benevolent queen and Gunner was a dragon attacking her kingdom of dolls. The only thing protecting her and her minions were walls of sofa pillows and a Frisbee drawbridge. They were both laughing endlessly because the dragon's name was "Burp."

Maddy looked at her father. "Daddy!" she yelled. "Gunnaw is a dwagon and his name is Bup!"

My children still roam in Eden, the voice said, using words he would never use. *The sarcophagi that hold each of us fast— constructed of oak, pig iron, cotton polyester blends, wedding vows, Sunday school, and nailed together with sales taxes— has not yet been cobbled together for them.*

"Daddy! Come see Bup!"

You need to start again.

"He's a dwagon that bweathes owange juice!"

Unfetter yourself and start again.

The next thing he knew he was on the porch under a steady rain, taking off his shirt and then his shorts. The warm water felt good on his shoulders and back. A crow hopped along the driveway with a worm in its mouth. The weather amplified the sound of a prop plane overhead making its way to Boston. He felt no shame.

"Yo. Neighbor." Kyle did not look to see who was speaking. "You feelin' alright?" He was too busy raising his arms to the sky as he had seen done in countless movies when characters had found redemption, including the one about the angels in Los Angeles starring Nicolas Cage and Meg Ryan. A friend told him it was a remake. "Your guy's showing. You should go inside with that," the neighbor said.

This is how it begins. The new you. Happy birthday, Kyle! How a propos that you wore your birthday suit!

Kyle could feel his children's gaze burning through his back, and it was not long before Holly closed the door behind her and was standing on the deck before him, mask still affixed and towel wrapped around her dripping body.

"Sorry," she yelled to the neighbor. "He'll be done in a sec."

"Done with what?" the neighbor asked.

Holly turned, looked into her husband's eyes and whispered. "Good question our neighbor has. What the hell are you doing?"

"The man on the beach today was right. I am not happy. I need to reset. Go back to zero. Shed everything, starting with my clothing. He deserved a bite of that tuna fish sandwich."

"Let me stop there for a second," Alex said. He looked at Harold. "Did you steal a bite of that dude's sandwich?"

Harold looked up at the ceiling as if deep in thought, but only for a second. He said, "It is hard to say. The details are blurry. But it sounds like something I might do."

Alex continued with Kyle's story.

Holly had packed up one of the two SUV's they had brought to the Vineyard and put the children in back. Kyle waved goodbye to his children and they waved back joyfully, now quite used to their father being naked. Holly said nothing. She rolled down her window as she backed out and said, "I'll be on standby at the docks for a long time. Call me if you regain your sanity." Her voice broke at the end and she peeled out of the circular gravel driveway.

He danced around the house, naked as a newborn, and he did so for hours. Until the sky outside grew dark. The rain worsened, and he watched ESPN while sipping from a bottle of Laphroaig he had liberated from the renter's basement. He had masturbated in the shower his entire life. This time he did it in the garage because why not? He fell asleep on the sofa to baseball highlights and slept until nearly eleven o'clock in the morning.

Upon waking, the room overwhelmed by the sound of rain hosing the windows, he wasted no time. He hopped in the remaining SUV and drove to the beach, looking for his hero, the visionary who had set him free. For the drive, he pulled up George Michael's "Freedom! '90" on his phone and blasted it. It reminded him of a time in high school by the reservoir with a cold sixer of Lowenbrau, when he had doinked Laurie Colavita in a patch of fiddleheads. Sweet memory. But then she told everyone he was terrible at it. He turned off the song and drove in silence.

There were about six people at the beach. All of them were gawking at the massive swells that had rolled in under an ashen sky. None of them appeared to be the old fat man. Kyle was cold. The wind and rain were balmy, arriving from the south, but the ocean mist held its winter cold and spat it into the air. He began to shake. Perhaps he would drive home and look for the man later.

It was then that he noticed the objects in the water. Two of them. The six people on the beach were all looking at them. And now Kyle was aware that the people were pointing at them, and yelling. They appeared to be black garbage bags, floating on the tide. He squinted and saw that they were not bags. They moved.

They were black dogs.

Kyle walked closer to the crowd. One woman was crying. Another man was braving the ocean up to his knees and vainly holding out a long stick, but the dogs were easily thirty feet out. They disappeared regularly behind the swells. Every time they reappeared, they were slightly farther from shore. Both dogs tread their legs furiously. No cries came from them. Or if they did, they were drowned out by the roiling sea.

"Let me look in the car," one man in a camo t-shirt yelled over the wind. "Maybe I can do something with one of my fishing poles." He ran off. No one seemed to care. The feelings of hopelessness and dread radiated out of everyone. Through their shirts. Their hats. Their very pores. None of them seemed to care about Kyle's nudity.

He had a brief hallucination. Or perhaps it was just a thought, but it was vivid and laced with nausea. 'Those are my children,' he thought. It was not the voice that had been speaking to him all day. This was just him, remembering the morning when his children had played aside the dangerous breakers while he yelled at the fat old man. These dogs were his helpless children, pulled out to sea on account of his neglect.

Then the alien voice returned. *What will you do now? You are a new man. What does the new man do?*

Gasps went up as the bystanders watched Kyle run full force into the ocean, diving headlong into the first hill of black water he reached.

That's right. Forget god. He will not rescue these dogs. You are god. Forget the kindness of others. It is a myth. Self-reliance, you sonofabitch! Save those dogs!

The ocean's temperature was painful. His lungs wanted desperately to inhale in response to the cold. The stinging in his fingers disappeared quickly, and that he knew was even worse than stinging. Walls of water slapped him from opposing sides while sand scraped across his face. Tiny bubbles fizzed in his ears. He had no idea where he was. When he came up for air, he saw neither the dogs nor the beach. He was in a deep valley of churning salt water, swells rising up on all sides. One of those sides collapsed and he saw the beach. One woman was looking at him and furiously pointing towards a spot to his left. Kyle took a deep breath and submerged. He did not find the first dog but rather slammed into it. Its brisket was large and its legs were moving with all remaining fuel. It had no idea what Kyle was or what his intentions were and so it lashed out, biting Kyle's shoulder. He let go of the dog and took in water as he screamed. When he came up for air, he was further from shore. The other dog floated into view, but Kyle avoided it for fear it would bite him too.

Oh well. Nice try with the new you.

It was time to die, Kyle thought. Drowned and eaten by confused dogs.

But that was not to be the case. A rogue wave, dark green and capped with white foam, rolled in and slammed the three souls onto the beach.

He was on all fours, catching his breath. His lungs stung. His knees and arms were scratched and bleeding from the tumble he had taken onto the shore. Someone slapped his back and said "Way to go, buddy! You're a goddamn hero. I'm gonna buy you a pair of pants! Anyone know who owns these dogs?" Kyle looked up, expecting to see the dogs lying on the sand, panting and wondering what had just occurred. But they were fully recovered and receiving tummy rubs from the crowd.

Racing to the ferry, he hoped to say goodbye to his children. By the time he arrived, they were gone on the last ferry out before the storm. He cried, but then stopped when he heard the voice again.

Say goodbye to them, young man. The new you has arrived. Let's commence to drinking. And then let's change the world!

"So the dogs were fine?" Gloria asked.

"Totally." Alex answered. "Some dog-loving Deadhead lady who saw the whole thing took over. Offered to find their owner and, if no luck, take them in herself. No questions asked. Now if you'll excuse me," he said as he rose from his chair, "I need to continue marinating these assholes with Wild Turkey."

"Sweet Caroline" by Neil Diamond was reaching its crescendo. The Black Goose's patrons started to sing along as the chorus approached. They all heard a transformer explode nearby and the music stopped. The room went black. People booed. One exceptionally drunk voice in the dark did not care and continued. "So good! So good! So good!" It was Nika.

The energy that had disappeared from the bar's wiring seemed to transfer into the musculature of Harold and Nika. They finally stood up to venture outside, brave the storm and get home. On the way out the door, a fight ensued between the three of them because Gloria wanted to look for Kyle. Harold wanted nothing to do with it. He was appreciative of Kyle's devotion and to his act of heroism, but, as Harold's rugged individualism dictated, Kyle was on his own.

The mood in the car was flammable despite the damp air. The space needed only an ill-deployed word to cause an explosion. Or maybe it was just Gloria. She could not help but project her bile onto everyone, even if Nika and Harold were chuckling away in the backseat. How, Gloria wondered, could her father not want to help the man who had saved the very dogs he had put into harm's way? Did he not want to pay someone back for causing them unhappiness? Was Harold's behavior in this moment the same sociopathy that left Gloria herself without a father? It seemed Kyle's pain was her own.

"Could you please put your seatbelts on back there?" Gloria asked as politely as possible. The giggling, whispering couple ignored her. "Hey!" she said louder this time. They looked up at her now. "Seatbelts," she repeated. "And stop giggling."

"I appreciate your concern for our safety but Nika and I are adults who can handle ourselves. Consider us states and you are Washington, DC. Let us govern ourselves. *Ungovern us*, young lady!"

A mockernut hickory lay across the road before them, its boughs blowing violently in the wind. The tree had landed on the roof of a parked pickup but Gloria could see no apparent damage. One brave soul in a yellow slicker was visible in the frame of their headlights. He had a chainsaw and was trying to disassemble the hickory before the storm was over. Gloria had no choice but to turn her father's car around and find another way out of town.

"Is pizza in this car?" Nika asked. "I'm so hungry."

"Alas no." Harold replied.

"What 'alas' means?"

"It means 'unfortunately.'"

"Why didn't you not say 'unfortunately'?"

Harold hiccupped. "Language is a party and I need to get up and dance."

"Language is not party. Language is tool. You need to cut wood, you get saw. You do not need saw with lights and bells on it. Just saw."

"Alas, I am marrying Wittgenstein!" Harold bellowed.

Nika leaned forward and yelled in Gloria's ear. "Hand me cigarette."

The request nearly caused Gloria to drive off the road in a suicidal-homicidal rage, but she squelched herself, reached over to the glove compartment, and pulled out a nearly empty pack of American Spirits. She blindly threw it in back.

Yet another route was closed to them. Police had put up sawhorses in front of the bridge to Vineyard Haven. Gloria yelled "Fuck!" and threw the car into reverse for a three-point turn. In the process of turning, her heart jumped. The headlights had picked up massive ocean swells mere yards from the car. The water was black and in it, Gloria caught sight of spinning tree branches, whorls of seaweed, and an empty two-liter Mountain Dew bottle rolling furiously along the surface. It seemed impossible to her that their own car was not washing across the road yet. They needed to leave the area immediately.

She knew of only one more route out of town. This was both bad and good in Gloria's estimation. It was bad because if it too was blocked, they would have no choice but to hole up in the dim Black Goose for the remainder of the storm, crammed into a flimsy shack with foolhardy inebriates and little food. It was good because if Kyle had not driven a car (she hoped he had not), they were likely to spot him along the road. Gloria pushed on the gas a little harder. More than before, she felt the urge to rescue the lost soul.

They made their way back towards town. Gloria looked in the mirror and saw Nika's head resting on Harold's shoulder and Harold's wrinkled knuckles wrapped around her arm. She felt nauseous.

Harold spoke up. "Gloria, dear. There should be a compact disc of Wes Montgomery in the glove box. Be a hero and put it on."

"Put your seatbelt on first and then we'll talk," she hissed.

"Never mind then! I can listen to Wes once returned to home and hearth."

"Put on radio then," Nika suggested.

"And again," Gloria said, "I will put on music when you put on your seatbelts.

Harold asked, "Why does it matter to you? You hate both of us overtly. Our demise would be your victory."

Gloria felt such sadness at that. Is that what he thought? Was her anger not obviously a cry for him to return? To return both mentally and geographically to the past? He had been a good father. He had been a jolly goofball of a father. She had been proud of him. She had adored him. When she was very little and the family had visited the town beach, her father would hold his arms out to their full extent and let Gloria and Seth hang from them. He could do that without dropping them longer than any other dad. And after he finally dropped them and the kids asked for him to pick them up and throw them as far as he could, he would honor their request, and Gloria was amazed that he could throw them further than any other dad. When they would go to their grandparents' house for dinner, Seth and Gloria would inevitably fall asleep in the car on the way home. Their father would take turns getting them back into the house and into bed. First he would carry little Seth in his arms. Then he would return to the car and gently rub Gloria's head. She was too big to carry. "Sweetie," he would say. "C'mon." And he would guide her, barefoot and half-awake, through the darkened house to her warm bed. Gloria wanted that person back in her life.

But saying that out loud was not an option for reasons unavailable to her. She considered herself someone who liked to speak her mind, but now, her mind recoiled from her intentions. Instead, it lashed out.

"Put on other CD in glove box," Nika slurred, still drunk and nodding off. "Carrie Underwood."

"No!" Harold complained. "Sanitized robotic country drivel."

"Before He Cheats! Before He Cheats! Before He Cheats!" She was awake again and waving her green plastic lighter in front of her face. She began to sing in perfect pitch, face aglow from the small flame. "I took a Louisville Slugger to both tail lights."

"Dad should know all about that," Gloria said through a humorless laugh.

Harold had been looking out the window but was now sober, wide-eyed and staring directly at Gloria, who was watching his change in condition through the rearview mirror.

"Gloria," he said.

No music was playing but Nika was bobbing her head to the Carrie Underwood in her head. She absentmindedly said, "What was that?"

Gloria smiled deeply and felt adrenaline release into her stomach.

"Oh come on," she said. "You have no idea why Dad's last marriage ended."

Nika had stopped moving her head around and opened her eyes, lighter still lit. "What are you saying? Harold told me." She looked at Harold. "You told me. She died. What of that is wrong?"

"Gloria," Harold said again.

Before this weekend, inflicting pain had not been one of Gloria's stronger suits. Her strength was easing the discomfort of others, often loading pain onto her own back. Somehow, in the warm, damp, claustrophobic environment of this long, long weekend, she had flowered into a master. Nothing felt more comfortable, even exciting, than what she was doing right now.

190

After training up on Scott, she was now administering a deadly punch capable of collapsing a windpipe. She could not help but turn her head completely around to deliver the blow looking at both of her victims in the face.

"Your fiancé cheated on his ex-wife!" she exclaimed with nervous excitement and something like glee.

The response from Nika was not what Gloria expected. The young woman screamed. It was not until both Nika and Harold put their arms in front of their heads (Gloria would always hold a flashbulb memory of the rash on her father's arm at that moment, the one he got from the jail) that Gloria realized, in the fleeting course of a nanosecond, that Nika's scream had nothing to do with Gloria's statement.

Time became confusing and knotted. In college, Gloria had learned that car accident victims usually do not remember the details of the event because their brains are too busy surviving—redirecting electricity and blood supply—to carve out new memories. This did not pertain to Gloria. She had just enough time before the car bounced through chokeberries and into a patch of oaks to register the object on the road that had caused her to swerve. It was a young man riding a bicycle along the center yellow lines. He was naked save the poncho blowing up over his head.

Sunday

Chapter Twelve

It was almost dawn, and brave, unknown men in the dark of the storm restored power to the hospital. No longer did burgundy emergency lighting illuminate the throngs of people in the waiting room— snoring or awake, curled up in sleeping bags or squinting at two-month-old magazines. Outside, the weather was still aggressive but the wind had subsided slightly and it still rattled the taped windows and whispered through sliding doors.

Harold would not look at Gloria, let alone speak to her. At one point, he had even tried to move to another seat, but Gloria had stood up and followed him. In a pathetic effort to avoid her, he had even flipped through the pages of a *Time* magazine, one of the "left-wing normative policy masters" he loved to eviscerate.

Amos walked into the waiting room and looked around. The place was so overwhelmed with people seeking shelter it took him a moment to notice Gloria waving her hand. The other two times Gloria had met Amos— both in the past forty-eight hours— he had seemed like the most centered person on earth. It was as if a wild panther could lunge from the shadows and he would do no more than raise a bushy eyebrow. That was not the case now. He was pale and sweated visibly, and his bloodshot eyes darted as his hands worried a clipboard.

Harold stood up, all six foot four of him, still wearing the clothing he had borrowed from the police station. The accident had not harmed him, save one scrape on his neck (which fit in nicely with the pencil hole still in his temple and the rash on the side of his face). The passenger seat he had tackled with his face sustained more damage than he did.

195

Gloria stood up with her father in solidarity as they awaited an update on Nika's condition. She massaged one of his shoulders but he snapped it out of her grasp. The urge to apologize rose in her again, like a verbal tic, but she held it down.

When Amos stood before them, Harold said, "You never lie. So speak with all candor and exactitude."

Amos rubbed his nose and looked down at his clipboard. "Well, she's going to be okay."

"Oh good! I may not believe in God, but the unnamable mysteries of the cosmos have worked in dear Nika's favor today!" Harold said as he exhaled in relief.

"Not so fast," Amos said. "The lighter she was holding did a number on her head. You said she was waving it around? Well, one in a million shot, but I guess when she went into the windshield, the lighter was at the right angle to enter her temple. It came out but left quite a gouge. The weather's too nasty to transport her to Boston, but we have time. It seems the heated end of it entered first and cauterized the damage. Good news there and even more good news in that she seems mostly unharmed. You know the story of Phineas Gage, right?"

As a psychology minor, Gloria did know the story.

"Enlighten us," Harold said.

Amos continued. "Gage was a railroad man in the nineteenth century. Also, a pious guy." Amos looked around the waiting room and brought his voice down. "There was an explosion on the line and a railroad tie went through his fucking head. Up under his cheek bone and out near the top of his skull. Anyway, he lived. He lived and had no cognitive impairments anyone could detect. Can you imagine. A railroad tie goes through your fucking head and you don't even walk away with a stutter? But while he didn't have any cognitive impairments in the traditional sense, some folks said his personality changed and he became an ornery bastard. Drinking, cussing, and so forth. Anyway, Nika may have had Phineas's luck, if you want to call it that, in that she's still alive and generally unharmed. And with Nika, we have no concerns about her becoming an ornery bastard because she's already there. No offense, Harold. Maybe she'll get ornerier, but we're now outside the realm of science. Anyone want to sneak out for a puff?" He patted his chest pocket.

Harold ignored the question. "Can we go in and see her?" His eyes were wide and to Gloria, he seemed sincerely concerned. She was not used to seeing this and it made her sad.

"Yeah, but I should warn you. We were pretty swamped with people here last night, sick and otherwise. People were sleeping here to take shelter...folks who didn't want to drive a few extra miles south to the school. So, well, like I said we were busy and, so, well. She's sharing a room." He looked at Gloria.

Gloria had no idea why he looked at her, and then it dawned on her. "With Scott?" she asked.

"Yup. Room two-eleven. Now if you'll excuse me." He patted his pocket again and walked through the automatic doors into the waning wind.

Gloria asked her father, "He put them in the same room just to make us uncomfortable. I don't want to see Scott!" She probably could have stayed in the waiting room and given her father and Nika privacy, but her urge to apologize to the young woman was growing.

Harold was already walking down the hallway. Gloria raced to keep up, pulling her purse up tight over her shoulder. The newly renovated space looked to Gloria like a country club, diverting visitors from the grieved reasons they were there. It

197

was a false haven of dark wood floors and pristine white walls adorned with framed photographs of famous celebrities. Jack Nicholson, Allen Ginsberg, Harry Dean Stanton. Privileged faces on privileged walls. But the fantasy was easily shattered by a simple glance into any door, where MRI machines, oxygen tanks, and biohazard signs awaited.

When they entered Nika's room, Gloria expected an immediate verbal assault. She even squinted and hunched her shoulders as if preparing for a physical blow. Harold was in front of her, also wincing. Instead, they were greeted with quiet sobbing. Nika's left hand was over her eyes but tears could be seen on her cheeks and the corners of her mouth. A bandage covered the location on her head where the lighter had made the gouge. It was clean, free of blood. A white curtain divided the room in two. If Scott was behind it, he was very quiet. Then Gloria heard his troubled snoring over the white noise of the equipment fans and air conditioning. Thank God, she thought. He's asleep. If we can just keep it that way.

When Nika dropped her hand and saw them, she did not yell. She continued to cry and said in a wavering voice, "I lost Russian."

"What? What does that mean?" Harold asked in a booming voice. Gloria wanted to throttle him but forced herself to put a calm hand on his shoulder and utter a gentle, "Shhh." Harold pulled his shoulder away from her. "Unhand me" he bellowed.

Nika's voice continued to crack as she spoke. "I call mother to tell her what happen. I am able to say in Russian that it is me, but when she speaks, it makes no sense. It is just...sounds!" She began to cry again, accompanied by low moans.

For a moment, Gloria was back in the windowless classroom in the basement of the psychology building at UVM.

When people learn two languages in youth, the professor explained, the same part of their brain is used for both languages. People who learn their second language at an older age jury-rig another part of their brain to learn the second one. So, in the case of a brain trauma, the person who learned both languages at youth will lose both languages. People who learned the second language at an older age may lose just one. It sounded like Nika, even more specifically, lost half of one language.

Nika regained her composure and spoke again. "I did not understand my father. Do you know what that is like? Can you imagine?"

Yes I do, Gloria thought. She found it difficult to see this formerly fiery woman in such a defenseless state. It must have been challenging even for Harold because he reached out to touch Nika's hand. She allowed it but turned her head away from him. The room was silent save the beeps of machines and the rain against the windows.

Snores continued from the others side of the divider.

Harold began to stammer but Nika spoke instead. "Do you know how your father and I met?"

"On the beach," Gloria said.

"Yes, but you do not know pretty details. You are like someone who knows only *La Boheme* is about poor roommates. There is so much behind it, Gloria."

Harold said nothing. He looked exhausted and his hungover, traumatized gaze fell on his crossed hands. Sleep was getting the better of him, but he battled valiantly. Gloria wondered if he had a concussion from the accident, but dismissed that idea as Amos had checked both of them and found nothing wrong. He was just bone tired from drinking, staying up all night, and coming down from the adrenaline rush of the crash.

Nika continued. "I kicked sand on him. It was accident but me and my girlfriends run down beach and we run too close to him, sitting in chair reading book. We are not naked. We think it is gross all the fat Americans have no shame. But we kick the sand on him by mistake and he gets up. He yell at us. I see he is reading book called *Lenin's Tomb*, because he is waving it around while he yells. I asked him about it. Harold changes right away. He tells me all about book. I tell him about Russia and my girlfriends walk away. We talk and talk, just standing there. Not sitting down. Not moving."

The words reached Gloria's ears but did little more. She was too focused on the white sheet and the snoring coming from behind it. Please don't let him wake up, God, she thought. I will never drink again.

Nika continued. "I wanted to talk to him more because he is smart. I ask him to put clothes on but he won't. I tolerate it. I tell him that I am sad because I am going home to Russia in two days because man harassed me at camp and I fought back. Harold got so mad at this. He throws book down and says, 'This will not stand!' I laugh at him. He sounds like he is on stage reading from terrible script. It is adorable. And he has told me nothing about himself. Such a nice change. Every man always talking about himself and all that he knows. It is like he is talking to objects in room, not to other people. But Harold is different. When he does talk, it is about the world and the way he thinks it works. Never about himself. I like this. The only thing he mentions is he has no money or he pay for lawsuit against camp for me."

Nika sighed and rubbed the bandaged spot on her head again. The hallway outside was empty except for one nurse who walked by infrequently, her shoes echoing on the grey and white linoleum. She was watering a plant at her station and reaching over to smell it. Gloria only noticed this pre-consciously, as she was now rapt by the story. Harold was awake but his eyes were closing and rolling back, and his head was falling forward before he would catch it and repeat the process. His hand still rested atop Nika's.

Nika's eyes widened when she spoke again. "Then I have idea. I grow up on American crime shows. We are going to pull a badger scheme on camp manager Barry! The plan was good plan. I go to camp and apologize to Barry for me kicking him in balls. I tell him I realize that I am actually hot for him and want to fuck his brains out. It was hard to say that because he has goofy face like Elmo the Muppet but bald, and he smells like McDonald pickle. I know he is weak in brain logic and strong in penis logic and his horny body will beat out his— what is in English— suspicion? So, I tell him to meet me at nice inn in Edgartown called the Daggett House. I reserved room. The plan is Harold waits in closet for me and Barry to show up. When we are naked, Harold will jump out of closet and take pictures. We will use pictures to blackmail Barry, a married man with three children. We will get money for Harold, and Barry will hire me again so I do not have to leave states. He is camp counselor but he is rich because his wife is rich. He is camp counselor for special needs kids because he say it is moral. He is really camp counselor to meet Russian counselors. Harold agree to this plan...I will humiliate Barry, and Harold will get money." Nika smiled and looked at Gloria. "It was so exciting! So bad but in good way! We are criminal team but with hearts. So much fun. So fun."

Her volume increased with the joy she was finding in the memory. Gloria tried too hard to listen but also keep track of the depth of Scott's inhalations and exhalations. This had become a hard task because Harold was now snoring as well, and his sonorous breathing canceled out the sound of Scott's entirely. Frustrated, Gloria snapped back to attention and tried to focus in on Nika's tale, heart and soul, so as not to be rude. "So what happened next?" she asked.

Nika continued, "Barry agrees to come to inn with me. Of course. Funny because he still walks with limp from when I put my knee into his balls. But when we get to front door of inn, Harold walks out. I ask Harold, 'What the fuck are you doing?' Barry is confused. Harold says 'I have better idea. Marry me.' 'Are you crazy?" I ask him. He says, 'Maybe but you can stay in America.' I am not sure what to do because Barry is there and confused. Barry is asking me who this old man is. I say to your father, 'But what about the money for you?' 'I do not care about pestilence of mammon,' he say like he quotes maybe Bible. Your dad also say, 'I care about you staying.' Barry is about to leave. I look at him and say to Harold, 'But I want this asshole to hurt more!' Harold right there punched Barry with all energy in the face. It was the most romantic moment of my life." Nika rubbed her head.

Outside, Gloria saw a band of light. The band was bordered by the horizon beneath and a severe cloud above. Morning was arriving, and along with it the possibility of an easing in the storm.

"At that moment, I decide I want to stay but not for camp but to be with your father. But you know what, Gloria? We are not lovers. We have never been. We are friends. He say when we drive home that day not to worry; he does not want to be with me that way because I am too young and that he just want company. I feel same way to him. We love each other but we are friends

202

only." Then Nika's face changed. Lines appeared on her brow and her teeth clenched. She extended her hand as far as it would go and slapped Harold hard on the leg. He yelled in pain as he awoke. "Old foolish man," Nika hissed. "I can accept you lie about being married before. But you cheat on her too?"

Gloria said, in a whisper, hoping to make others whisper too, "Wait a second. Your marriage is just to keep you in the states. It's a sham. Who cares if he cheated on my mom?"

Nika practically yelled, "I have dignity, idiot. It does not matter why we marry. It will be marriage with trust. He lied to me. Two times. It is over. Zero trust. We are done."

Gloria was in a panic at the noise, looking over at the white screen, wanting to put her hand over Nika's mouth. She moved right up to Nika's face, finger to mouth, and shushed her over and over. "Sh sh sh sh sh! Please! Sh sh!"

Harold said, "But I have told you everything. I have confessed."

"You have confessed nothing!" Nika howled. "Your daughter who I did not know to exist until two days ago confess for you! I want you to leave, Harold!" Gloria had given up trying to silence the girl and put her head in her hands. Nika was crying again as she said, "Now I go home to Russia and see mother and father." She stopped for a moment, touched her bandages and cried so hard she moaned, "and I will not be able to understand them." She continued to cry with her arm over her face. She stopped long enough to scream, "Get out!"

Amos popped his head in the door and raised an eyebrow. "Is everything okay in here?"

"No," said the voice of an old woman from behind the white screen. "These people are noisy."

Gloria walked past the screen and saw an African American woman at least seventy years of age lying on the bed with a neck brace. "Who are *you*?" she asked Gloria.

"Oh! I'm so sorry," Gloria said putting up her hands and retreating.

Nika screamed at her guests. "Get. The. Fuck. Out!"

"Please quiet down," the old woman said. "I don't want to hear every detail of your-"

Nika interrupted, yelling past the screen. "And you shut the fuck up, old woman!"

"Young lady?" the old woman asked.

"What?"

"Got a light?" She chuckled at her own words and Nika said nothing.

Upon seeing the old woman, Gloria noticed in herself a kernel of a notion. It was a tiny notion, bouncing about, one of many. Like a single pachinko ball's manic trajectory, nearly unnoticed among many machines among many parlors. But Gloria noticed it. *I'm disappointed to see this old woman because I was kind of hoping to see Scott.*

Amos, Harold, and Gloria walked down the hallway as the lights went out again, replaced by a dim red glow.

Gloria turned to Amos. "I thought you said you never lie."

"I don't. What are you-"

"You said Scott was in there."

"I thought he was. That's not a lie. That's a mistake. You know how overwhelmed we are?"

204

The three of them walked out into the daybreak and across the parking lot, Amos to his jeep and the Gombergs to Harold's Camry with the smashed-in hood and spiderwebbed windshield. The wind was still strong, but not enough to carry debris, and the rain had stopped. Harold took off all of his clothes, leaning with difficulty against the driver door to remove his shorts. He grunted both times he had to raise a knee.

"You guys shouldn't be driving anywhere," said Amos as he passed them, blowing smoke out the window of his red Jeep. "I hear this is just the eye."

The Gombergs said nothing as they got in and fastened their respective seatbelts. They drove slowly back to the house. Gloria tried to turn on the radio once, but Harold immediately turned it off. Feeling awkward and unsure what to do, Gloria fished one of Nika's cigarettes out of the glove box, but removed it from her mouth when she spotted the bloody lighter at her feet.

The body count continued. But now, Gloria was one of the killers.

Chapter Thirteen

Harold opened the fridge and leaned down to investigate its contents.

"Do you want some brussels sprouts?" he asked over his shoulder.

Growing up, Gloria's mother had done almost everything around the house. She had defied her moneyed upbringing and scuffed her knees scrubbing floors, hurt her back loading the dishwasher, and screamed herself hoarse getting the children ready for school. There was one exception, and that was the cooking. Harold had always been a master chef, a hobby he had picked up from his own mother nearly sixty years ago in a claustrophobic kitchen in New Haven that also included the family tub. From those humble beginnings, he had broken from the old-world traditions, leaving behind the boiled meats and cabbages of Eastern Europe, introducing flavors unimaginable to the elders in his neighborhood who knew only ingesting food as a means of surviving Polish winters. Harold was experimental to the marrow and so could not resist preparing a crepe with lobster and fava beans or a homemade turrón. Gloria knew that he had cooked heaping pots of brown rice, broccoli, garlic, and ginger for his fellow hippie activists in college, that he had prepared homemade desserts for his coworkers at the advertising agency, and that even on camping trips with Rachel before they had children, the young couple would eat better than people worlds away at Tavern on the Green.

In many ways, cooking replaced words for her father. Where he stumbled in verbal displays of affection, he compensated by preparing a meal. So, when her father said, "Do you want some brussels sprouts?" Gloria knew that this was the closest she was going to get to hearing her father say, "I still acknowledge you despite you nearly killing my fiancé."

Power was out in the house. Her father used an old single-burner camping stove to prepare the food. Such stoves were meant to be used outdoors given the danger of tipping over, but Harold did not seem to care.

The two ate in silence. As Gloria expected, the brussels sprouts were delectable. He had used nothing but salt, pepper, and butter, but, as Harold once put it, "salt, pepper, and butter are the workhorses of cooking." Gloria did not realize her hunger until she was eating, and now she gracelessly rushed the food into her mouth, ignoring both etiquette and food temperature. Sun streamed in through the kitchen window, only the second time it had appeared since Gloria's arrival. The exhaustion in her muscles from a night without sleep made her want to walk over to the couch and close her eyes without taking another bite, but hunger won. Their forks clinked against the small plates Gloria remembered from summer vacations in her childhood. Confident that the storm was over, Gloria had cracked open one window by the front door as well as the sliding door on the beach side, allowing a cross breeze that smelled of cool spring air and the bounding ocean. It mixed with the deep mildew of the room. Gloria loved the mildew. It was redolent of summer vacations in her youth. The ocean still crashed and churned, whitecaps tumbling down swells, but the world immediately above the water seemed to have moved on from recent business.

On a purely sensorial level, the moment was divine. Beyond that, the joy ended. Gloria had no idea what to say to her father. She had mangled his car— and his life— the night before, almost killing the three of them. She had apologized over and over when she had driven the sputtering car from the site of the accident to the hospital. Nika had been mildly conscious and moaning in the back seat and Harold had tried resting her head on his lap, but she had withdrawn. "I'm sorry, I'm sorry, I'm sorry, I'm sorry, I'm sorry, I'm sorry," Gloria had said. Like so many other times in her life, Gloria had apologized so much and with such a staccato delivery that it became transcendental, like the state attained by Hasidic Jews bowing in synagogue. Its impact on others was less relevant to her.

Now at the breakfast table, with the sun shining on her father's face, his mouth full of food and her own belly sated, she was struck dumb. She looked around the room for something to spark an idea for conversation. Commenting on any of the books on the shelves would be a bad idea because they would all lead to a screed from her father about the magic of privatization. She did not want to speak of the jazz records lying about because nothing bored her more than jazz. She also did not want to speak about the bong because it would lead to her father reminding her that she had buried his "Vital Effects" container. And, of course, she could not stay silent, because that was not in her nature. To gloria, silence in the presence of others was never silent. It was a dark, damp cellar where more ghosts flooded in with every passing moment.

So, she focused on the wood burning stove.

Smiling, she said "I still can't believe that stove. It's way too heavy for this house to hold. I can't imagine how much you bribed those guys to assemble it for you." She chuckled. "You're so funny. You wanted the stove and you got it. Who cares if it cracks the floor? 'I want a damn stove!' Mom would've loved that. Grandma and grandpa too. They would've flipped their wigs knowing you put a half a ton of stove in their house regardless of what the floor can hold."

A smile crossed Harold's face, and in a voice hoarse from no sleep he said, "Oh stop! You are not a nuisance in the least."

"I'm sorry?"

"You certainly do not have to leave. You can stay for months if you would prefer." He rose and began to pace the room, his hands clasped above his bare buttocks.

"What are you talking about?" Gloria asked.

He put his hands up as if to stop discussion. "There is no need to apologize about the accident. These things happen."

"I did apologize."

"I mean, I understand your need to apologize more because a thousand times, in your mind, is not enough. And it was a pretty horrendous situation. But really, it is fine. And of course, there is no need to explain why you came up here in the first place, completely unannounced!"

"I came up here to tell you I was getting married."

Harold was not looking at her as he spoke. He was looking past her.

He asked, "What was that again?" He pointed at her, or a bit past her. "That thing you just said there."

"I said I came up here to-"

"Oh right. Scott not being your type of man. I noticed that too. But I assumed you were…what?" Gloria had not interrupted him. "Oh, your choice of men had something to do with *me*?" He put his hand on his chest.

Gloria felt a wave of panic. If her father saw how far out of her way she had gone to hurt him, to the point of choosing a spouse for that purpose, she would be mortified. It was probably too late. He was speaking like he already knew the lengths to which she had gone.

She made another effort to deflect his line of questioning, but all she had was, "I don't know what you're talking about. I loved Scott." But something about this rang false to her ears. Either she did not love Scott or she did and had erroneously used the past tense. Who could clear this up for her?

An aggressive wall of wind blasted through the kitchen and knocked over a roll of paper towels.

"Oh my," Harold said. "You picked a spouse you thought would get under my skin? Oh, sweetheart. Oh, don't cry. Sure that is a little extreme, maybe bordering on pathological, but hey, who is perfect in this multiverse, right? But stop! You do not have to leave right this instant. I know your mission to get under my skin is complete, but *do stay*." He said the last two words with an exceptional amount of venom, and he spat a little saying them.

She thought she would be embarrassed by her father's exposing of her intents, but instead, a heat rose in Gloria. "Fine," she said. "You nailed about half of it. But you missed this: I'm here to find out what the fuck your game is. I don't even know who you are anymore! You lost sight of your family. Seth. Me. We're still alive and you left us! Why? For what? For some ascetic philosophy that makes hardly a lick of sense, smoking bowls and shutting out your children? What the fuck? Your focus on it is so damn singular. It's monomania. You're like Ahab with this philosophy!"

Harold looked straight at her now. "Trust me, there is more than one Ahab in this room."

Gloria did not speak. He was right.

Harold continued. "But I refuse to be your white whale. You can pack your things, and Scott's, and I will drive you to the ferry. I am done being under your microscope. I have things to do."

The sun was gone and wind gusted through the open window.

No matter how embarrassed she was, she was not ready to relent. "So, you just won't tell me."

"Tell you what?" he asked as he walked to the window to witness the clouds returning.

"What happened to my dad, goddammit? The one who drove me to summer camp and sang along to 'Sympathy for the Devil' when it came on the radio? The one who took me and Seth to this very house for summer vacation when Mom was sick with pneumonia." She pointed out the sliding door. "You cooked us lobster in a huge metal pot right there, boiled in saltwater with seaweed. Where is that dad? You killed him. Where did you hide the body? Where is he, Dad? Where? The one-" she had trouble getting the words out. "The one who called me 'the princess and the poet.'"

Harold did not look at her as she spoke. He only looked out the window. Then he turned, his eyes bloodshot. Gloria wanted to think it was from tears, but she was confident it was just the need for sleep.

Walking to the bong, Harold asked, "Do you remember the last movie I ever saw?" He picked up the bong, possibly remembered that his "vital effects" container was buried on the beach, and put it back down.

It was a strange question he had asked, because he knew the answer. She had overheard him discussing it with Scott only two days earlier.

"Yes," she said. *"The Prince of-"*

"The Prince of Tides! Precisely! A kewpie doll for you! Now, one more question. More challenging this time. Do you know why *The Prince of Tides* was the last movie I ever tolerated?"

Not only did she not know the answer, but she did not care. A more critical subject was being discussed.

"Let me tell you why *The Prince of Tides* was the last movie I ever tolerated. The film in question revolves around a man whose sister has attempted suicide. The man, I cannot remember his name, let's call him Bobo, enlists the help of his sister's psychoanalyst, played by Barbra Streisand, in an attempt to collaborate on the subject of his sister's unhappiness. Instead, Bobo succumbs to the psychoanalyst's Semitic bloom, and they begin a courtship. As their flirtation intensifies, Barbra turns her keen analytical mind on the man before her rather than the dead sister. She is interested in the tragic mechanisms that steer the whole of his family, but ultimately, Barbra cares most about the tragic mechanisms that steer Bobo himself because it is with Bobo she hopes to spend the future and fructify the world with offspring. Are you with me so far?"

"I suppose but I'm not sure why."

The sky raced by, the cloud ceiling so low Gloria thought she could reach out the kitchen window and touch it.

"So," Harold continued, "after multiple sessions of her digging into his psyche, she uncovers the problem that makes Bobo such an impenetrable soul, a man whose emotional range includes only barking at people. A man who can only think to crack jokes when cornered with the grim details of his life. And do you know what she uncovers? Do you know what his cathartic therapeutic breakthrough is? The thing that drove the whole family's misery for so long? The mushroom of an idea that grows in the darkness of the unconscious per Freud? Do you know?"

"I can't remember. It was a long time ago."

Harold laughed. "They were raped by escaped redneck convicts. The whole family!"

"I don't see what's so funny about that."

"When is life that simple? What family is so fortunate that they can pin all of their unhappiness on being collectively raped by escaped redneck convicts?" Harold moved to face an imaginary person next to him. "'Why is father so emotionally distant?'" Harold then moved to face where he had been a moment before. "'Well, it is certainly not his fault because the family was raped by redneck convicts.'" He moved again to a new position and looked elsewhere. "'Why is Junior failing all his classes and being sent to the principal for texting pictures of his doodle?'" Harold moved again. "'Have you not heard? The whole family was raped by escaped redneck convicts.'" Harold began to dance around the room and sing in a conga rhythm, "Raped by redneck convicts! Raped by redneck convicts!" Each time he said 'con' and 'victs,' he stuck his bottom out to the left and right, respectively.

"Stop that," Gloria requested as calmly as possible.

"Raped by redneck convicts! Raped by redneck convicts!" He opened the sliding door, danced out onto the deck, and began to dance down the steps. The force of the tide had carved out a massive drop-off in the sand halfway between the shore and the house, but now the ocean was hitting the drop-off with all of its force, sending walls of water yards into the air.

"Raped by redneck convicts! Raped by red-"

Weakened by the storm, the step beneath Harold gave way, as did the three subsequent steps on which he tried to land. Harold came to rest on his knees in the wet sand.

Gloria felt a wave of dread run through her. There was no way she was going back to the hospital a fourth time. She carefully descended the steps that were intact and jumped down the remainder to the ground.

Harold rose as if nothing had happened. The two of them were now closer than they had been in ages. He investigated her eyes and wagged his finger at her.

"Redneck convicts. You are not going to get that kind of easy answer with me young lady. For most souls, me included, going mad is a process." He poked her sternum. "It is not one event that does you in. It is the imperceptible drubbing of years. The violence is glacial. The redneck convict hides in the everyday. In the stain on the carpet from the coffee you just spilled. In the splinter that slides underneath your fingernail. In the sarcastic tone. In the greying hairs that fall off in the shower. You see? The murderer is everywhere and so he is nowhere. The murderer is life, in the billiard room, with the disappointment. And unless you accept that solution, I am so sorry to tell you that you leave here empty-handed." He turned to the sea and began to walk away. "Your mystery goes unsolved."

She could hardly hear him as he walked through the seagrass, looking this way and that, so she followed him again. "What are you doing now?"

"Solving my own mystery," he said. "Looking for my weed."

Offering up the location of his container might have been the right thing to do, but she had no interest in doing the right thing.

He ran over to the storage closet beneath the house, returned with his shovel, and began to dig in an arbitrary location. "This shovel is not from that local hardware store on the island that is open about two hours a week. No, I went to the mainland to give Home Depot my business." He stopped digging where he was, moved about three feet to the west, and began digging again. "They are open many hours, employ many people, and have everything." He moved and started digging again. "You lefties hate the box stores because they ruin communities. But what is so objectively great about communities? Isn't a job and a roof over your head more important? You say 'the good old days' is a crypto-racist term justifying old prejudices, yet you cling to the good old days of communities. Communities kept groups separate. There's your crypto-racism. Let the box stores come and employ people! Black and white alike. And perhaps even Orientals. Do you know what the big corporations of today are? Planets! Planets formed because tiny flying objects began to be pulled together via gravity, and the bigger these clusters of small objects became, the more powerful their pull." He stopped digging and wiped his brow with his bare forearm, sweaty despite the wind. "And you know what? Move forward billions of years, and you have nine planets and a far less violent solar system, cleared of debris. General Electric is Jupiter, ExxonMobil is Saturn, and so forth. Accretion. Clean. Simple. And neither good nor evil. Just a fact of the physical universe. So anyway, I bought my shovel from a box store." He went back to shoveling.

"You're unbelievable," Gloria said.

He continued shoveling, ignoring her.

"Talking corporate acquisitions and libertarianism at a time like this. What a strange defense mechanism. You're standing there buck naked but God forbid you reveal a single thing about yourself."

"There is no god."

"I don't care. I can still say 'God forbid.' I don't remember much from college but I do remember what Voltaire said."

"Voltaire? Look at you!"

"He said that if there isn't a God, it's important to create one. Voltaire probably knew selfish jerks like you when he wrote it. So, pre-existing or man-made, I choose to believe in God."

"If there is a god, then who is his progenitor? Surely for a god to exist, he must have-"

"What are you, in tenth grade and high?"

"I would like to be high but you-"

"Shut up. Stop talking, for once. Who cares who made God or if someone even did? You apply your human rationality to a discussion of the Creator, like a child who brings his toy hammer to help his father fix the car. Rationality is a puny human instrument."

"But if you dispense with rationality then the-"

"Why are you always talking? I'm talking now! I don't know what happened to you, but you're a miserable man now. And clothing serves a purpose. So does government. And so does God."

Harold slammed the shovel down to the ground.

"I will tell you what, young lady. Let us see if deities exist. When I say the name of the Abrahamic god, Yahweh, should a vehicle come into sight moments hence, I will not only believe, but I will depart this waterlogged bastion of liberalism and join you in New York, yet another waterlogged bastion of liberalism. Are you ready?"

The ocean advanced, and the bubbling, seaweed-laced edge of a breaking wave brushed Harold's big toe. The wind collected sand, became a tangible thing with coarse surfaces, and scraped against father and daughter's cheeks.

"Dad. Can we just move on? Give me the keys to your car and I'll drive to the ferry dock, leave your car there for you, and wait for the next boat to take me home."

"No no. I want to play this god game. Anyway, my car is dead. All thanks to you."

"Then how did you expect me to get out of your sight?" she yelled back toward the water.

Another wave crashed, this one reached past Harold, submerged him to the ankles, and drenched Gloria's open-toed sandals.

"I had not thought that through. Hitchhike? There is also a ten-speed in Dick and Prissy's storage shed. Now come back here and let us play at the god game. Again, I yell, Yahweh, and if a vehicle appears, I will believe."

The game was foolishness, she knew, so she walked up the stairs to the house, prepared and longing to take a nap. The thought of the humid-but-cool feather pillow was more enticing than any cigarette had ever been. At the top of the stairs, she heard her father's laugh over the waves and then the sound of him yelling, "Yahweh!"

The tops of two charter buses appeared over the pitch pines, lumbering down Moshup's Trail. Gloria was terrified because she in truth did not believe in God; she had lobbed her earlier arguments at her father for an omniscient being merely to anger him.

Harold could be heard yelling, "Coincidence! Coincidence! That is all! A damned coincidence." Fear fading, Gloria jogged to the end of the driveway, soaking her bare feet and the bottom of her jeans in deep puddles of warm rainwater. At the end of the driveway, she walked out into the street and waved her hands over her head. The buses came to a slow halt with brakes that whined. The massive rigs were white with black tinted windows. There was no writing on the sides, only some blue wavy lines of detailing.

Harold was walking toward the scene with the patience of a man who had no interest in arriving at his destination.

There was a hiss of compressed air and the door of the first bus opened. A muscular black man in a windbreaker and baseball cap stood up from the driver's seat and descended the steps.

"Morning," he said over the wind, smiling and tipping his hat.

The hat read 'FEMA.'

The man lost focus on Gloria and his smile disappeared. His eyes worked their way up and down something behind Gloria. Her father.

"Is this man bothering you, ma'am?" the bus driver asked.

She wanted to reply 'yes' because the man was indeed bothering her. Gloria looked behind her at Harold standing in the driveway. If it was possible, the all-nighter had him looking more naked and disheveled than normal.

"No," she said. "A ride would be good. To the school. Would that be okay?"

A wind snapped across the road, sending Gloria's wavy hair into her face and causing the bus driver's cap to fly off. He deftly caught it and replaced it on his head.

"This bus is for the Wampanoag. For the folks up at the Aquinnah reservation. It's dedicated to them, but of course, emergency situation like this." He looked at the sky to the south, growing darker. A crow on the phone lines overhead complained and took flight inland. "Backside of this storm's supposed to be worse than the front. This is the beginning of it. Hop in."

"Thank you very much."

Harold said "I am not getting on that bus."

The bus driver said, "I don't talk to dudes with their peckers out. Put on some chinos and we'll have a discussion."

"I am not speaking to you, you glorified Ralph Kramden. I am speaking to my daughter. I do not care about what I said earlier regarding the next vehicle we see. This bus is chartered by FEMA, the most nefarious arm of Leviathan. I would not step foot-"

She turned to look at her father. "You're confused. I didn't ask you to join me on the bus. Last night, when I suggested you come to New York? That was small talk, but you were too dense or drunk to recognize that. Just leave me alone. Both of my parents are clearly gone."

"Whoa shit" the bus driver said as the ocean found its way between the small dunes, rolled beneath the Gomberg household, fanning out across all visible land before reaching Moshup Trail Road. The water hit their calves with force, sending foam up Gloria's shorts and nearly toppling her. The water was frigid, pervading sinew and gnawing on bone. Gloria gasped deeply. It felt like death.

The bus driver continued over the din. "We need to leave, pronto."

Gloria turned and entered the bus. Her brain was working so hard and the adrenaline pumping through her system so mightily - not from the encroaching waves but from the way she had just spoken to her father - that every piece of information coming through her senses about the walk up the steps was being processed and stored. The "Watch Your Step" sign, the corrugated rubber on the risers and the treads, the smudged handrail; all of these things were as vivid as a fireworks display. She felt her heart thumping as if she had run a marathon. The words she had just spoken and current sense information accounted for so much of her thoughts that it took her a moment to decide her next move, which was as simple as sitting down. There was a spot in the very first row, next to a young woman with long black hair wearing a blue windbreaker. She was typing into her phone, and looked up only momentarily to take in the new rider. Gloria finally sat.

Over the engine, she heard the bus driver yelling to her father, "I don't know what's going on with you two but this storm is serious. Sure you don't want a ride? This could seriously be a life or death decision, sir." She could not hear her father's response, but the bus driver said, "Well, then get your naked ass under a mattress because it's gonna get ugly." The driver then rose up the steps, took his seat and adjusted the lever that closed the door with a hydraulic hiss.

Rain began, moving horizontally off the ocean, and it pelted the bus windows mightily. As they pulled away, Gloria saw her father through the psychedelic patterns of meandering raindrops. The old man was standing motionless in the driveway, his expression utterly blank. A massive wave knocked away a long section of the rotting beach fence and over the course of seconds carried it to the bus. The wave covered Harold up to the knees and made him stumble for a moment and look around at his predicament. The bus rocked slightly as the water passed beneath it. The driver visibly tensed his arms to keep the steering wheel straight. A few fellow riders, who Gloria noticed for the first time now, stood looking out the windows and pointing in surprise.

Why did she feel guilty right now? Why did she want to have the driver stop the bus so she could apologize? No, she thought. Your rage was justified this time. You did exactly what you needed to do. And it was Harold's decision not to get on the bus. Take deep breaths and move on.

You've killed your father, she thought.

Uncomfortable with silences, she looked at the woman next to her and said, "Hi."

The woman looked up from her texting and said, "Hi."

"I'm Gloria."

"Marie. How are you?"

"Oh. I've been better." Gloria gave out a nervous laugh, which Marie shared. "And how are you?"

Marie looked around, then looked back at Gloria and said, "I'm a Native American person on a vehicle chartered by the U.S. Government. You tell me."

They laughed again and shared some small talk about the weather. When the conversation paused for thirty-two seconds, Gloria fell fast asleep on Marie's shoulder.

Chapter Fourteen

He's back there drowning, she thought. He's drowning in
frigid seawater. She knew it as surely as she knew his face. And
it was her fault.

The smell of the gym reminded Gloria of her very early
school days in Norwalk. It was that time in life when everything
she experienced carried significance because it was her first time
experiencing it. The gym at her school had seemed like the
biggest possible room in the entire world. It had also cast a spell
because it was the one place the children could break from the
dogma of the classroom.

Looking at the legion of people now taking shelter, she was
reminded of one specific event in that gym of her childhood. It
had been the winter of her first-grade year and a blizzard raged
outside. The children were packed in, sitting "Indian style" on
the floor for an all-school assembly. A magician was scheduled
to entertain the kids, but the principal warned them he was late
due to the weather and that he may not make it. Two hundred
kids fidgeted and yelled, throwing wadded up paper and standing
up for no apparent reason. The teachers did their best but it was
bedlam.

The magician did arrive. He stepped into the room and
began setting up props while some of the more gregarious
children made running commentaries about his lavish clothing,
magic rings, and mysterious boxes. He had a female assistant.
She had shoulder-length blonde hair that flipped up at the end
from under a wool winter hat, and she was wearing a glittering
silver dress mostly covered by a down parka. Gloria was in love
with this woman who was more elegant than anyone she had

ever seen. The woman helped set up the props and every time she came close to Gloria, who was sitting quietly and respectfully in the first row, stale cigarette smoke and a case of the hiccups filled the air.

Finally, the principal announced that the show would begin and the kids cheered. The assistant unraveled a large tapestry that said "Magic Merv" in gold script. Magic Merv bowed to the audience and began to speak. He had a boisterous voice made to cut through the heckling of children, and it boomed from out of his massive head that sat atop a morbidly obese frame. He seemed as big as the gym itself and he completely commanded his audience. Starting off with guessing cards and making pennies appear from behind teachers' ears, he quickly let the act grow in spectacle, and soon enough he was making his assistant— whose name turned out to be "the Lovely Miss Violet"— hover three feet above the ground.

Gloria was overwhelmed. Her mind raced, trying to figure out how Merv was making these things happen, trying not to worry about the rabbit when it disappeared, and figuring out how she could quit school and become a magician.

It felt like the show was winding down, and Merv went silent. He shushed the children and told them in confidence about the mysterious Sarcophagus of Ra, which he had stumbled upon in his travels through the deserts of Egypt. He moved the sarcophagus forward on its squeaky wheels, turning it in the process and exposing the front to the audience. The box stood as tall as Gloria's very tall father and maybe even wider than him. It was black except for a gruesome painting of a mummy with glowing red eyes. Gloria kept herself together but just barely. She was not used to such morbid imagery and she felt that a true threat had entered the room. Merv told all of them to watch quietly as the lovely – and fearless - Miss Violet walked into the sarcophagus, which would most assuredly "swallow her very being!" And with these words, Miss Violet approached the box and Merv held her hand as she stepped up and in. Gloria was too terrified to cry out. She wanted to yell, to beg the elegant lady not to be crazy.

Merv closed the box with Miss Violet inside. He spoke words—an Egyptian curse, he explained— and smoke rose from the back of the box. Many of the children jumped, including Gloria. When Merv opened the box, breathing heavily due to his weight and efforts, Violet was gone. The children did not clap but gasped instead. The claps only came after some teachers started them off, and even then the response was anemic. This event was beyond their ken, and for Gloria it was far out of her comfort zone. She cared for the Lovely Miss Violet in a way she could not explain to the children around her, so instead she sat quietly, holding back tears.

"Worry not, children. We can retrieve Miss Violet back from the clutches of Ra with a simple incantation that we will all say now in unison!"

At that moment, the principal interrupted the act, and said that due to the blizzard, there was going to be an early dismissal. Some kids cheered while others booed. The principal continued. Everyone was to return to their classrooms immediately, collect their things, and wait for their parents inside or get on the buses that would arrive ahead of schedule. The power went out as they began to leave.

"It's okay, kids," Merv laughed as he daubed his brow with a red velvet handkerchief. "We'll continue this another day!"

224

Gloria panicked. She was being ushered out of the gymnasium, hundreds of small feet squeaking on waxed wood. Gloria looked over her shoulder she saw no sign of Miss Violet.

Gloria was inconsolable. Her teacher, Mrs. Coker, could not convince the sobbing child that the Sarcophagus of Ra was a silly prop. Without asking for permission, Gloria sprinted out of the classroom, down the hallway, and out into the frigid parking lot, wearing no coat and buckled shoes made for better weather. She immediately saw what she was looking for. It was parked only feet from the school entrance. She approached the white van, its lower half brown with mud and its wheels buried in a drift. The side read in large purple script "Magic Merv" and below in smaller script "For all of your important events!" The motor was running. The exhaust pipe vibrated and expelled grey fumes. Gloria ran around to the driver's side and there was Merv, wearing a ski hat, leather gloves, and a long wool coat. He was smoking a small brown cigar and bouncing up and down to keep warm.

He looked at the girl, smiled and said, "Hey there, little lady. Are you supposed to be out here?"

Gloria could not answer because she was too overwhelmed. She began crying again.

"Hey, hey, hey. It's okay," he said. "Whatever it is, it's okay." He flipped away his tiny cigar and knelt in front of her, so close Gloria could see the individual snowflakes caught in his mustache. "What's this all about?" he asked.

Gloria slapped his chest with her ungloved, freezing hand.

"You made Miss Violet disappear! She's gone. Ra's got her!"

Merv's face went from concern to a grin. He chuckled. "It's okay, kid. It was a trick. She's alright."

225

"No she's not."

"I'll tell you what. Come here a sec." He took her hand and walked her over to the driver's side door.

"I want you to say these words. Now I'm only telling you these words because you're special. Ready? Say them after me. *Alaba.*"

"Alaba."

"*Anubis.*"

"Anubis."

"*Baboo!*"

"Baboo."

With that, Merv picked her up from under her arms and lifted her to the driver's side window. On the passenger side sat Miss Violet. She was tuning the radio and holding a steaming Styrofoam cup. She looked over at Gloria, gave a quick wink, and went back to tuning the radio.

When Merv put Gloria down, she hugged him around the legs.

That night, Gloria pleaded with her parents to have Magic Merv perform at her birthday, and her parents approved. Gloria told all of her friends at school, even ones she was not inviting, that Merv was coming, and she whispered to Mrs. Coker that she was not afraid of the Sarcophagus of Ra anymore. Gloria would have trouble falling asleep every night until her birthday, thinking about Magic Merv summoning an oversized ace of spades card out of thin air and the Lovely Miss Violet stepping gracefully into a box of certain death.

Then, one week before her birthday, Merv died. He had suffered a massive heart attack while driving.

Rachel went to work behind Gloria's back, making secretive phone calls, stretching the cord to its limit so she could talk behind the basement door. Two nights before the party, Rachel sat Gloria down, stroked her bowl-cut hair, and surprised her by telling her that the Lovely Miss Violet was stopping by in a few minutes because she was in the neighborhood. Not knowing what to do with her excitement, Gloria ran around the kitchen screaming and kissing her toddler brother who was too busy eating spaghetti in his booster seat to notice.

Violet arrived just as her father was walking out to buy groceries. The exquisite lady, dressed more commonly now in grey polyester slacks and white cable sweater, gave her coat to Rachel. She greeted the shy young girl with the biggest "Well, hello" Gloria had ever heard. That was also the first time Gloria had heard Violet's voice. She had a southern accent that was exotic to the child's ears.

After accepting a cup of tea from Rachel, Violet sat down with Gloria on the plastic-covered living room couch and asked her all about her favorite parts of the act from the other week at school. Gloria recalled the highlights and the two of them had a lively back and forth. When the first lull occurred, Gloria remembered it being easily a half-hour in, Violet looked over at Rachel, cleared her throat, and then explained in a hushed voice that Merv could not make it to her party.

When she heard those words, Gloria felt like something was physically removed from her body, something vital to existence. A lung perhaps. She was dizzy. But at the same time, she wanted to be tough and cool in front of Violet, so she remained still. And she listened. Violet said that Merv could not be there because "well, he went and did the darnedest thing and, and…" Violet again looked up at Gloria's mother, who did not hide her nod very well. Gloria saw the interaction. Violet continued. "Silly old Merv made himself disappear! Can you believe such a thing?"

Gloria could not. However, rather than address the pain and call Violet on the lie, she chose to believe it.

Gloria's mother said, "These things happen from time to time, sweetheart. Magicians do this, either on purpose or by mistake."

"Exactly," Violet added. "They do it, and they come back when they feel like it. So don't worry, sweetheart." Gloria saw a wetness in Violet's eyes. "He'll be back someday. Until then, I know a great magician named Bill Hall who will be great at your party, okay?"

The name 'Bill Hall' did not summon visions of reality-bending feats the way "Magic Merv" did, but she accepted the news and let Violet leave without further inquiries. The lady took her coat back from Gloria's mother and Gloria never saw her again.

That night in bed, Gloria repeated the incantation under her sheets, over and over, deep into the night. "*Alaba anubis baboo. Alaba anubis baboo. Alaba anubis baboo.*" They had to bring Merv back. Violet was safe, but Merv had to be as well. "*Alaba anubis baboo. Alaba anubis baboo. Alaba anubis baboo.*" She said the words until she was too drowsy to say them anymore.

Her last lucid thought before falling asleep was not about the loss of Merv, nor was it about her love of Violet. It was about her mother. She reflected on the fantastic lengths the woman would go to hide bad things. She was not sure if she loved or hated her for it. Either way, it would not be the last time Rachel Gomberg would distort the truth for her children.

Chapter Fifteen

'Under every deep, a lower deep opens.'

The quotation came to Gloria suddenly and then was squelched by thoughts of her surroundings. Its meaning and the reason for its rise to consciousness remained uninvestigated.

She walked the perimeter of the high school gym looking for a place to sleep. It seemed like all of the cots in the center were taken. She noticed Kyle standing by the folded-up bleachers, wrapped in a blanket and nothing else, chatting up some people from the Asian tour bus. Gloria felt so stupid not knowing what country in Asia they were from. Even though she could not hear what Kyle was saying, it was clear he was having a go at speaking their language. Several members of his audience nodded their heads in recognition. His eyes caught Gloria's and he gave a polite wave. Gloria waved back but with little enthusiasm. After the previous day's accident, Kyle had stumbled serpentine over to the smashed-up car and asked if he could be of any help. Gloria had rejected his offer because she considered it worthless, given that he had been drunk, naked, and riding a bicycle at the time.

Dick Hoyt was also present, standing among his own circle of chatty people, sipping on coffee and chuckling about something Gloria could not hear. Dick had clearly just changed into a fresh pink polo shirt and white shorts that contrasted with his bony, tan legs, but his hair remained as confused as it had been the previous morning when Gloria had seen him last.

Prissy rolled up from nowhere. "Well, hello stranger," she said, playfully elbowing Gloria in the arm. "Fancy seeing you here. Where's that exhibitionist father of yours? Oh, he is such…a…stitch!" This did not amuse Gloria at all, as she knew that Prissy would love to see her father dead or at least evicted.

"He decided to stay with the house."

"Brave man. They're saying this storm will probably going to go down as one of the most damaging because it's staying put. It just won't leave!"

Gloria related to the storm. She negotiated with it. 'If you leave then I'll leave. How about it, sister? We should both know when we're not wanted. I don't even need to go back to New York City. Let's just hold hands and stroll off into the North Atlantic together.' In her head, the one-way conversation with the storm ended and she found herself being pulled down a third time by Prissy's small talk.

"…coffee is abhorrent but so many nice people here that I never get to catch up with. That tall man leaning against the bleachers with the white hair? Handsome, isn't he? That's Paul Pierce. He was Case's teacher at Choate who retired to the island. He's the one who suggested Lehigh to her! Don't tell Dick, but I am sure warm for his form." She chuckled and scanned the gym with the confident air of someone looking upon a wine tasting they are throwing at their own home. She blatantly pointed at a tired-looking woman in a white Black Dog sweatshirt and sweatpants, brushing her short grey bob. The woman likely saw Prissy's gesture as she too was scanning the room. "Angie Yarrow over there?" Prissy whispered through breath that smelled of gin. "Total lush." She brought her voice back up. "But so nice. I was in a book group with her and some other ladies from Moshup Trail but it broke up because no one was reading the books and then Angie over there got so lit up on Merlot she laughed a little too hard at something I said and wet herself. Mortifying for everyone." She looked away from Angie and back at Gloria. She sighed. "You know who would have loved that book group?"

"Who?"

"Your mother." She did not elaborate on this and simply said "Well, off to make the rounds. Find yourself a comfortable cot and make yourself at home!" Prissy walked in Angie's direction, using Gloria for balance as she stepped over someone's duffle bag.

Gloria's exhaustion manifested itself in a loss of body heat. She picked up a random blanket from the floor and wrapped it around herself. The only sleep she had achieved was an hour or so on the bus. She still needed to close her eyes but she knew herself well enough to understand that no sleep would come to her in this brightly lit space full of echoing chatter. She made the decision to tour the school in search of peace. A pair of white, windowless double doors in the corner of the gym beckoned.

The sound of the crowds disappeared as the doors closed behind her. Lockers lined the dark corridor in which she now stood, and Gloria was finally alone save one teenage girl sitting cross-legged against a wall, texting into the light of her phone. When she heard Gloria enter the hallway, the girl rose and went back into the gym, looking at her phone the whole time.

There was complete silence, low light, and isolation. It was exquisite. Gloria reveled in the calm for a moment, walking as slowly as possible so not even the squeak of her shoes on linoleum could interrupt. The only sound was the wind making its way through duct work.

Flyers for end-of-year events hung on cork boards, alongside reminders about a delayed yearbook release date. A poster hung on the wall of a classroom door. It showed a rocky cliff, topped with impossibly green grass beneath a blue, cloudless sky. A waterfall spouted gloriously from the cliff face. In the top right corner of the poster, in a white, scripted font, it read "Somewhere, something incredible is waiting to be known." The quotation was credited to Carl Sagan.

Smart man, Gloria thought. But another quotation was stuck in her mind at that moment, and it blocked the optimistic Sagan words from taking root. It was one she had glimpsed in a book her father had read in her childhood, and it had stuck with her, popping into consciousness at opportune times. Being in a school setting now unleashed it. As she thought about the miserable trajectory of the past weekend, as she compared her original goals to the grim outcomes, to the unexpected missteps and booby traps and further missteps within the booby traps, the quotation had taken hold and become a dull roar in her head. "Under every deep a lower deep opens." Whatever Emerson's intent, positive or negative, it summed up recent events so well that Gloria wondered if *that* should have been printed on a poster in scripted white text next to an image of a waterfall.

She continued to look for somewhere comfortable to lie down, maybe a nurse's office or a couch outside of the principal's office. So far, there were only classrooms. Her mind wandered to the music of the Emerson quotation repeating in her head. Nika was in her thoughts as well. Where would she go and what would her future hold now that she was released from being a Gomberg chess board pawn? Nika, now physically, psychologically, and psychically scarred would likely return to her place of origin, railing in Russian about Harold and Harold's daughter who had nothing to do with the invention of Red Bull. Nika would explain all of this to her parents and never understand their consolations.

And what of Scott? Dear Scott. She had thought she could pop the relationship like a balloon and it would be gone. There is no such thing as a half-popped balloon. So why was she thinking about him regularly? Had there been something more in them than weapon and weapon owner? Was the fact that they had both tragically lost their mothers enough of a mortar to hold them together? Or perhaps it was like Prissy had suggested; just finding a decent human being was enough, and Gloria now believed it. She dug her fingernails deep into her palms until the pain overwhelmed her thoughts.

It was then that she smelled the marijuana and saw the smoke, billowing out from a classroom door. She peeked in and saw the silhouette of Amos Andrews, sitting on a desk and exhaling out an open window. His flipped-up collar was dancing in the wind entering the room. Gloria opened the door and the odor increased threefold. Amos was backlit by the stretch of windows, and the room was mostly shadow. The desks were set up in a circle. A considerate teacher or parent had donated a rug to warm up the space. It rested on the floor within the ring of desks. Gloria recognized it as the same kind of rug her parents had owned in the living room when she was a child, oriental with a medallion of gold and burgundy in its center, its pattern rearticulated in the corners, a complexity unimaginable. Gloria walked in and stood in the center of the desks, also centered on the rug. She looked at the whiteboard, upon which was listed points of story structure— introduction, complication, climax, denouement, and coda.

"Howdy," Amos said, reaching out to offer Gloria a drag of his joint.

"No thanks," she said.

"Suit yourself." He took another hit.

233

"Why are you here? Shouldn't you be healing people at the hospital?"

While he held in smoke, he croaked, "They wanted a person here, just in case." He exhaled. "Easy gig. No one has even a cold. Thought I would hide a while and find some peace." He looked at her. "You look exhausted."

"Thanks."

"You're welcome."

"And, of course, I know you mean it because you never lie."

"Correct. But you also look very pretty despite your being exhausted. You're a very pretty woman."

"I appreciate it, despite the robotic itemization of my physical traits."

"You're welcome."

Gloria looked around and realized she had nothing more to say to him and so began to turn.

"Your father loves you, you know."

"Excuse me?"

"Your father loves you. It's just that for such a talker, he doesn't know how to talk."

Gloria had not expected this. And it was then she realized the value of this man in front of her.

"You always tell the truth."

"We've established that."

"Not just about yourself, but about others as well?"

"I suppose."

Gloria felt an excitement build in her. She was again a detective assigned to a murder, and now she had found the ideal witness.

"Why did my dad cheat on my mom?"

"Aw man. This seems wrong."

"Truth, Amos."

Amos took another hit, exhaled and said, "Alright, but before we go down that path, just so you can have faith I'm not bullshitting you, I want to tell you my last and only current lie. I swear I tell the truth all the time except this one."

"What is it?"

Amos looked out the window at the dying wind and said "I'm not Wampanoag."

"What?"

"I'm not even Native American. I'm a guy from Madison, Wisconsin of Huguenot extraction."

This was not any path Gloria had expected their conversation to take and she felt impatient. "I don't care."

"I only told the lie to your dad, in the heat of the moment when we first met. He was picking on me for not being from the island. I guess I could have just told a normal lie and claimed I *was* from the island, but I doubled down. Said I was not only from the island, but one of the original inhabitants of the island."

"Does my dad still believe that?"

"I have no idea. He pretends he does. Might make him feel like no one can call him a racist because he hangs out with a Native American. But that won't work because everyone else on the island knows I'm not from here. Anyway, there you go. It's all out. I am fib free. So, what were we talking about?" He took another drag off his joint. "Oh right. Why did your dad cheat? That's easy. She cheated on him first."

Gloria responded before she had even processed the information beyond a superficial level. "*Bullshit!*"

Amos jumped a little. "No, ma'am. Not bullshit at all."

"You're just trying to pin the blame for his awful behavior on her, making it sound like it's her fault."

Amos flicked his joint out the window and stood up. "I'm not saying anything's her fault. You think someone just has an affair out of nowhere? Rachel, sorry, your mom, did not have an affair while sleepwalking or because of a nervous tic. It had precursors. The universe is a complex system. Each effect spurred by an earlier cause. Your mom's affair was not the first event in the universe."

Gloria thought about this.

Amos walked into the circle of chairs, feet from Gloria, and continued. "You're looking for the source of a river that has many tiny tributaries. Give up the search. The river's source is unknowable. It's probably unknowable even to your father."

Gloria sat down on the rug. "He's never talked about it to me."

Amos sat as well. "Probably trying to protect you. I don't know."

"I've given him shit about his affair for years."

"So he tells me."

"He never said a thing."

Amos patted his breast pocket. "Do you have rolling papers on you?"

"She never said a thing either. Well, not about her own affair. Just his. What a bitch."

"Whoa. I just said she was driven to it by…"

"Stop explaining shit to me like a typical man."

"I *am* a typical man."

"Work on that."

"Do you have any rolling papers?"

"I have a right to be mad at my mom, you know? She never told me. And hey why is my dad telling you this stuff and not me?"

Amos found some rolling papers in his wallet. He pulled a small Ziploc of marijuana out of a cargo pant pocket and began manufacturing a joint. He answered. "Well, he had had a really, really bad day. Like a life-changing bad day. So bad he needed to open up about stuff."

"Are you going to tell me about this bad day?"

"Yes. You may be surprised to hear this, but your dad decided he was going to actually get a phone installed in the house, rejoin society. Make a try to be communicative. Around the time Nika came into his life and he was a little happier. Phone company came and did the work. Within days, though, the automated calls came, telling him he owed money on this, that, the other thing. One in particular kept coming in about a loan he had taken out for fixing some wear and tear on the house."

"That doesn't sound so bad. Definitely not a 'life-changing' bad day."

"Well, the problem was the voice on the calls. It was your mom."

"Mom?"

"Yeah. You know she was a popular voice talent, and after she died, I guess the loan company didn't change their phone system, starring her. So, your dad just kept getting hounded by these haunted calls, his dead wife taunting him about his financial failures. I came over one afternoon to play chess and he was sitting on the deck, not in a chair but on the wood, naked and pale on a beautiful summer day. Your dad is never pale. He looked at me like a man who'd just witnessed his own death. Right then the phone starts ringing again. He looks at me and says, 'Pull that phone out of the wall and throw it into the ocean.' I did. And then he starts telling me about his past in lurid detail. Ergo, I know about the deceptions."

237

This was going nowhere, Gloria thought. She was gathering information, but nothing that was hitting the nail on the head. Perhaps, she thought as she rubbed her own stiff shoulder and considered Amos's eyes, I am not asking the real question. It was obvious to her what the real question was, but it was hard for her to ask. The words seemed like something a child would ask, a selfish child who had not yet learned to apply feelings and motivations to others. And with that question came the feelings of a child. Raw, unwelcome feelings. She felt a pain in the back of her throat, as if the collective words were pushing the aggregate of their weight against her tongue, straining to make it move. Her eyes watered.

"Can I have a drag of that joint?" she asked Amos. She was not sure where *that* question had come from, because it was certainly not the one that had caused her to choke up.

Amos handed her the joint and she inhaled. She coughed for what seemed like the remainder of the day. Not having thought about a drink or cigarette for a few days since the storm began, she now wanted every vice possible. Once the coughing had subsided, her head light as a weather balloon in the stratosphere, the true question came.

"Why does my father hate me?"

"Hate? Big assumption there. Why would you think he hates you?" Amos croaked while holding smoke in his lungs.

"He's cut off all communication with me."

"Silence doesn't mean hate. Silence has no meaning in and of itself. It could mean nothing and it could mean anything. You're painting the color of that silence."

"Okay, so what does he say about me to you?"

"A lot." He pointed to the front of the classroom. "I could practically draw out a timeline of your life on that whiteboard.

Seth's too. The times you would go to the supermarket with your dad holding paper on a clipboard and you would walk around checking items off for no reason. I could name all of Seth's four children and the risk management firm he works for. I know about the time you wet your pants on the first day of camp. Or the time you ran up on stage with your boyfriend's band in college to sing a Bee Gees song –"

"'How Deep is Your Love.'"

"'How Deep is Your Love' and some skinhead threw a beer bottle and it hit you in the head. Your dad drove up to school in the middle of the night to visit you in the hospital. He tells me everything about both of you. Your life is on his lips nearly every day."

She rose and looked down at Amos. Now extremely frustrated and perhaps a little stoned, she said, "That's very sweet, but then why doesn't he talk to me? Why no visits?"

Amos stood as well.

"That's where my information runs out. I can't tell the truth if I don't know the data." He walked to the window and opened it further. A very gentle wind entered the room. Nothing blew off the walls. All that moved was Gloria's hair. A strong smell of spring replaced the room's marijuana stench. Amos continued, "But I can give you my opinion. If you don't mind another guy pontificating."

"Go ahead," Gloria said, watching as Amos began to walk toward the door.

Before exiting, his eyes bugged. "Man," he said. "I probably stink of weed. I better air out." He crossed back to the open window, stepped up on the radiator, and put his foot through. With surprising agility, he began to slip his body through until his feet were planted in the grass outside. "Ah! I'm in a puddle out here. My feet are soaked."

Gloria was exasperated. "What's your opinion, Amos?"

"You remind him of her."

"Who?"

"Lady Bird Johnson."

She was lost.

"Rachel Gomberg. You remind your father of your mother. It's too painful for him to be around you."

Gloria considered this.

"To him, you're another automated phone call from beyond the grave. He's pulled the phone out of the wall and thrown it into the ocean."

She had nothing to say.

"Now if you'll excuse me, water's pouring on my back from the gutters. Catch you later."

Trying to avoid puddles, Amos was walking like the earliest animated cartoon characters, his legs making sweeping arcs beneath his bouncing body.

Then he returned and popped his head through the window again. "By the way, would you ever want to get dinner?"

Gloria hardly heard him. She was staring at a blank spot on the cream-colored cinder block wall. Amos's voice seemed to be coming through cans tied to a string, stretching from Jupiter to Earth. It took some time for her to look at him, let alone respond. Finally turning and taking in the view of his dripping, bald head sticking through the window, she said "Of course not."

"Why?"

"You're my father's drug dealer."

"Fair enough" he said. "By the way, where *is* your dad?"

Gloria could have sworn she had heard *dead* instead of *dad*, but assumed she had mistaken the sounds due to the whistling winds.

"At the house," she said.

"Whoa. Hardcore," Amos said, and again he walked into the waning storm.

Gloria was now alone with these new thoughts. It took only seconds before the tears came. She openly sobbed. They were not tears of sadness. They were tears of letting go. They were tears of acceptance. They were tears of exhaustion. It was clear to her now that her father did not just live far away with minimal means of communication. He lived on another plane of existence, across a chasm as grand as the one between the living and the dead. And she was on the side of the dead. By being here on this island, she was trying to punch through quantum foam to enter his universe, and that was simply not possible.

Or was he the one who was dead? Abandoned by his daughter in the storm?

Emerson had been right. There was always a lower deep. But she sensed that she had just reached the frozen floor of the abyss. And perhaps, just perhaps, Amos was her bald, stoned Virgil, pointing her toward the exit out of Hell.

Chapter Sixteen

"I hope your dad's not dead" Kyle said matter-of-factly.
Unlike Scott's station wagon, Kyle's SUV was clean to the
point of being antiseptic. It smelled of new leather. There were
no Cheerios in the children's car seats and no empty coffee cups
in the holders. Marlo Thomas's *"Free to Be You and Me,"* CD
was placed in its jewel case and neatly tucked away in the netted
passenger door pocket (Scott's jewel cases had always been
cracking beneath Gloria's feet). When she closed her eyes, she
felt she was escaping her personal lunacy and supernaturally
inhabiting the life of a normal person, breathing their air in their
own cadence, thinking their thoughts, and enjoying their
successes. Then she opened her eyes, turned and reviewed her
naked unwashed driver, and was reminded that this pristine
world was already tainted by proximity to her father.

Kyle drove the SUV down debris-strewn roads like a cruise
ship on calm seas. Water-logged tree limbs and even a twisted
metal porch glider were easily bested. The ride was downright
pleasant. The air whispered out of the vents and Gloria felt
herself falling asleep again. Eyes closed, she slurred, "It was
really nice of you to give me a ride."

"Least I could do after causing your car accident yesterday.
Besides, I'm looking forward to seeing Harold while I'm sober.
He changed my life."

"Sorry to hear that," she yawned.

"Well, I'm thrilled. I was so buried in my sarcophagus.
Those clothes were a metaphor for so much, you know? They
were a flag. The flag of an oppressed nation called Kyle! Well,
welcome to New Kyle. The nation of New Kyle's got no flag,

sister. No threads on my back anymore. No government either. And God, well, I guess he's still with me. That's a tougher thing to shake off. Grew up Catholic. Holly did too."

The windshield began to fog.

"I know," Gloria said. "She mentioned it more than once at work."

"Our kids were both baptized. Shedding God. Not easy. I need to have a talk with Him. Until He goes away."

Gloria understood this sentiment. She had grown up Jewish, and even though she had turned her back on God much like her father, some part of her still believed. To turn your back on something, you still need to believe it exists. Despite being highly rational, at least in her own opinion, she could easily allow for God by compartmentalizing Him and placing Him outside and above the gossamer of logic. But removing Him entirely from her thinking process, that was unthinkable. The thought of simply vaporizing God, not unlike what she did to Scott, was not an option.

Kyle looked over at her, started to say something and then stopped. Then he tried again. "Look, my marriage is pretty much over. I know you're older than me, but are you..."

Gloria's eyes opened. She interrupted him. "Are you fucking kidding me? No. Don't even finish asking, Nation of New Kyle."

Kyle slowed the car down. "Whoa! Sorry. I'm just a little confused with everything that's going on." He accelerated back to their original speed. His hands aggressively worked the climate controls, maximizing the defog and turning on the windshield wipers.

Guilt coursed through her reflexively. "I'm sorry."

For the life of her, she could not figure out why she was apologizing, other than that she had apologized for all things she had done and for all things the people around her had done. It was in her nature and it would never go away. Gloria, she knew, was forever Gloria. Maybe she had been that way before she had even existed. Some Ukrainian Jewish girl a century earlier had been apologizing to the Cossack who kicked her father in front of her. Maybe a fish swimming the Paleozoic oceans apologized as it entered the green muted shadows of a whale's mouth.

She thought about the nesting dolls again. The Glorias. The murky origins of her guilt were locked in those Glorias. In her smallest Gloria. Buried so deep she would never know it. But even if she did find the wellspring of the problem, it would probably not make any sense to her. She thought back to when her mother took her to see "Cats" where she learned that cats have three names: The one given to them by humans, the one they use with each other, and then their true unspeakable names. Gloria felt that the origins of her character were like that third cat name. Cats know their private name. Gloria did not know hers. She could call it Guilt, and she could explain it with mythical narratives of psychoanalysts, but its honest nature skulked outside the kingdom of words.

Sun broke through as the car pulled into Harold's driveway. When she opened the passenger side door, the smell of the ocean air was blissful, as if the storm had churned up all the ambergris in the ocean. A kind breeze greeted her and blew grey strands of hair into her mouth. Kyle waited in the car as she ascended the stairs of the house to grab her things. She would also bring Scott's suitcases back to New York and maybe - just maybe - take that moment to discuss matters with him.

The front door was unlocked as usual. She entered and the house was still.

"Dad?" she called. No response. The kitchen window had cracked, shards scattered across the linoleum. Beyond the porch's sliding door, the ocean foamed. Sunshine lit up the pile carpet and jazz albums lying in disarray everywhere. As she approached the stove on her way to the living room, the floorboards beneath her creaked angrily. She felt one of them bow, perhaps loosened by the storm. She became conscious of the fact the house was on stilts and that there was a considerable space between her feet and the ground below. This sudden awareness made her heart race. A room she had known since childhood suddenly seemed unlivable and dangerous.

She went about collecting her things. Toothbrush. Tampons. Her clothing was strewn about the guest room, and she shoved it chaotically into her duffle bag regardless of cleanliness. Her wallet had not been on her person for days. She picked it up off the chest of drawers, a surface still noticeably devoid of family photos. Their absence still attracted her focus, feeling like a phantom limb. As she walked by her father's room, she noticed the tapestry over his window flapping about like a tie-dyed flag of some borderless, anarchic nation. Broken glass lay all over that floor as well.

She eyed a pack of Nika's cigarettes on the kitchen counter and shoved them into her purse. It was then, as she was picking up the cigarettes, that she saw her phone. It rested on the counter next to the stove, clearly untouched by the elements. It had never been in the ocean. Gloria walked over to it, picked it up, and held down the power button. It came to life with one-percent battery. The phone vibrated in her hand with the notification of a new text message. She hoped it was from her boss, maybe rethinking the firing. Even better, it was from Scott, or as she had labeled him in her phone, "Studley McPhishLover." She punched in her passcode and brought up the message.

She was immediately confused. There was a back-and-forth in the thread she did not remember, full of comments she had never written. Scrolling up, she read from the last part she could recall.

11:03 pm
Hello

Hello

Hey

Hello

Amusing speech recognition so forgive any weird words

Who are you it says love dove

Very funny

I have not made a joke

Mr. Gomberg?

Yes

Why do you have glorious phone?

How does this working am I doing this correctly Houston there is trouble

I think it's you stun weave a problem

It is most certainly not that why do words show up I did not typist

Auto correct. What are you doing with glorious phone?

*She absconded with my
Alaskan thunder fuck and in
trade I told her I threw her
phone into the briny deep
which of course I did not
donut seeing as you and I are
exchanging bone motors
currently*

I wouldn't call these Bond Mose.

Nor would I

I want to know if Gloria wants to talk

*I am certain I do not
know so you should ask her*

I can't

Why not

Because you have her phone

I see

*Can you just please tell her I still
lover but need to talk*

That will be a challenge

Why?

*She is gonad and I do not
in vision herring returning as
she abandon me in the
hurricane*

Thank you Mr. Gone Berg

Goodbye Tim

Before she could process the dialogue, the house groaned again, as if every plank was buckling and every stilt was rusting out. A wave of panic hit her. Where was her father? Was he

247

dead? He had stayed with the house throughout the storm. Until this moment she had assumed he was immortal, and that no storm could touch him. But where was he? She ran back to his bedroom. The tapestry continued to rustle, and when it flapped up and light shone through the room, she could see that he was not in the unmade bed. Gloria stepped across the hallway to the tiny bathroom. It remained empty.

"Dad?" she asked the house again. There was no response. Within seconds, she was across the kitchen and living room and pulling open the sliding door. It resisted; further evidence the house was moving, shifting, failing. Her father was dead. She knew it like she knew his name. She could picture it perfectly. He had tried to make it to town by bicycle, to apologize to her for his neglect, and been washed away into Menemsha Pond by the swollen waters at the herring run. His death was her fault. The guilt she had suffered her entire life had been a prescient notion, foretelling her role in his death.

She ran out onto the porch and saw her father sunbathing on a faded Little Mermaid beach towel. He was using a broken boogie board for a pillow. Gifts spat out by the sea. An open book rested on his chest, the pages probably soaked through with the sunblock in which he was slathered. The storm had dug a chunk out of the sand, leaving a six-foot cliff where the ground had once been smooth, and the old man rested on the cliff's precipice. Driftwood, a car tire, seaweed, bleached soda cans, and an infinite count of whelks, moon shells, and smooth pebbles covered the beach. Next to Harold was the 'Vital Effects' cooler, wide open, and the outsized bag of marijuana sat next to it. She looked over to the storm-flattened seagrass and noted the six or seven holes her father had dug and the shovel he had used to dig them. One hole lay beneath the broken porch steps, right behind where they had once met the sandy ground.

Clearly her premonition of her father's death had been incorrect. There he was. But the notion had been so strong. 'So who is dead?' Gloria thought. Was she the unwanted specter bringing her father misery? Or was he in fact dead, gone from her life, and responsible for the haunting? One thing was certain: Gloria needed eight hours of uninterrupted sleep.

She walked down the porch stairs, jumping down the broken steps at the bottom, and walked out to meet her father. When she reached the storm-carved precipice, she stood over him. Her shadow crossed his face and he opened his eyes.

"Cagey girl," he said. "Burying the cooler beneath the porch steps. Not unlike Poe's purloined letter. I was impressed. Nonetheless, I won the day and found it on the seventh try. I just smoked a doobie the size of a dirigible to celebrate my advantage."

"I'm leaving, Dad." She waited for an unlikely response and as expected, none came. "I understand the distance between us now. I understand why you're angry at the world and I understand why you don't like being near me. And I think I even forgive you for it. But I can't be around you anymore because…" She felt herself about to cry, but stopped. She had practiced this back in the school before asking Kyle for a ride. "It hurts too much to be near you."

He was quiet. For once. He did not move a muscle. Then he asked, "Do you have a ride?"

She knew anger should have been her response to this empty question, but something was shifting in her. She was not angry. She was bored and ready to leave.

"Kyle's here. He drove me up and said he'll give me a ride to the ferry."

"Kyle, eh?" He stood up, his height always surprising to Gloria. "I should sue him back to the Earth's Hadean Period. He put my old lady in the hospital! Where is he?"

"He's in the car but let it go. Let's not get litigious, please. If we were, I could sue you for setting a mad dog on *my* old man."

"Oh please. Your Steely Dan loving drone bee was not associated with you in any way. There was no emotional attachment and anyone could see that. And anyway, I should be suing you alongside Kyle because you were not looking at the road when the accident occurred."

If their usual script had been followed, Gloria would have taken this moment to defend herself and then shoot back some barb in the hope of drawing blood. But again, she felt nothing but an urge to flee. "Goodbye, Dad," she said. "Good luck with everything." She began walking to the driveway.

As she passed the 'vital effects' cooler, its lid wide open and the bag of weed unpacked next to it, she noticed something at its bottom catching the sunlight. She stopped walking and knelt beside it. Looking back up at her was the framed photo of her mother that had been in the guest room. The woman seemed to be looking back up at Gloria, across time and space, with a smile of approval. Gloria reached in and pulled it out. Beneath that was the other missing picture, the one of Gloria and Seth next to the girl they no longer knew, waiting in line at the Flying Horses. She picked that one up as well. And beneath that, she saw what she had been sure was long gone, what should have been sold at a yard sale decades ago and stowed away in the basement of a stranger. It was the Glorias, resting inside a womb of meticulously applied bubble wrap and tape.

"Enjoying the clown car of history?" her father asked.

"Vital effects." Gloria said through a lump in her throat.

"Oh, please," Harold started, but then he said no more.

Both were silent for a time as Gloria replaced the items in the cooler. She stood up and began walking again.

"Do you want some pie before you go?" her father asked. "Rhubarb. I made it from scratch."

Gloria smiled. She was about to turn when, in front of her, the wood-burning stove fell through the floor of the house and crashed to the ground twenty feet below. The noise was painfully sharp and it repeated in the pieces that broke apart and shot everywhere. The flue collar sparked against rocks in the driveway and the baffle hit the Camry. No cloud of sand rose because the ground was heavy and wet from rain.

Gloria was about to turn to her father again when one of the stilts under the house buckled, and the porch and part of the living room collapsed. Puddles of water that had been beneath the house compressed and splashed. Gloria felt the beach vibrate beneath her, and then it did so again when a second stilt cracked and the kitchen came down in its entirety. The cataclysm made her step back instinctively. On the ground before her were piles of broken, non-descript structures that resembled things she had known her entire life. Above them was the interior of the house, devoid of a fourth wall, a stage set. And then that collapsed too.

When she was finally able to move, after her legs regained their strength, Gloria looked back at her father, but he was gone. It took her a moment to realize that he had fallen off the newly formed sand cliff. She ran to the edge and saw the man slowly rising, spitting out sand and brushing seaweed off his arms.

When his gaze took in the wood heap that used to be his home, his mouth opened. The surprise on his face was something with which Gloria was unfamiliar. Nothing had ever caused him to be so utterly unbalanced. He listed to one side, and then another, his mouth never closing. A shell detached and fell from his shoulder.

"Wow" he said.

And then he looked up at Gloria, and his mouth opened again. This time, it was not a look of surprise. He was trying to say something. And he was failing. He began to croak some syllable but it was gone. And then he tried again and finally it came out.

"Take me with you?" he asked.

Of course, Gloria thought. Of course, he is asking me now. His house has disappeared. This is not some soft spot in his heart that has finally been unearthed. No, this is a pragmatic, opportunistic move. He needs a home so now he is willing to join her. To Gloria this was so obvious.

But then it wasn't. She looked into his eyes, which appeared to be wet. Or maybe they weren't. She could not tell as his face was in shade. But it was the words and how he uttered them that made her suddenly trust his intentions. They had seemed raw in a way she had never heard from him. They sounded free of review and revision, devoid of artifice, as if they had escaped the detection of one thousand guards and sprinted across an open portcullis to green fields and freedom beyond. They sounded liberated.

They sounded ungoverned.

Monday

Chapter Seventeen

"I am exhausted," her father said, yawning in the passenger seat. "Forgive me while I retire to the back seat and rest in the arms of Morpheus." With that he rose and shifted his frame in an unfortunate manner, hovering his bare bottom inches from Gloria's head.

"God, Dad," she said.

"You will live through this," he grunted as he brought his leg over the seat back and landed in the rear of the SUV. Within a minute, his snoring could be heard over the quiet engine.

They had been in line to get on board the ferry for hours, throughout the night. Luck would have it that the dock had been re-opened only minutes before they arrived, and they ended up receiving an enviable position near the front of the line. Kyle had a reservation for the ferry that day, and given they were in Kyle's car at the moment, they *were* Kyle as far as the Steamship Authority was concerned. However, he had neglected to tell Gloria or Harold where the boarding pass was. Shaped by the pain of her experience with Scott at Woods Hole days earlier, Gloria had immediately dropped the sun visor when situating herself in the driver's seat of the car for the first time, and lo and behold, the pass had dropped down into her lap.

She had slept that night on the dock but her father had not, and now he was finally giving in. The weather outside had turned yet again. While the hurricane had gone out to sea, a more subtle misery now dominated. When the morning light finally arrived, the world was grey and soaked in a relentless drizzle. Thousands of people were trying to leave the island, and the traffic backed up off the dock and a quarter mile down Seaview Avenue. A bleak line of foiled vacation plans and frayed nerves.

Gloria felt her eyes begin to close again and her head bob on her neck when a white vehicle passed by her. It was an ambulance. Dock workers directed it to the front of the line. This activity brought Gloria back to attentiveness. An EMT with a crew cut and bushy black mustache got out of the driver's side door and made his way to the back. When he opened the rear doors, Gloria saw Nika on a dolly, sitting up with her head still bandaged. The young lady probably did not recognize Kyle's car and missed Gloria staring at her through the morning rain. She considered waking her father, still snoring in back, but decided against it. Instead, Gloria watched alone in silence. Nika looked lovely despite her injuries and despite the fact she was yelling at the EMT about whatever was the content of the insulated water bottle she held in her hand. Perhaps it was not Red Bull. The mustachioed man closed the doors and Nika disappeared from Gloria's life.

After the house had collapsed and her father had begged for rescue, Kyle ran up to them, naked except for a Black Dog baseball cap. His eyes were focused on the smoking pile that had moments earlier been the Gomberg residence. This distraction led Kyle to trip and catch himself several times on his way. "Guys! The house collapsed! Did you see that? Holy shit! It just...kuh-blam!"

Kyle's approach had allowed both Gloria and her father to change focus. And change focus Harold did.

"You!" Harold boomed as he dug his way up the sandy cliff. "I plan to summon mer-lawyers from the vasty deep and they will shake you down for all you are worth." Gloria could tell he had been smoking.

Kyle got down on his knees and yelled, "I'm sorry, sir. Please forgive me."

"How about a trade?" Harold had asked.

"What do you have in mind?"

"This plot of land for your car."

"Done."

They had exchanged title and deed, the former in the glove box and the latter being inside "vital effects," however legally sketchy the transaction had been, and sealed the deal with a handshake.

Harold spoke while their hands were still locked. "Safeguard this bastion of liberty, Kyle."

"I will, sir."

"Spread the gospel. The world needs to know. You are now the New England arm of our movement. I will go to New York City and begin our work there. And will oversee the funds we will gain from my plans for a cemetery that is also a garden."

"I'm honored." Kyle gestured back to the remnants of the Gomberg summer home. "What should I do about the house pile?"

Harold broke their handshake and saluted. "It was great knowing you, Kyle."

The first ferry to arrive once the water permitted passage was the *Island Home*. The vessel creaked and yawned in the agitated sea while cars entered her hold. A Steamship Authority employee directed Gloria and Harold to their parking spot behind a muddy Jeep with a "COEXIST" bumper sticker, each of the letters represented by a different religious symbol. Gloria

257

thanked heavens her father was asleep to miss that. She pulled up the parking brake and killed the engine. The world shifted relentlessly as the ferry slammed into one wingwall of the dock and rebounded, only to be slammed into the opposing wingwall. Gloria worried the ferry would not make it safely to the mainland forty-five minutes away. She had no plans to leave the car until they were safely on the continent.

The creaks and groans scared her. They were too loud. Occasional snapping sounds could be heard. They had not even left the dock yet. Her heart raced as she envisioned the worst; salt water rushing across the floor, shallow at first, then exploding through every orifice in the ferry's hold. It shatters car windows as bolts shoot out of the collapsing metal walls like bullets, killing those who have not already been sucked out into the raging green deep.

The troubling sounds were impossibly close. As if they were in the car. Then Gloria realized that much of the din *was* in the car. Her father's snores blasted out of his mouth. Air stopped for seconds on end, only to be released in a manic array of whistles and fricatives. He sounded like a pinball machine.

"Dad," Gloria said softly.

No response.

"Dad, turn over. You're-"

She looked up from her father and out the back window. The word "ECNALUBMA" stared back at her. It was not the ambulance with Nika in it. That one had boarded before them. She knew immediately that this one contained Scott and her heart doubled its pace.

Walking to the back of the ambulance required gymnast-like balance. The ferry, now making its way across Vineyard Sound, listed hard before righting itself and overcompensating. Gloria imagined the irony should she slip and fall, suffering the same fate as Scott. This possible future motivated her to keep her balance and tread carefully, ultimately allowing her to make it to the back of the vehicle unscathed.

Peering inside, she saw that the overhead light was on, and it shone down on Scott, as expected. All she saw of him were the bottom of his bare feet sticking off the end of a gurney, and further on along the gurney, white casts holding up both of his arms. No one else was in the back of the ambulance.

She knocked. There was no response other than Scott wiggling his fingers. She knocked again. A woman's head appeared in the window between the back of the ambulance and the front seat, then it disappeared again. Gloria heard a door slam and she waited for the driver's head to manifest itself atop a body next to her. As she waited, she held onto the door handle to maintain her balance.

The woman did appear, all five feet of her. Hair back in a severe red ponytail, her bone-white face was annoyed and expectant. Gloria looked down and said "Hiiiiiil. I am so sorry to bother you, but the man in-"

"Does this look like the Disney monorail?" the driver interrupted, zero patience in her voice.

"No."

"It's an ambulance. You don't just get in. There are sick people in these things."

"I'm sorr-"

"Hold on." She opened the back door. "Mr. Simon, there's someone who wants to see you."

"Hiiii" Gloria said. She heard nothing from the ambulance for a period that felt too long.

Then "She can come in."

259

"Go on" said the small woman.

"Thank you so, so much" Gloria replied, as she placed a foot on the back bumper and lifted herself inside. Again she almost lost her footing and held onto the other closed door for support. Once in, she heard the door slam behind her.

Fluorescent lights bouncing between off-white walls hurt her eyes. She squinted in order to see her ex-fiance. And there he was, still wearing a neck brace and arm casts. He had two black seat belts crisscrossing his chest. In contrast to the antiseptic environment of defibrillators and cabinets of plastic-wrapped medical implements, Scott was a mess. His hair was a tangle. His bloodshot eyes sat beneath puffy eyelids. He had grown stubble that looked kind of fetching on his lantern jaw.

He looked at her without moving his neck. Then, very slowly, he raised up his two middle fingers at her. She laughed. He did did not.

"You're a jerk" he said.

"I know! I am so so sorr-"

"Don't say that word. Please God. I know how little value it holds with you. Stop carpet bombing the world with empty apologies."

"Fine, but let me say I was in a stressful situation when I said the things I said."

Scott gasped. "Oh, did a dog try to eat you too?"

The boat heeled hard to port, and then to starboard. The movement forced Gloria to drop down into the blue vinyl seating behind her. She had never been seasick before but now felt her stomach contract and her throat open and close involuntarily. The feeling went away as quickly as it came. Scott stared at her.

Gloria said, "With everything going on with my dad and then with my job and then with you, I just kind of flipped out. I

260

became focused one-hundred percent on destroying my father. I lost perspective. And I was drunk too. Or hungover. I don't know."

"Look," Scott said. "It's fine. What's done is done. It's over. Behind us. Tomorrow is another day. I'm just trying to think about the future. Recuperating. Getting back to work. The past sucks too much. I can't consider it anymore."

There was no evil in him, she thought. No urge to hurt her. No effort to throw back the garbage she had thrown at him two days earlier. Good old Prissy Hoyt, she thought. There was something to what the old lady had said. I shouldn't be looking for a guy who sends me over the moon. And it's okay that I originally chose this guy partly because my dad would hate him. He is a good man. We need to be together. Starting now.

Let's do this, she thought.

"Listen, Scott. I need to get my dad settled somewhere else. I haven't figured out where yet. Somewhere nearby in New York. Believe it or not he actually asked to stay with me. But I'm done with his shit. So I've got to figure it out."

"Damn. Good luck with that fun," Scott said.

"Yeah. But look." She paused. The Bigger Gloria appeared and looked down over the moment. Returning so soon after its recent appearance at the bar. She saw things from on high, where she had a view of herself at all ages of life. The little girl whose father had turned to her on the beach and dubbed her "a princess and a poet." The child who had lost Magic Merv. The teenager who had turned to booze and smokes after watching her father disintegrate along with his marriage. The young woman who had alone watched her mother die, and only then realized that she had been abandoned by every blood relation, either by geography, madness, or the grave. And seeing all of those

261

renditions of herself, she saw this moment as what it was. The turning point. The moment when she stopped letting the world disappoint her and she navigated her own course. Forget the efforts to recapture her father. That had been a fool's errand, not a navigated course at all. It was time to stop the ocean swells from having their way with her. Now she would cut through them like Moses. The bigger Gloria looked over the moment and approved.

She continued. "So when I get that all squared away with dad, let's maybe get a bite and figure things out. Get things back on track."

Scott laughed, and said "Sorry?"

"Let's do this. Let's get things moving again in the right direction."

"I, um. Hm. How do I put this?"

"Put what?" She felt her stomach turn again.

"Well, the short answer is 'no.' The long answer is 'no way.'"

"What do you mean?"

"I mean no way, sister. If you had suggested this twelve hours ago, it might have been a possibility. But not now."

Gloria fell forward onto Scott's legs as the ferry lurched. Looking behind her, she saw that the vinyl backrest had shoulder straps. She slipped her arms through them and, not seeing how to loosen the straps, sat bolt upright. Her current situation reminded her of movie soldiers lined up in the backs of bombers, strapped into lines of seats, steeling themselves for the big drop.

Scott continued. "So yesterday, I'm in the hospital, and - I mean no shit, right? Where else would I be? Bowling alley? So I'm at the hospital and the nurse comes in and says a woman's downstairs who wants to see me. Name's was Peggy Amblin. I had no idea who she was, but the nurse told me this lady had Logan. She had him! So I told the nurse hell yeah! Let her up. So she comes up and sure as heck she has Logan in her car. Some guy had rescued him in the ocean during the hurricane."

Kyle, Gloria thought.

"And Peggy's there and sees it all, and she's an animal nut and she offers to temporarily take in the dog - and some other dog - and find the owners. She brings me an iced coffee to sip through a straw while she's there, and we get to talking."

I hope you both die in a fire, Gloria thought.

"I mention being a Phish fan and she's not only a huge Phish fan, with tickets for nearly every east coast stop on their current tour, but she's in a jam band herself! One I've seen before. A couple of times. All-girl outfit called Sister Soul Stirrer. You'd love them. Anyway, they're opening for Phish at one of their Boston shows! Amazing."

"Who?"

"Sister Soul Stirrer."

"Mouthful" Gloria said through another wave of nausea.

"So look. I think you see my point. I want to try to look into this other thing. Peggy's interesting. We have some stuff in common. She lives in New York too. So in terms of getting back together? Soft pass."

"Nice try," Gloria chuckled.

Scott frowned. "Excuse me?"

The ferry dipped forward and the driver could be heard to say "whoa."

"Nice try," Gloria repeated. "I buy that part about someone having Logan. I know he was rescued. I even met the rescuer. But there is zero chance some pretty lassie came into the hospital who plays whatever in an all-girl jam band. That's a little too neat."

"What the hell are you talking about?"

"Peggy Amblin? We're in an *ambulance*. Amblin. Ambulance. That was the first name you thought of. You're like a lame version of Kevin Spacey in The Usual Suspects."

"What?"

"And 'Soul Sister Stirrers?' That's the worst name I've ever heard. There's no fucking band called that. The word 'stirrers' is hard enough to say on its own. But 'Soul Sister Stirr-Stuhhhruhrrs? See that? I have to say it like one mile an hour to get it out. Try harder, Scott. You want to play hard to get? Fine. But don't give me this bullshit."

"You're certifiable," he said.

"I'm not the one making shit up like a teenager."

"Maybe you should go."

Gloria felt a burp in her throat laced with stomach acid. She held it in.

The *Island Home* leaned so hard, she swore she could feel the ambulance's chassy distance itself from the two right tires. Water is going to break the glass any moment, she thought. I can sense it like through a third eye.

She unstrapped herself from the seat and began to get up, holding onto anything in sight.

"I'll be in touch soon. When you're ready to give up on these stories and get back together, you know my number."

"Sure."

And that was it. "Sure" was how he left it.

As Gloria made her way slowly back to Kyle's monstrous car, knowing full well Scott was done with her, she took some comfort in knowing that Peggy had the other dog too. Logan's lookalike. That beast lurked in the dark corners of Scott's future, ready to have another go at his trachea.

And then she vomited.

Chapter Eighteen

"THURSDAY, FOR ONE NIGHT ONLY, PHISH AT
FENWAY" the radio blared. "WITH OPENING ACT, SISTER
SOUL STIRRERS. DOORS OPEN AT-"

Gloria turned off the radio.

They passed through the rotaries of Route 28, as if passing
through airlocks, returning to livable atmosphere. She turned the
radio back on for company and fiddled with Kyle's confusing
tuner. WMVY played Rickie Lee Jones, while Boston's WZLX
was mostly static, although Roger Daltrey's screams
occasionally forced their way through.

Gloria thought about Scott. She had always believed that a
person gains something from every relationship. It might be a
new understanding of how people can interact, not through
words, perhaps, but through touch. It might be another layer of
emotional armor. A way of dressing. A style of comic delivery.
A sudden openness to a sexual kink. There was always
something. So, what did she gain from her time with Scott?
Nothing came to mind as she looked at the Bourne Bridge,
growing in the distance.

Then the music on the radio changed, and with it came the
realization, and it was so small and so huge at the same time she
nearly drove off the road. It was Scott's music. She hated all of
it. Phish, the Grateful Dead, Widespread Panic. It was all
terrible. Worst of all was Steely Dan, that over-calculated,
pretentious nonsense. But within that garbage, they had one lyric
that Scott always sang, and at this moment, as it played on
WZLX, it meant everything.

"Any minor world that breaks apart falls together again."

266

It gave her an idea that she had to act on immediately.

Harold woke in a panic, yelling.

"The monkey is the lodestar! What?" He looked around, drool on his chin. It did not take him long to get his bearings, and when he did, he quickly ascertained that something was wrong.

"Where are we?" he asked. "This is not Connecticut. Why are we on 90? You and your mother! No sense of direction." He sat back, rubbed his belly, and yawned. "I suspect that evolution did not grant women that faculty because they never left the hut. The men needed to know their way around as they were the ones tasked with bringing down the ibex."

"We're not going to New York," Gloria said, aggressively ignoring her father's take on the sexes and navigation.

"What are you talking about?"

"We're going to California."

Harold leaned forward, unencumbered by a seat belt. "I beg your pardon?"

Gloria smiled. "We're San Francisco bound. I'm dropping you at Seth's."

"No."

"Actually, yes."

"My cemetery! I cannot be expected to work the system if I am that far-flung."

"The cemetery idea is shit, Dad. Consider this as my rescuing you from the cemetery." She was calm as she spoke. "We need to see Seth. Be a family. At least for a little while. Spend a few days together. We haven't done that since Mom died. Consider it a reset. For all of us. And then I'm going back to New York. Alone."

"A reset? Folderol! And who are you to call such shots? When you were born, this seating arrangement was quite the reverse. I was driving the car and it was you who was helpless in the backseat. What cheek to turn the tables on me like this. A bloodless coup!" Harold kept opening his mouth as if to argue further. He looked around the back seat, like the words he needed were dyed in the car's ceiling fabric or sewn into the seat upholstery. But nothing came. Then his movements slowed. A peace came to his face, the furrowing in his brow easing, like waves in a storm coming to calm. He looked out towards the fresh leaves on the oaks and the aster growing wild along the highway shoulder. His arm reached and his finger pressed the button opening his window. He closed his eyes and inhaled deeply through his nose. The air in Gloria's ears pulsated unpleasantly from the rush of wind flooding the car. The breeze made Harold's thinning white hair blow behind him. He opened his eyes, closed the window, and was silent for a time, still looking out at the passing flora.

They passed a sign saying "Welcome to New York, The Empire State" and when the off-ramp arrived for the southbound side of the thruway, Gloria did not waiver. She kept the car moving forward.

Harold spoke. "When your mother died, everyone was angry with me for not being by her side. And not attending the funeral."

"I don't know if everyone was angry. But I sure was."

"I swear to you that I did say my goodbyes to her."

"I don't care, Dad."

"Remember that story I told you about the time I snuck into her window when we were first courting and pitching woo? How

I broke my teeth with the champagne cork? And we got caught and had to sneak out another night? And then we created you?"

"Mom told me the story."

"It was a fantastic moment for us. We had many fantastic moments after that. But those nights, young and serenaded by every star? That was the crest. And you were the result."

He continued looking out the window, a smile on his face.

"When your mother had her stroke and the embolism robbed her of consciousness, I had no interest in hovering around her bed with other people. Why would I? What would we all say or do except look around dumbstruck, like fools? I paid for the medical necessities per your requests, but kept my distance otherwise." A conspiratorial grin crossed his face, and he leaned forward as if he was concerned unseen strangers would hear the next part. "But do you want to know what I did? I orchestrated a repeat performance of our apex. I drove my car to her house late at night. You were not there. Ruby Fontana from mother's book group was not visiting with her rum cake. Jesse Rothenberg from the synagogue was not mowing the lawn for her. It was very late and it was dark, save the low light from a waning crescent moon. Only the hospice nurse was there, watching television in the dark. Some tripe involving people putting tarantulas on their faces for money. I grabbed the ladder from the garage, put it against the house, and climbed up to her room. Our old room. Just like the old days! It was warm and the window was open."

He smiled even bigger now, and looked at the car floor. "I got in bed with her and lay by her side for the night. She was clearly gone, but it did not matter. No champagne cork to the teeth this time. And now there were no parents to rush in and discover us. We spent one last night together in peace. Then when the sun was rising, I kissed her on the head and left."

269

Harold put his head back and closed his eyes. "We said our goodbyes the way we should have. Alone. Together."

The drizzle returned, but the grey of the sky caused the colors around them to show more brilliantly. Yellow wildflowers on the highway berm seemed lit from within and red barns glowed like embers.

Harold coughed and then said, "Most people pack clothing and cash before a cross-country trip by car. I have neither."

"I have five bucks. We'll figure something out."

"I doubt it. We will die from exposure before we reach Ohio. They will find us huddled around a gas-soaked tire which we failed to set alight."

Gloria laughed. "I'll be clutching my last cigarette which I never got to smoke."

"And I will be wrapped in a length of upholstery which I tore from the car and tried to fashion into a parka."

"Am I still the princess and the poet?"

"Excuse me?"

Gloria took her eyes off the road and looked back at him. "The princess and the poet. You once called me that. When I was little. I was looking at your book on Emerson and asked you what a line meant about a lower deep opening." She looked back at the highway but her eyes peered into the rearview mirror repeatedly. "You said I was the princess and poet. So? Am I?"

Harold met her gaze in the mirror, and said, "Yes. You are."

The two of them closed their mouths and took in the scenery.

Harold asked, "Did you ever untangle that sentiment? 'Under every deep a lower deep opens?'"

"I never read the text around it so it's hard to say. I thought it meant something bad. But maybe not. Things are just getting deeper and deeper, and things go on forever? I don't know. Whatever."

Harold chuckled. "Precisely. Whatever."

And then Gloria said, her voice warbling, "I miss her, Dad."

"I do, too."

The road stretched out before them and they fell silent. Gloria found herself thinking back, it seemed like eons ago, to when she overheard her father saying something about life being a trip eastward, and the landscape getting duller and the future being eternally mundane. Yet here they were, defying time, moving backward, giving what was left of their broken world a second chance.

Then it was back to more practical thinking, and Gloria wondered whether her father could get away with wearing her paisley print blouse and yoga pants into a Waffle House.

Acknowledgments

This book would not have happened without the outsized contributions of several people and groups.

The kernel of the idea arose from a late-night, bourbon-fueled conversation with Kirk Wood Bromley across a campfire at Martha's Vineyard Family Campground. Roughly six years later, Kirk also reviewed one of the final edits. His unique insights and lunatic spirit were completely essential to the creation of Harold Gomberg.

Nancy Bloom, aka my mother, read an early draft and pointed out those times when I had left things unclear or unresolved.

Marietta Zacker was kind enough to review a nearly-completed draft and give me the tough feedback I needed when I was losing sight of my audience.

I'd also like to thank Alex Johnson, Joe Lemonnier, Todd Chapin, Chad Gracia, Pete Lepeska, Michael Lisk, and Roberto Pieraccini, dear friends, artists, and lovers of the written word, for providing their insights.

A big thank you to the Aquinnah and Edgartown Police Departments for not hanging up on me and answering all of my weird questions about squad cars and booking procedures.

The character of Amos was tricky. For people reading the story for the first time, they will think Amos is a member of the Wampanoag Tribe. He is not, which is revealed near the end. My hope is that if any member of the Wampanoag Tribe of Gay Head / Aquinnah reads this book, they will see Amos for the lost person he is, and not take him as a commentary on their beautiful heritage. I would like to thank the Tribal Council for answering my calls and graciously taking my questions.

An extra-special thank you to the hyper-talented and unstoppable Heather Kern at PopShop Studio for the cover design. The quality far exceeds the book's contents.

Finally, this book would not exist if it weren't for my dearest Tricia Bloom. She was impossibly patient reading multiple drafts and talking through character and plot issues. More generally, she was kind enough to emotionally and intellectually invest. I love you with all I have.

Made in the USA
Middletown, DE
29 March 2019